THE

CRYPT

a novel

by

Jonas Saul

PUBLISHED BY

Imagine Press

ISBN: 978-1466484825

This book is dedicated to my readers for all their support. Your love of Sarah has inspired me to continue this series for many years to come. Sarah Roberts Book 4 is due out early 2012. Happy reading.

JONAS SAUL

Chapter 1

Sarah Roberts stood on the darkened street in the eighth district of Budapest and waited to be attacked. This was her third time venturing out in the middle of the night in search of a would-be attacker.

She'd been in Budapest now for over four weeks and her sister Vivian hadn't said anything since her arrival. All she had was the final note her dead sister made her write telling her that Armond Stuart had fled to Hungary. Sarah had no specific idea where Armond was either.

At war with herself and out of communication with her parents and the few people she had grown to trust, Sarah felt truly alone.

It was just after two in the morning. She hoped that the dress would attract the wrong kind of attention. She wasn't trying to look like a prostitute, just vulnerable. The knee-length dress was decorated with a pretty floral pattern. This was the shortest dress she would ever wear. No miniskirts. Not even for this. Her top wasn't revealing at all. The red angora sweater gave nothing away. Jeans were her norm, but sacrifices had to be made when one wants to be attacked.

Weapons were easy to come by: knives could be had at any corner store; forks were nice to jab into an opponent's skin or eye; but a gun was what Sarah needed. She had trained with them over the last four years at various firing ranges. She had done well a few months back staying alive while dealing with Armond.

Now it was all about hunting him down and killing him.

That was it.

Cold blooded murder.

Armond Stuart had raped and killed her sister Vivian when Sarah was still a child. Since then he had developed a kidnapping ring and a human trafficking business that spanned the world. How many girls had been harmed, and how brutal that harm had been, Sarah could only wonder.

Killing Armond in cold blood was the only answer.

That was what started the internal war she had with her conscience. How could she just walk up and shoot him in the face? That's not what she was about. Sarah was about helping others. She began saving people almost five years ago. In that time she couldn't count how many had walked away from death or worse.

Breaking up Armond's organization in America a few months back had set many young girls free. What Armond had done was unacceptable. He had to be stopped. A man like that cannot be rehabilitated. Death is the only way.

Yet she didn't know if she could do it. When the time came, would she pull the trigger? Or did she have to wait until she caught him in a compromising situation to justify the kill?

And why wasn't Vivian giving her any messages? The last one was in the States. Was it because she was overseas?

Sarah shook her head at that notion. *No way. Couldn't be. Vivian's dead. She's on the Other Side. My sister can travel wherever she wants to be with me.*

A soft scuffling sound interrupted her thoughts. She looked around but couldn't see anything or anyone close. She leaned back against the wall where she'd loitered for the past hour.

Why had there been no communication? Could it be because in the States when Vivian gave her direction it was more about saving those girls while here it's all about killing Armond? Is that it? If she's just hunting the man then she's no better than a mercenary or an assassin hired to execute another? Would Vivian sanction that? Or were there others involved on the Other Side, directing Vivian now?

Sarah looked up at the dark summer sky and asked out loud, "After all the evil Armond has done, isn't this still righteous? How come it was okay to kill him while he was in the act of harming someone but now when walking through the park it isn't?"

She had come to Hungary because of Vivian. She took the money from her father for the ticket. He believed in her. And now, after a month, she was no further ahead despite taking a crash course in Hungarian, which seemed to be the hardest language in the world to understand. At least they had North American restaurants and the hotels were quite similar.

But that introduced another problem. She could be found here. In the States she could use motels that took cash. Here she had to use her credit card and show her passport routinely. Anyone who wanted to find her, could. She felt too exposed. Maybe Armond was watching her right now while she hunted him.

How crazy my life has become.

Sarah stepped out of the shadows and edged closer to the street. Online she had read that the eighth district was the most dangerous part of Budapest. She was sadly disappointed. Nothing at all had happened each of the nights she had come here looking to be mugged or attacked.

She brought no weapons of any kind. Her hands were fast enough. She had learned a few pressure points on the human body to know exactly where to touch a two hundred pound man. With her thumb alone she could have a man on the ground choking on his collapsed trachea after having applied the proper pressure.

Yet no one challenged her.

Nearing the street Sarah saw a little Lada Sputnik go by. She watched its taillights disappear down the road, leaving her alone again.

She started the quiet walk back to the Best Western hotel. The stupid heels she wore were getting caught on the uneven pavement and making her stumble. She stopped, reached down and took them both off. Barefoot, she continued walking the empty streets of Budapest.

What about saving people?

Why wouldn't Vivian send her something so that she could do a few tasks, something to make her feel useful? After all, she was an Automatic Writer. Her sister had been using this talent for many years, saving so many people...and then as soon as she landed in Budapest the well went dry.

Something had changed. It was different now. Maybe the rules on the Other Side had been altered? There was no way for Sarah to know. She would just have to wait. Eventually Vivian would use her again. She'd make contact or Sarah would be forced to fly back to the States. What a waste of time this trip would be if she ended up at home having accomplished nothing.

She turned a corner and slowed up. Three men were whispering to each other on the opposite side of the street. They stood in the shadows under an awning.

Could this be a waste of time? Would any of them have a weapon?

She continued walking. But this time she acted afraid that they might see her. She stayed on her side of the street and even added a little skip in her step. As she passed the three men they turned as one and began walking on their side of the street.

Got their attention. Good.

She kept going, walking so fast now that she was almost doing a slow jog. Up ahead she saw a busier street. It had to be around three in the morning and yet every few seconds another car would pass by.

With the aid of a window in the side of the building she was passing Sarah could see the threesome were crossing the street behind her. They were closing the distance quickly, hoping to stop her before she got to the busier intersection.

Something else caught her eye. A man was leaning against a light post across the street. From the reflection in the window it appeared he was watching her.

She spun around and stared at him. She couldn't see his face in the dark. He wore a hat with a small brim. After a moment of staring at each other he lowered his head a little and raised his right hand to tip the corner of his hat.

The three men were almost upon her now. She had to move.

One thing she really hated was being followed. By now she would normally have turned around and allowed them the chance to run, but she needed them close.

"Hey baby," one of them yelled.

She turned to look at them. They were about ten feet behind her. Two of them were of a darker skin color.

Gypsies.

She'd been warned about them. These gypsies were getting a bad name for themselves in Hungary. There was a small group of men who hunted gypsies. They committed horrible crimes, even killing gypsies. All that perpetuated was more violence and then they got themselves arrested. Who was better with that rationale?

Sarah faced the trio as she started to walk backwards. The busier street was just over a block away now. Even if she ran, they'd catch her.

The time had come.

"Do any of you three speak English?"

The white guy in the middle nodded and smiled. "I speak fluent British English. My two friends here don't but they can basically understand you. Now tell us, what would you be doing in a neighborhood like this, dressed like that? Are you for hire?"

"Fuck you."

"Oh, a feisty bitch. I like that."

She was still walking backwards. She looked for the man in the hat who had been leaning on the light post but he had disappeared. A quick look over her shoulder revealed a drop off in the sidewalk coming. Sarah hopped over a little to her right and used the street. In that second the trio moved as one to close the gap even more. Now they were four feet from her.

"You wanna have some fun with us?"

"Sure, but not tonight. Maybe some other time. Leave me your number. Maybe I'll call."

"No. You don't come down here dressed like that and expect us not to notice. You came looking for some action. We've seen you around a couple nights in a row. What else would you be here for if you're not hooking?"

Even though she knew he was right because she knew how men thought, dressing the way she did was never an open invitation. That was the part of men she hated.

"Hey, asshole. No still means no. It doesn't matter how a girl dresses."

One of the gypsies smirked.

"Do that again and I will break your fucking nose," Sarah said.

The gypsy turned to the leader. It was evident to Sarah that the guy in the middle who'd been doing all the talking was the one they looked up to.

She held both her shoes in her left hand. Without looking down she adjusted the heel of one of the shoes to angle outward and the strap of the other to dangle loosely off her last two fingers.

She had stepped back a few more times. One fast look over her shoulder told her they were running out of time if these boys wanted to dance without being seen by the numerous drivers racing by. Maybe fifteen feet separated her from the sidewalk of the busy street.

She stared at the leader. He was smiling like he knew they had her. He looked confident and filled with attitude. He had to play the part for his boys. She'd seen this all too often.

Sarah slowed her step and then stopped walking about ten feet from the corner. They hadn't tried anything yet. They'd waited too long. These guys were barely hitting their mid-twenties and were too afraid to outright attack her. Maybe a warning was what was needed. They should learn not to follow girls like they just did.

There was no way they were packing a gun. They weren't tough enough. This had been a waste of time.

She needed a shot of whiskey and her bed.

"Okay, here's how we're going to play this. You three turn around and go back to wherever it is you crawled out of and I am going back to my hotel. That is the only way no one gets hurt. We all act like we didn't meet each other at all tonight."

The gypsy smirked at her again but this time he laid his head back, looking down at her along the bridge of his nose.

She'd warned him to not do that. He was taunting her. It was like he raised his nose in the air on purpose to offer it to her. *Here, break it. Show me what you got,* was written all over his face.

Well fuck him. He just bought a free ride to the local hospital.

Sarah lunged forward with one quick step and raised her right foot into the guy's stomach. The blow caused him to fold at the waist as the wind was kicked out of his gut. In that brief second, Sarah was already lifting her right elbow up. His face came down and forward as he folded and made contact with her elbow, snapping his nose with an audible crack. She extended her arm fully, using the back of her fist to smash into the side of his head.

The smirking gypsy fell to the ground half moaning, half squealing while he tried to breathe through his wrecked nose. Blood was already oozing down his face as he rolled on the ground.

This all happened in less than four seconds. The only brave one to stay close and not fall back was the English-speaking guy.

Sarah raised her left hand and presented him with the heel.

"Step up motherfucker. Step up and this heel goes in your eye hole."

He paused a second and then stepped back, his hands out in front of him in surrender.

The guy on the ground moaned increasingly louder.

"I warned him. Now I'm warning you. A woman can dress any way she wants. Just because I have a nice red top and a dress, it doesn't give you the right to assume I am going to be a willing victim. How do you *not* know that I'm lost. My husband and I might have been out on the town and I got lost."

"You don't have a wedding ring," English said.

"Smart. Okay, be smart. We both know what's going on here. You three followed me and tried to scare me. That shit is old. It doesn't work on me. But the problem is, other girls would be afraid. Seriously afraid. Either get jobs and do something productive with your life or you won't live long."

What am I doing? Giving motivational speeches to street thugs at three in the morning in downtown Budapest? Better yet, why am I doing it? I can't save the world. Maybe my sister needs to make contact so I can stop looking for a fight.

"You are fucked," English said. "We do have jobs. Good stable ones. We weren't going to do anything. We were just following you. Taunting, teasing. We aren't gang bangers as you call it in America. And now you've really hurt my friend. Just get out of here. Leave us alone."

Sarah stepped back. Was she losing it? Is that why Vivian hadn't been in touch? Did her sister feel she was unstable? Had the pressure been too much? She always thought she could handle it. Why would Vivian start sending her messages in the first place if she felt Sarah was too weak?

Still, these three men had made the wrong choice. They could've let her pass. They could've continued talking among themselves. But instead they had started to follow her. They had crossed the street and actually made her turn around to watch their progress as they got closer. The street was relatively dark. It was the eighth district. Gypsies had a nasty reputation. It all added together and came out with nothing nice. Any other woman would've been terrified. They made the wrong choice.

Fuck it, they deserved this.

"Are any of you three carrying a weapon?"

English looked at his other pal standing to her left. He looked back at her and shook his head. She couldn't tell what he was feeling. It wasn't confidence anymore. It was more of a knowing look. Like he'd seen her before or maybe he recognized her. After the Mormon compound was raided, Sarah's face was plastered on the front pages of hundreds of newspapers across North America. Maybe even parts of Europe reported on her too.

The English-speaking guy did say something a moment ago referencing America. Did he guess based on her look or her voice? Or did he know?

The gypsy on the ground wasn't moaning as much anymore. He'd rolled onto his side. One hand was still near his nose but his other hand was close to his abdomen. He cupped something in his palm.

Before she reacted adversely, her mind registered his hand was holding a cell phone.

In the distance Sarah heard a police siren wailing in the night. She guessed it was at least five to ten blocks away.

English whispered something to his friend.

"What was that?" Sarah asked.

He looked back at her. "I told him in Hungarian to help me hold you down if you try to run. The police are coming. You are in a lot of trouble."

Sarah stared at him. There *was* something she didn't know. Not that they were withholding information on her. It was more of a feeling, intuition. A change in the air. Like they had the upper hand and they knew it.

She scanned the immediate area. Was anyone coming out of the shadows? Was it the man with the fedora leaning against the light post?

Or maybe they were friends with the police? Could the officers responding to the scene tonight be their pals and they were going to conspire to really fuck her over?

Whatever they thought they had on her she was sure Vivian would've sent a warning. Silence for a month didn't supersede Sarah's safety.

Vivian would've said something. Sarah would stake her life on it.

"I'm not going to run. You needn't worry."

"You will be arrested," English stated in a matter-of-fact voice. "You attacked our friend without provocation."

Without provocation? Fuck you. I was being followed.

Sarah nodded. "Maybe you're right. Let's just wait and see."

The sirens were at least a block away now.

The rotating lights on the top of the little police cars could be seen bouncing off the walls of the building up ahead as they approached.

Now was the time.

Sarah raised her right hand, fingers splayed out and struck herself across the face hard enough to leave a serious red welt.

"Hey, what the hell was that?"

Sarah smiled his way. "I've been doing this too long."

The police car rounded the corner and began to slow as soon as the driver saw them all in the middle of the road. The car stopped behind Sarah and the driver stepped out.

He addressed everyone in Hungarian. A ramble of monotone gibberish went back and forth for half a minute. Sarah waited until they were finished.

The guy on the ground started moaning louder again, rolling around a little, holding his face with both hands.

The officer turned to her and said in English, "What is your story?"

"I can't sleep. I was out for a late night walk when I noticed these three guys were following me." She heard one of the gypsies grunt as if she was lying. "I tried to get to this busier street." She turned and gestured behind her. "But they got really close. I don't have anything to defend myself with, officer, so I removed my shoes. They said, dressed the way I am, that I was asking for trouble. This guy," she pointed at the gypsy on the ground. "He stepped up and slapped me hard across the face—"

"That's not true!" English shouted.

The officer turned toward him and spewed something in Hungarian lightning quick. English dropped his head a little.

"Continue," the cop said to her.

"After he slapped me, in my defense, I tossed my elbow in his face. I think I accidentally broke his nose. I'm sorry, officer. I just wanted to go back to my hotel. I was scared."

English spoke first. "This is all lies. We were following her, but that's because it's our job—"

"Hey!" the cop yelled. "Enough out of you."

Job? What the hell was he talking about? Could he have misused the English word and he meant something else? If not, then who hired them? Who wanted Sarah followed?

That must be what she felt earlier. It was like they knew something and she didn't. These three had purpose. They'd seen her before. They'd watched her before. These three posed a danger to her now. Something was going on that was deeper than Sarah knew and Vivian wasn't informing her.

What the fuck could it be?

"Look miss, you're going to have to come with me. I will take your statement at the police station."

"I'm not going anywhere with you. How do I know you aren't all in this together?"

The officer stared at her. "In what together?"

"English boy over there just said that it was his job. What the fuck does that mean? Who are you people? No one follows me. You will never get the drop on me."

English turned away. He was evidently pissed that even a portion of the truth had been revealed.

"In America you may have crooked cops but over here I am a member of the *Rendorshag*, the Hungarian police. I do not consort with the likes of these men."

"Bullshit," was all Sarah said under her breath.

The cop looked surprised. "Okay, you're coming with me."

"Try it."

"Try what?" he asked.

She could tell her confidence was keeping him at bay. But how far did she want to push this? She was in a foreign country. She didn't know anyone. What would Hungarian jails be like? What was she even doing here in the first place?

"I was obviously followed by these three men. I was hit in the face and I defended myself. I am a small girl out walking alone. Three men attacked me and you want to take me to your police station? If that doesn't reek of corruption then I don't know what does. I'm not going anywhere with you."

"How could you possibly stop me? There's three of us still standing."

"As I said a minute ago, try it."

The standoff didn't last long. The officer stared for a moment and then stepped toward her.

He reached back for something on his belt. Possibly handcuffs or wrist ties. All that mattered to Sarah was that he left an opening. His chest and face were unprotected.

Without thinking of the consequences, acting only on her inner call to violence that seemed to never be satiated, she lunged forward and jammed her thumb into the base of the officer's throat in the center of where the collarbones meet.

He instantly staggered back, mouth open and began the horrible sounds of choking for air.

She knew she'd jabbed hard, but not hard enough to kill him. It would leave him gasping for a minute or two.

The normal reaction for the person choking was for both hands to raise to the area of the neck. The police officer didn't disappoint her.

Her left hand dropped both shoes to the pavement as she bent at the waist, leaned forward and snapped the clip holding his gun. With deft hands she had the weapon lifted out of its holster and in her palm aimed at the other two men in less time than they had to react to her attack on the cop.

"Stay back," Sarah said as she aimed her new weapon in their general direction. In the same movement she flipped the safety off and slid her index finger inside the trigger guard.

The officer was breathing better. A wheezing, raspy sound emitted from his mouth as color returned to his face.

"I'm done for the night. I will back away and leave you to do as you please. If anyone tries to follow me I will take it as a personal threat to my person. In my defense I will be forced to shoot my would-be attacker. Are we clear?"

The officer nodded right away. He wasn't stupid. He knew who held the gun.

English and his gypsy friend who still stood off to the side behind the cop only stared at her.

"I asked, are we clear? Don't be a fucking idiot. Answer the question or I will be forced to make you hear me. You don't want to piss me off. I get ugly when I'm pissed off."

The cop turned to both men. He mumbled something unintelligible.

English looked at Sarah and nodded almost imperceptibly.

"No, you answer me. Are we clear? That is the last time I ask."

She still held the gun out at arm's length. She adjusted its aim to focus on English's face.

He waited another moment and said, "Yes. We are clear. No one will follow you again tonight. But I will be watching you."

Threats really pissed her off.

"You will not be watching me. No one *watches* me." She stepped forward into his space, placing the gun at his belt line. "Threaten me again and you will be eating your next meal with no teeth."

Being this close offered her a chance to remind him of who was in charge at the moment. A quick drop of her head, hard enough to matter but not hard enough to break anything, and English felt her forehead connect with his nose.

He staggered back and grabbed his face. His voice nasal, he asked, "Why'd you do that?"

"No one threatens me. I told you, I get quite pissy when that happens."

She backed away and only lowered the gun when she was twenty feet from the four men who still stood in the middle of the road, watching her retreat.

What just happened there?

English had said something about him doing his job. The cop wanted to take her to his station. He probably wanted to take her somewhere else, rape her and leave her by the Danube River for the night.

Nothing made sense.

Sarah knew she had gone too far. She had stolen a gun from a police officer. A Hungarian police officer. She couldn't do that and remain in Hungary.

At this point she would be labeled an International criminal or something. She had to leave Hungary.

"Damn," she said as she slammed her fist into her hand.

Nothing was going as planned. She had come here as her sister had asked her to. She had done everything she was supposed to do. But now, four weeks into her stay in Hungary, she was no further ahead.

She felt like she was losing her mind.

Could she be losing her edge, falling apart? After all that had happened to her in the last five years, was she fucking up? Did she really attack a cop and steal his weapon? She'd stolen a cop's car before but never a weapon.

Whether she was going crazy or not, she knew one thing for sure: she had to leave Hungary as soon as possible.

And who was the guy with the fedora hat? Why was he watching her?

Stakes are about to be raised and I'm going to do the raising.

THE CRYPT

Chapter 2

Sarah finished packing the one small suitcase she traveled with and set it by the door of her hotel room.

She'd stayed at this Best Western since the day she arrived. A Do Not Disturb sign had remained on her door the whole time. Having a maid enter her room wouldn't work with Sarah. She made her own bed, and once every three days, she grabbed the towels and garbage, entered the hall and changed them with one of the maids working in the other rooms.

When she got back to the room last night she was too tired to imagine leaving right away. The officer would have to report his weapon stolen. Forms filled out, paperwork filed and a description sent out to other officers. By the time the day shift came on, Sarah would be on all their computer screens.

All she had to do was take a cab to the Budapest Liszt Ferenc International Airport, buy a ticket to somewhere in Canada and board that flight. She'd decided on Canada to avoid the American authorities if they were tipped off and told to watch for her. Could she get to the Budapest airport without the authorities warning airport security? If she was destined for trouble, wouldn't Vivian have made contact?

Of course she would have.

She entered the bathroom, balled her hair into a bun and tucked it up under a pink baseball hat.

No make-up, a baseball cap and a stupid T-shirt that only a tourist would wear. It had a picture of Budapest on it with something about August 20th and how last year's party was a blast. Above the city in the picture a Malév Hungarian Airlines jet soared over the Danube River.

She looked down at her shirt. A rush of sadness enveloped her. She'd failed. Armond Stuart was here and she had nothing to go on. He was getting away. He would get away. In the coming years he could abuse hundreds of more girls unless someone stopped him. Sarah had come close in the past but he got away from her and he was doing it again.

Epic fail, she thought as she turned from the mirror and walked back out to her luggage.

One final check on the gun and she was ready to go. The weapon sat in the waistband of her jeans, at the small of her back. The slight bulge it made was covered by her carry-on luggage, a backpack she had slipped her arms into.

She checked the peephole in the door: no one on the other side.

Sarah opened the door and stepped from her room.

She let the door close and started for the elevator.

In under a minute she was walking through the lobby toward the counter to hand in her key and have a cab called.

The Best Western had an impressive lobby with many couches and lounge areas. Sarah scanned the large room. No one seemed out of place. Maybe they weren't onto her yet.

She waited behind an older couple checking out at the desk.

A part of her was happy to be leaving. This had been her first trip to Europe and it had come as a shock. The differences to North America were mind-blowing. She missed home. She missed the familiarity.

The couple ahead of her moved to the side. When they did, she turned to look out the front doors of the hotel.

Two police cruisers sat parked behind the four large columns that denoted the entrance to the hotel.

Shit.

Could they be here for her?

Of course they are. Who else would the police be calling upon at ten in the morning with that many cars?

"Just a sec," she motioned to the clerk who had been waiting patiently for Sarah to respond to her.

Sarah nudged her luggage up against the counter, grabbed a hotel brochure and headed for the back couches. One man wearing an expensive suit sat reading a newspaper along one wall.

Halfway to the back Sarah glanced over her shoulder. No one had entered the front doors yet. The old couple who were ahead of her had exited already. Even the clerk had stepped away somewhere.

She reached behind her and removed the police gun she had stolen last night. A burgundy couch sat facing the rear of the lobby. As she passed it, she pretended to trip. Her hand shoved the weapon in behind the cushion as far as she could. Still on her knees, she made sure it couldn't be seen or felt when she readjusted the cushion into place.

She stood up, looked around and then turned and continued to walk to the back of the lobby.

After taking off her backpack, she unzipped it and withdrew the book she was reading.

If the police were here for her, then she would never be able to leave Hungary, let alone the hotel.

If they had another purpose, she would sit idly by until they had left and then she would continue on her journey to Canada.

She only got to the second page before five men entered the lobby. Two were wearing suits, two were in police uniforms and one of them wore civilian clothes.

The one in civilian clothes was English from last night.

So they were here for her. They had already found out the hotel she was staying in. It wasn't hard to track someone down when European law required all hotel guests to register using a valid passport.

What now?

Why, in my moment of need, have you abandoned me, Vivian? What have I done to deserve this?

English turned toward her. He tapped the shoulder of one of the men wearing a suit and pointed at her. The group of five started her way.

She leaned forward and slowly placed the book in her backpack.

"Sarah Roberts?" one of the suits asked.

"And you are?"

"My name is Imre Mátyás. I'm with the Budapest police. This man here," he pointed to the man behind him also wearing a suit, "is with our immigration office and you can tell who the other two police officers are as they are in uniform. Finally, the man in the back there is János Csaba."

The man from immigration was smiling like he knew something. The kind of smile that said he was winning and he knew it. He had something planned for her. She could feel it.

Maybe one day I'll find out what your problem is and wipe that fucking smile off your face.

"How can I help you?" She asked.

No one offered hands to shake. No one moved to exchange air kisses on their cheeks.

"Are you Sarah Roberts?"

She nodded and said, "Yes."

"You will need to come with us to police headquarters."

"I'm not going anywhere with anyone until I see some identification."

Her stomach was rolling. It wasn't the tension from the confrontation. She'd been here too often to be bothered by that. It was them. She hated cops. Always did. There were five of them. She was in a foreign country. There was nothing she could do. Even if she could get away, where would she go? Every border crossing would be watched. Every plane, train and automobile would be inspected.

It was over. They'd caught her. At least she had respect for them. American police would not have been able to pull this off as fast as they had.

Both suits had flipped out their wallets. Their IDs looked genuine enough.

Two more tests.

"What district is your police department in?"

"District thirteen. Now please stand up. We can continue our conversation in privacy."

"One last question. What is the common name of your police department?"

The suit turned to his men, a look of exasperation on his face. János shrugged his shoulders in an *I told you* gesture.

"It is nicknamed the Police Palace. Now, are you going to come with us willingly or not?"

"Am I being arrested?"

"Not right now, but that can be arranged. Will you come with us or will you force me to detain you?"

Sarah dropped her hands to the armrests of the chair she sat on and nodded again.

"I will come willingly."

She stood slowly so as not to alarm them. Each man stepped back. *Good, English must've wooed them with stories of our skirmish last night.*

"Turn and face the wall."

Sarah looked him in the eye. "I said I would come willingly. That means no restraints. I either leave here unrestrained or I leave here on a stretcher."

The suit stood back and sized her up. "I like your fire, young lady, but no, I will not be using cuffs of any kind. I simply need to pat you down. An officer has reported his weapon as missing. I would hate to have that weapon show up in your hand. Neither one of us would want that. So turn around and allow me to frisk you."

Sarah watched them all for another moment and turned, spreading both hands on the wall.

By now a small group of five or six people had gathered in the lobby to watch.

I guess the police arresting someone is more exciting than checking out of your hotel. Assholes.

The suit was quick about it. He found no weapon. He grunted an *okay* and Sarah turned around.

One of the uniformed police picked up her backpack and the group walked through the lobby toward the front doors.

The lone man in the expensive looking suit had set his newspaper down to be nosy.

As they reached the front door the other uniformed police officer grabbed her luggage and rolled it out behind them.

Sarah got in the backseat of one of the cruisers and waited to be driven to the police station.

The gun was safe.

She had only defended herself last night. That would be her story. Whatever English had told them she could refute.

However all this came out, what would be the worst that could happen?

The American Embassy would help. She was an American citizen. They had just released her picture a month ago detailing all the help she gave them in breaking up the Mormon Compound.

Sarah Roberts was something of a celebrity back home.

Wouldn't that count for something in a Hungarian jail?

Probably not.

Chapter 3

The Hungarian police assholes were no better than the criminals they strove to protect the public from. It had been over four hours since she had last seen one. Were they attempting to sweat her? At twenty-three years of age, Sarah had been interrogated many times. The benefit of being questioned by the police was they had rules to follow. They couldn't shoot her if the answers sucked.

Her last interview was with a guy brandishing a whip. She had a gun to her head and he was firing randomly with one bullet in the weapon somewhere.

Nothing would be as brutal as that today, she thought to herself.

She leaned back in her chair. Her bladder was about to burst but she knew they'd let her out when they were ready. There were more important things at work here than urinating.

There was so much to think about, so much to deduce. She would probably be taken to the American Embassy and then on the next plane home, which was fine with her. She was on her way to the airport when they stopped her anyway.

The only real problem would be if they decided to arrest her for the theft of the police officer's weapon. Sarah had a great chance to beat that charge as she could describe the scene as four men against her. Then the cop wanted to take her *somewhere,* which caused her to feel suspicious of him. She did what she had done out of not just self-defense, but self-preservation.

She heard noises outside the door.

Someone was coming.

When she was placed in the interrogation room, she had turned the lone chair in the room around and sat facing away from the two-way glass. No way was she going to let them watch her face.

A pad of paper and a pen had sat on the metal desk in front of her.

Maybe they thought she would write some kind of confession before they were to begin with the questions? Or maybe Vivian would attempt contact and she'd have something to write on?

Not fucking likely. Vivian is gone.

The door opened. Sarah turned and saw the man in the suit who had talked to her at the hotel. She'd already forgotten his name. Imre something or other. Hungarian names were hard to remember.

He held two steaming glasses in his hand.

"Coffee?"

"Sure. But before I add more liquid into this little body, I need to use a bathroom or give me about ten more minutes and we could just mop my urine up."

The cop set the two glasses down and looked at her. "Are all you Americans so dramatic?"

"It's my way of saying, thanks for not offering a bathroom for me to use for however fucking long I've been stuck in this metal hole. Because of how disrespectful *that* was, I was seriously tempted to piss in the corner. I can fuck around right back at you."

"That kind of attitude won't get you far in Hungary. It may have worked in the United States, but it won't here. We're tougher than they are."

"Two things. One, no you're not. And two, I would be dead many times over if I didn't have this kind of attitude. Now, last chance: bathroom or floor?"

He turned and gestured for the door. "Let's go."

He walked her down the hall and punched in a code at a lit panel on the wall. A door opened and he ushered Sarah through it. A bathroom door was on the right.

In minutes they were walking back to the interrogation room without either one of them saying a word to the other.

She sat in her chair after spinning it back around and began to sip the coffee that he'd offered her moments before.

"Where's my luggage?"

"No questions from you. I ask the questions here. But first we wait."

Sarah set her cup down. "Wait for what?"

"My colleague."

Sarah smiled. "I know this is juvenile, but I just got you to answer a question not three seconds after you said *no questions*. Pretty good huh?"

He stared a hole through her. *This guy was too serious,* she thought. *I wonder if he's married.*

"You married?"

He didn't respond. To be doing something, he lifted his cup and sipped his coffee.

"I only ask because you look really uptight. A wife can help with that. Loosen things up a little."

"So now you give relationship advice? A girl who has reportedly never had a boyfriend. Why's that? Was it because just a few years ago you were a victim of *trichotillomania*? Come on Sarah. Don't assume we're stupid. I know everything about you."

Sarah was stunned. For the first time in a long time, she was surprised. How could he know that kind of information? Pulling her hair out had been a long time ago. She'd stopped doing it when she was nineteen. Since then it had grown in lovely. By looking at her now, you could not tell that most of her hair had been missing years ago. When she was kidnapped at eighteen years of age, her kidnapper asked what was wrong with her. He described her as a cancer patient after the chemo treatments. That's how bad she looked. But not now.

The Hungarian cop knew a lot. He'd done his research. But could he have found all that out since she'd been here? Or were they following her since she'd arrived in Budapest?

Then it hit her.

English had said something about doing his job last night. He was with the officers this morning at the hotel. She had originally thought he was there to aid in the identification of the suspect, but he was there in an official capacity.

English was a cop and he and his cop buddies had been following her. The Hungarian police had been onto her for weeks now, watching, researching and keeping tabs on her. She was sure of it.

But why? What had she done? Nothing on their soil yet. She hadn't even helped an unsuspecting accident victim or saved anyone's life because Vivian hadn't been in touch.

Her head shot up. She snapped her fingers and smiled.

That had to be it. Vivian was quiet because she was being watched. Vivian didn't want the watchers to learn anything more than they already had. I'm sure of it.

The cop had been watching her as she ruminated. He jumped a little when she snapped her fingers, but remained quiet.

"You seem to know a lot about me," Sarah said.

"Not really. We ran your passport and got the usual basics. Hometown, parents, schools, you know. Although we did find something out that was quite unusual."

Sarah sipped her coffee again.. She didn't know when she'd get another one that tasted this good. "What was that?"

"You've been a busy girl. You're something of a hero back in the States. You want to tell me about that?"

"Nope."

"Why not? It may help you here."

There it is. They want information on her Automatic Writing. They want to know how it works and why she was in their country. Was she here because she knew something?

Her abilities scared people because they weren't something that most people had encountered. The unknown always did serve a dish of nerves to the ignorant.

That was why she tried to remain an unknown. She had tried to keep under the radar for so many years. It was people like Parkman who had hunted her down and kept tabs on her activities for years. Once he'd compiled an accurate picture of her and what she had been up to, all it did was pique the interest of everyone from psychics to scientists.

"I did nothing wrong in your country. We have nothing to discuss. When you're done here, you will either drive me to the airport so I can continue my journey or you will deliver me to my embassy where I will continue my journey. Either way you play it, I'm leaving this fucking place and heading home. So go ahead. Give me your worst."

She sat back and took a couple deep gulps of her coffee, draining half of it. The warmth soothed her.

She felt better. Much better. If they had been watching her, that meant they probably bugged her room. They may even have cameras in her room the fucking perverts. That was why they would know she was in the eighth district for three nights in a row. English and his crew could have been watching her for days and she wouldn't have known if they were really good.

Sarah knew she wasn't as talented as an international spy. She was quite aware of her abilities. If professionals were following her, there was a high chance she wouldn't know they were there.

Unless Vivian told her about it. But she hadn't. Other than her parents, only Parkman knew how she worked and that Sarah and Vivian's only goals were to stop criminals or to save people from dying who weren't supposed to go yet. If it wasn't their time, Sarah was dispatched. It was that simple.

But she would never be a lab experiment. And if that's what was happening here then Vivian had saved her by staying uncharacteristically silent.

Sarah had to remember that there may be times when things were at work that would be greater than her. Things that even she had to figure out. She had to learn to trust.

That sucks. Trust is fucked. I trust no one.

Trust had always been an anonymous rotting corpse. You know it once lived somewhere, but you can now see it's only good for worm food. Worthless shit.

Imre stood up and left the room without another word. She could only assume he was watching her from the other side of the two-way glass.

She lifted her paper cup and drained the rest of the warm coffee. It tasted great as it was probably after three or four in the afternoon and she hadn't eaten anything since the continental breakfast at the hotel.

The door burst open after about a five minute wait. The noise and speed at which the door opened made her jump back.

Reflexes were great but sometimes they sucked too.

"Lucky for you I wasn't still drinking my coffee."

"Threats? Is that how we're going to start our conversation?"

The man speaking was the immigration officer she'd first met at the hotel. The one who had smiled like he was up to something. Like he knew something.

Behind him stood Imre.

"Is this the bad cop, good cop routine? Come on, do something else. I've seen this a thousand times. You're going to yell and curse and then threaten me with a bunch of unfounded charges and try to scare the shit out of me. Then he," she pointed at Imre, "will offer me a deal for a confession and everything will go away and be all right again."

She paused and looked directly at the immigration prick.

"Let me save you the time. I know what you're up to. I also know that I haven't broken any of your laws. So arrest me or let me leave because you're not just wasting your time, you're wasting mine too."

The immigration officer only moved to look back at Imre. For a second she actually thought she was getting to them.

The asshole smiled and looked back at her. He leaned down and placed both hands on the table.

"Have it your way." He stood back up, adjusted his suit jacket and said, "Arrest her."

Sarah's eyes widened a little. "On what charge?"

"Conspiracy to commit murder and attempted murder."

"What? That's ridiculous. You can't prove any of that."

"Oh yes I can. We have everything we need on you to prove that you are hunting a man by the name of Armond Stuart. You went to great lengths to nab him in the United States before you came here and now you have crossed International borders in your pursuit of hunting a known fugitive of the law. You are not a Federal agent or a police officer in any capacity. Therefore, your search for Armond has only one goal. And your attempt to steal a weapon last night was only to further your aims. I know all about you, Sarah Roberts."

He stood back up to his full height.

"You will be in a Hungarian prison doing hard labor for dozens of years when I'm done with you."

Chapter 4

The prison cell was cold and damp. Sarah knew this was all part of their goal to unsettle her by putting her in the farthest jail cell at the back of the building. It was the lowest spot in the building. The stone floor collected moisture like it was perpetually thirsty.

The single mattress was stained and smelled of urine but it was softer than the damp stone floor. She laid back on it and focused on not inhaling too much of the acidic odor.

I've been in worse places. This is a Holiday Inn compared to the shed with the hole in the ground I escaped from months ago.

She lifted her shirt up over her nose. Breathing got easier as the aroma in the room filtered through her own clean smell.

How long would this charade last?

If there was one thing Sarah had learned in the past, it was that things were not always as bad as they seemed. Something was up with that immigration officer. He had a bone to pick with her somehow. Whatever his problem was, he was the least of her worries.

Her family didn't have the money for lawyers. If these Hungarians really wanted to throw the proverbial book at her, she didn't know what she could do. Although, they *would* have to prove those charges...and - her status being what it was in the States - she was sure her embassy would get involved in any court action, if it ever got that far.

The problem was she actually *had* come all this way to find and kill Armond but she wasn't sure how they knew that, or what intelligence they had to back it up.

Maybe this was an intervention. Sarah knew that it wasn't who she was as a person. Her inner struggle since she'd been here was how could she pull the trigger? If she found Armond walking down the street, how could she just walk up and shoot him? She saved people. She helped people. Her goal was hope. Hope for the human race. Not murder.

Too lofty, she thought.

But that was why she had to kill Armond. To keep safe the other girls he would attack and kill. Sarah knew that a man like Armond would never stop. The recent debacle at the Mormon Compound would only slow him down.

Somewhere along the way, Sarah had to stop him.

A door opened down the hallway somewhere. She could hear multiple pairs of shoes echoing along the chamber.

No one talked.

Maybe she was getting a cell mate? With men you never know what they'll deliver. She wouldn't put it past them to give her a rapist for a cell mate and in the morning say sorry, they made a mistake. That kind of thing would fuck her over and keep their hands clean in the process. Then they'd have her for murder.

The rapist would be the one fucked over in this case.

As the footsteps neared she had gotten off the bed and edged back into the corner where a small amount of moisture had pooled into a tiny puddle.

Then a trio of men stepped into view.

All three she recognized. Imre the arresting detective, the immigration officer and her personal stalker: Officer Parkman.

He stood there with a half smile and a toothpick in his mouth.

"Are you serious?" Sarah asked.

Imre was reaching for keys but stopped. "What?"

Sarah continued to stare at Parkman. "All this way?"

Parkman shrugged his shoulders and tilted his head. "I know, I know."

"All this way and you still eat those fucking toothpicks like they're made of chocolate."

Imre turned and looked at Parkman. "You fly from the States, take a leave of absence and vouch for her and all she has to say to you is something about your toothpick?"

Parkman turned to him. "You don't know Sarah. This is her way of showing she's happy to see me. If she wasn't, she'd attack the bars trying to get at me. She's quite the girl. I've never met a tougher person in my life. And that goes for cops. What she's been through—"

"Hey!" Sarah yelled. "Enough. If you've come to get me out then let's do this. But don't come down here and treat these men with fictitious stories of bravery. Anything I've been through in my life any other person could've done." She stopped, stepped forward and raised her index finger as if testing the air. "This isn't Sarah Day, is it? Because if this is Sarah Day, someone should've told me."

All three men stared at her. Imre still held the keys in his hand. No one moved.

Finally Parkman bumped Imre's arm. He jolted and mumbled something.

After trying two keys, Imre got the cell door open and beckoned for Sarah to follow them. They left the dank basement cells behind, processed her paperwork and gave her luggage to Parkman.

"Where will you be staying before your plane leaves?" Imre asked.

"Back to the Best Western for another night and then we're gone."

"Don't deviate." Imre warned.

The immigration officer was strangely quiet the whole time. When Sarah got to the exit doors she turned back and looked directly at him for a moment. The look on his face was brutal and told her a story. She was only twenty feet away from him and she could see absolute fury on his face. Something was definitely wrong. He couldn't just hate her because of her reputation. She'd done nothing personally to him. But that couldn't be right. This ran deep. This was personal *for* him. He had a stake in her somehow and Sarah was determined to find out what it was before she left Hungary.

Outside in Parkman's car, he turned to her and asked, "You hungry?"

"Sure, since we're in Hungary, let's be Russian to Turkey and…" She looked up at him. He wasn't smiling. "Okay, I know, juvenile, but when I was a kid it was funny."

"You were a kid once?"

He put the rental in gear and pulled away from the curb.

"What happened? What did you do? You know how hard it was for me to get you out of there?"

Sarah shook her head.

"Hard."

"Oh," was all she said.

"At first they said they had all these charges and then after a little scrutiny I found out they actually had nothing on you. They couldn't even find the gun they claim you stole off one of their cops last night. They had no proof but I still had to threaten to bring in American lawyers from the embassy. I explained that holding you would create an international incident. Which one of them would want to lose their jobs first, I asked them. For a minute I thought I would be arrested myself. It was Imre who relented. That immigration officer was a prick all the way. Did you do anything specific to him?"

Sarah leaned forward and pulled down the sun visor as the setting summer sun was coming straight in at her.

Parkman looked over. "What's that smell?"

"Urine."

"You piss yourself?"

"No. The prison cell was covered in piss."

"Oh. Great."

He lowered his window a little and spit the toothpick in his mouth out into the road. He looked over again. "It started to taste like piss."

"You know what piss tastes like?" She smiled.

"Glad to see you've got your humor."

"How come you're here? And why did you vouch for me?" she asked.

"Oh, hey, thanks. You know, I could've left you there."

"How could you get here so fast? It's a ten hour flight. They put me in that cell two hours ago."

"After I met with your dad I decided to come out here and find out what you were up to. I took a leave of absence. I've been in Budapest for about two weeks. It wasn't until today that I found out where you were."

"You serious?"

"Yes."

"They knew where I was the whole time."

"I don't have their resources. Remember, this isn't my jurisdiction. They aren't going to let just anyone in on their investigations because I'm a cop." He paused and looked sideways at her again. "Wait, what do you mean they knew where you were?"

"They've been watching me. They know everything about me. Even my issues with hair-pulling from years ago."

"But why? As far as anyone in Europe should know, you're just an American girl traveling within the Schengen Area. You get up to three months in the Schengen Area without a problem on your American passport."

"They've been following me and watching me, but from afar. I've been here for over a month and I just found out. They're good. Too good. I need to find out why."

"Oh no. We have to leave Budapest. Every day you stay here is ammunition for them."

Parkman turned onto a busy street, dropped the Opel into a lower gear, ground the gear and then hit the gas, shooting them forward. He eased it back into third and cruised again.

"Sorry, not used to the stick shift. Couldn't rent an automatic for the prices they were asking. At least not on my salary."

"What are you doing here? Seriously. I do appreciate being out of jail, but why come in the first place?"

"You have an uncanny ability to find trouble. I think sometimes you need backup."

"I do pretty good on my own."

"I know. But ask yourself. What would've happened if I didn't follow those leads to the compound a few months back? Your wrist was broken. You had hair missing and you were shot and bleeding."

"The hair was my doing so that doesn't count."

They stopped talking. He looked at her sideways. She avoided his gaze.

A few blocks from the hotel, Parkman pulled up at a pizza take-away joint. Hungarian pizza took some getting used to but Sarah devoured her slices without thought of quality.

"Thanks," she said.

He looked up at her and nodded.

"No, I mean thanks for being there for me. You know I appreciate it. I'm just no good at letting people know it."

He slowed his chewing and looked up at her. With a mouthful he mumbled a *you're welcome.*

Back in the car, Parkman turned away from the Best Western and drove deeper into the city center.

"Where are we going?" Sarah asked.

"To the Hotel Erzsebet. It's near the center of town, close to the popular Váci street. It's also close to the main shopping areas and near the Great Market Hall."

"What? We're tourists now and not terrorists?"

"Sarah, we have to show them that you were here for fun and to get away from the shit in America. After a day or so we will grab a flight back to the States and everything will be over. Besides, they shouldn't get all fucked up about it because you're hanging out with a cop."

"It won't be over for me."

"I know. If they really were monitoring you, then they would have the Best Western bugged better than a stakeout on the mafia while looking for Hoffa's remains."

Sarah turned to him and frowned. "What?"

"Nothing. Look, this is safer."

"Two rooms?"

"I'd have it no other way."

She saw his smile. With no toothpick in his mouth it was a rare full smile.

They checked in, got to their rooms and said goodnight. Both of them had agreed to leave the door adjoining their rooms unlocked just in case.

Exhausted, Sarah sat on the edge of her bed and stared at the television. Turning it on would've been more entertaining but she hadn't gotten around to it quite yet.

A shower was first. Then new clothes. Maybe a drink from the minibar and then sleep.

Yeah, sleep. Who knew when she'd get another full night of sleep.

Shit was getting real, and fast.

That immigration officer was coming after her. She could feel it. When the time came she would have to deal with him.

Her arm twitched.

What? No fucking way.

Her arm went numb. She stood up, grabbed the little pad of paper and pen on the desk and sat on the floor.

Then a dark mist enveloped her vision and Sarah blacked out completely.

Parkman's voice woke her.

She opened her eyes and looked around. The room was the same. The only difference was Parkman. He sat on the edge of her bed. He had the pad in his hand.

She lifted her head and then got up on one elbow.

"Wow. It's been over a month since that's happened. I forgot how debilitating it can be. It really knocks you out."

"I knocked a few times. You didn't answer. When I came in, you were just dropping this from your hand." He looked back at the paper he held. "I think you better read it."

She got up off the floor and sat on the bed beside him. He handed her the pad.

I'm sorry. I should've made contact sooner but they had a camera on you and parabolic listening devices. They were watching for contact from me. I think someone wants you for a psychic awareness government project of some kind. I'm looking into it.

Armond is in Budapest.

Tomorrow, 2:12pm, at The Great Market Hall you will see his new face by the red Ape.

Warning: It all ends at the Crypt. Only nine days left.

I'm so sorry Sarah…see you soon.

Chapter 5

The sun lit the sky with a bright purplish color as it rose on another summer morning in Budapest. Sarah had left the hotel at five in the morning while Parkman was still sleeping in his room.

They had talked for over an hour about the message from Vivian and the futility of hunting Armond. Their best course of action was to give the information to the police, so they would know where Armond was and arrest him. Killing Armond was murder and there really was no way around it.

Sarah had listened to Parkman, had considered her options. But during their conversation she came up with an altogether different plan.

Parkman went to his room and Sarah slept. Now it was close to 5:30am. She'd left their hotel and was just now approaching the Best Western.

As far as she could tell, no one was watching the entrance. With her gone their surveillance would have been pulled. She waited for fifteen minutes, watching the vehicles passing. She checked the parked cars in the area and saw they were all empty.

Time to go. She crossed the street, stepped in the front doors and made her way through the lobby to the couch where she had stashed the gun. The night staff behind the counter had nodded at her and then turned away as she was preparing coffee. No one else was in the lobby.

Sarah grabbed a newspaper that sat on a nearby table and eased herself down beside where she'd stashed the gun.

She opened the paper and began scanning the Hungarian news even though she couldn't read a damn thing.

One last look around the lobby confirmed no one present. She was completely alone.

With her right hand she reached down behind the cushion and into the back of the couch feeling around for the steel grip of the weapon.

Her fingers brushed something. A metal wire or the gun?

She lowered her shoulder as she half-turned and kept a watchful eye on the front desk. At this hour the hotel traffic was minimal which was one of the reasons she choose to leave her hotel at five in the morning.

Her fingers came into contact with the cop's gun. She wrapped her hand around the butt of the weapon and began lifting it. Using her left hand she folded the newspaper in half to use it as a shield for the gun.

In one quick movement she slid the weapon out into the open and under the cover of the newspaper.

Perfect.

In that same moment a man entered the lobby from the outside. She stared at him, waiting to see his intentions. He only had a few choices. Go to the front desk and make an inquiry or walk through to the elevators. Anything other than that and her radar would be pinging.

She stood up and then stopped. Where had she seen him before? A quick look over her shoulder and she remembered. He was the man watching English and his two gypsy friends follow her the other night. He'd tipped his hat at her.

She stepped over to another couch and sat where she could watch him.

He looked like he dropped out of the fifties. As he shuffled along toward the counter, she took in his suit and spit-polished black shoes.

His beige fedora struck her as very "Cary Grant". He looked like a 1950's FBI agent.

She waited and watched.

He made it to the main desk. The woman stepped out from a room behind the counter with a new coffee in her hand and said something in Hungarian. From where

Sarah sat watching, all she heard was a whisper of their conversation.

Fedora Man reached in his pocket and produced a wallet of some sort. He showed it to her and the woman turned from him and walked back into the room behind the counter.

Then Fedora Man spun on his heels and stared directly at Sarah.

It's on, she thought. *This guy is here for me.*

Whatever they want to do or however long they want to do it, they will never quell her desire to exact justice on Armond. All these assholes getting in her way were only distractions.

The man started walking toward her. Sarah stayed perfectly still, the newspaper folded in her lap with the cop's gun hidden under its shelter of ink.

One flip of the edge of the paper and she'd be arrested again as the incriminating weapon was now in her possession.

Yesterday they could prove nothing until they found the gun. She led them right to it. And then this ass waited until she had it in her hand to make his move.

Fedora Man stopped six feet from her, reached up and tipped his hat. Just like the other night.

"Good morning."

Sarah nodded.

"May I have a seat?"

Sarah nodded again. It was killing her. Why so polite? Why not drop the ball and get on with it? She was also surprised with herself. Maybe all the years of violence and confrontations had hardened her because she didn't feel the least bit nervous. Cops had rules they had to live by. She wasn't going to be killed or attacked. All they could ever do was talk a lot and remove her liberties, but as O.J. proved, with enough money and a good lawyer, many liberties could be returned.

He sat across from her, adjusted his jacket and leaned back into the cushioned softness of the leather couch he occupied.

If anything, Sarah was intrigued by his entrance. There was something dangerous about him because he exuded a power only serious confidence could create. This was a man who got the job done. She didn't know who he worked for but whoever it was they had someone solid here.

What he didn't know was that Sarah had more confidence. There was almost nothing he could do that would surprise her. She sat poised and ready to strike at the first movement she didn't like. He was the one who needed to be on guard. She had a weapon at the ready.

"What are you planning?"

"Excuse me?"

His English was American. She was sure of it.

"I'm a friend."

"Then explain something to me," she said.

He lowered his head enough to see he was attempting a slow-motion nod.

"Explain what?"

"How come I don't know you? I know my friends. If you're a friend, then why don't I know you on sight?"

He lifted his head and stared at her. "Not in that sense. I'll say it differently. I'm a friendly. This means—"

"I know what it means, but thanks anyway. Don't need friendlies."

"Sarah, I think you do."

Mr. Mysterious was starting to piss her off. Sarah felt her temper rising. Playing riddle man, and acting like this dance was a game, only served her a cold plate of *fuck you*. Time to draw him out.

"Either state your business or fuck off. I've got some touring of the city to do before my flight back to the States."

"You're not going back to the States."

"Okay, the only way you could know my personal agenda is if you're some kind of God. Since you're not, then you've got a pair a balls the size of Texas. Either tell me your business or I'm leaving, Fedora Man."

He brought his hands together and tented them in front of his chest. He appeared to be contemplating what to tell her and what to leave out.

"Okay, Sarah, you win. My name is Rod Howley. I'm with the Sophia Project out of the University of Arizona."

"Come again? What's that?"

"One of our main purposes is to investigate the experiences of people who claim to channel or communicate with deceased loved ones. Our ultimate goal is to investigate if these communications can be validated under controlled conditions."

Sarah had never heard of them before. Having spent a considerable amount of time with Dolan Ryan and Esmerelda she thought she would've heard of the Sophia Project. From her high school studies she knew the name Sophia meant *wisdom*, but that was the extent of it.

"I've never heard of you or your little group. But the important question is, why tell me?"

She knew why. They had to have gotten wind of what she'd been doing for the last five years or so and wanted to learn more from her. The proper words here were, *use her as a guinea pig*. But their timing couldn't be worse. This was no time to be hanging around doing psychic tests while Armond was on the loose, even if she wanted to. The only way anyone would get Sarah and Vivian to perform like circus psychics was if they forced her and forcing Sarah to do anything would be a trying task.

"Sarah, we both know why I'm sitting here. You're a very active girl. As I understand it, Vivian gives you messages and you act on them for the good of humanity. Very noble of you. But this latest job has crossed the line. We need to talk, find a resolution and continue your mission with more control involved."

This guy knew more than she was comfortable with. Tossing Vivian's name in to subtly display his knowledge only pissed her off further. He talked about her dead sister like she was a card being played in this game of chess he started as he strategically placed himself near a check-mate.

Wrong move asshole.

"Unless you say something to convince me to continue talking to you, I am going to stand up and walk out of here. Try to stop me. Please do. I usually wait for provocation."

He untented his hands and showed her his palms. "I'm sorry. I can see I'm upsetting you. That wasn't my goal."

He paused to remove his hat. Sarah took the opportunity to scan the lobby. It remained empty as the clock behind the counter said it was coming on six in the morning. The female hotel clerk was nowhere to be seen.

"Sarah, Parapsychology research—"

"Stop using my name so freely. I don't know you. You don't know me. We're strangers. It will remain that way."

"Okay, I'm sorry."

She could tell that was hard on him. There was something peculiar about this man. He looked like a caged raccoon. Seemingly innocent enough but get too close and he'll attack. She decided to listen a little longer. She wasn't psychic in the traditional sense but she could tell when someone was on the edge of a fight and Fedora Man really wanted to do some damage. It oozed off his skin. He didn't seem comfortable sitting and discussing things. It made her think he was an interrogator and not an explainer.

"Parapsychology research is conducted in over thirty countries worldwide. The term parapsychology was first coined in or around 1889 by philosopher Max Dessoir."

"Why the history lesson? Under other circumstances I love to learn new things but you walk in here, use my name and say you're a friend. I ask for you to tell me what's going on and you're giving me a history lesson. Time is running out."

"Fair enough. Do you expect me to take you seriously Sarah?"

Her finger itched to slide into the trigger guard of the weapon that still lay concealed on her lap. *I'll show you just how serious I can be,* she thought.

"Absolutely. My sense of humor is like a court jester. Not seen much anymore, but when it does come around we all laugh. Today I'm serious and you should be aware that serious, by definition, actually means dangerous."

"Then I expect you to take me seriously too. I only have a few more things to say and then you can decide."

"Decide what?"

"Decide whether or not you will accompany me back to America where we will really do some good."

She leaned forward slightly. "Are you saying that I'm not doing good on my own?"

"The direction this conversation is going isn't good. Will you allow me to continue? I only need a minute more."

Sarah leaned back and sized him up. He was American. He held no authority in Hungary. She had the gun. He only wanted to talk. She wanted to know more about the man who seemed to know a shit load about her.

She nodded for him to go ahead and then scanned the lobby again. No one around. They'd been talking for a few minutes now and no one had entered the lobby. She was starting to find that strange. If someone didn't come through any door soon, she felt the rope of the noose would tighten.

"The Society for Psychical Research was founded in London in 1882. The American Society for Psychical Research followed suit and opened their doors in New York City in 1885. By 1911 Stanford University became the first academic institution in the United States to study extrasensory perception, better known as ESP. Finally, in 1930, Duke University followed."

He stopped to gauge her response. She offered nothing so he continued.

"My organization usually has volunteers but sometimes we search out people who we have heard of. People who display a talent far beyond usual parameters."

"Your organization? You mean the Sophia Project?"

Sarah looked behind him. No one in the lobby at all. The noose tightened. Something was wrong. She had to leave.

"Sort of."

Sort of? What the fuck is that? He just said he was with the Sophia Project but now he's sort of with them?

"You might want to qualify that comment. Do it quick. I'm about to leave."

"I'm actually employed by the United States Government. My organization works in conjunction with the people at the University of Arizona."

"So you're not actually with this Sophia Project?"

"My employer is the government. I am employed to work with the people at the Sophia Project. Let's just say I'm their recruiter."

"While you talk in circles I'm leaving. Rarely do I meet someone who is so full of shit that they've lost sight of the piss they spew." She paused for a second and wondered if he was armed. As a recruiter was he supposed to take her in? There could be no time for surprises. Not today. "Stand up."

"You're making a mistake. I'm the only friend you've got."

"Wrong thing to say. Stand up. Last chance."

To his credit he took her seriously.

"Now step away from me."

She didn't even need to show him her weapon. He complied without protest.

Once he was over ten feet away Sarah stood and folded the newspaper and its concealed weapon under her left arm giving it easy access for her right hand.

"You are making a mistake. It will be much harder for us to talk when you're in a jail cell. I also would find it difficult to get you back to the States once incarcerated."

"Wow, you've got big plans for me. Remind me again, who put you in charge?"

"Sarah, this is your last chance. Listen to me. Come with me. Your life will get a lot easier. Defy me, and your life will not only become more difficult, it will become unbearable in a short while."

She dropped the newspaper and pulled the gun out, flicking the safety off in less than a second. It was so fast that Fedora Man stepped back.

"You want to threaten me? Threats only anger me. Is that your goal? To anger me? Don't make me angry Mr. Howley, you wouldn't like me when I'm angry."

He slowly raised both hands, keeping his eyes on the weapon.

"Sarah, you will have no choice soon. I'm a recruiter. It's what I do. I'm here to recruit you with or without your consent. I thought we could be civil about it."

Her peripheral vision told her the lobby just filled up. She took a step to the right and angled herself to be able to see the front desk without taking her eyes off him.

Seven men, all dressed in suits had emerged from numerous parts of the lobby of the Best Western. They looked the same like cops in uniforms except these men all wore suits, stood with their arms crossed in front of them and they all had slicked back hair.

"What the fuck is this? A Brylcreem convention or are you all just fuck buddies?"

Everything made sense now. These men were the reason no one had entered the lobby. Mr. Rod Howley had come with backup.

Without waiting for a response, Sarah stepped toward Rod.

"I should shoot you in the foot to see how well you follow me after that."

"Do it and more like me will come. Eventually you will have to come with us. You can't continue this way. It's too dangerous."

She got close enough to place the tip of the weapon under his chin.

"Tell that to the people I've saved over the years. Tell them it's too dangerous that I'm out there helping people. Bullshit. Who are you to tell me I'm too dangerous?"

"Examine your current behavior."

She dropped the weapon and leaned in with her elbow all in one easy motion. Her elbow slammed into his left ear with enough power to double him over. As she righted her arm, she brought the weapon up to aim in the general direction of all the men standing twenty feet away near the main desk of the lobby.

"Please, someone pull out a weapon. Do it! Let's all show Mr. Howley here how dangerous people can be when they're cornered. When the odds are overwhelmingly against them and they're told that they must succumb to the wishes of a complete stranger who happens to know too much about them." Her teeth were clenched and she felt spittle shoot through them.

All seven men stood statue still. Anyone could see how angry she was and no one felt sure enough to challenge her.

Rod was standing straight again, holding his ear. "Okay Sarah, you win. Today you get a free pass."

She edged around him and started for the front. As she neared the men, they moved away from her, their backs to the elevator hallway. When she got to the front exit door she scanned the outside. Another man in a suit stood with his arms crossed holding back six people with luggage.

These men had successfully cordoned off the entire lobby of the Best Western hotel, downtown Budapest, so that Rod could talk to her. How powerful were these men? Better yet, *who* were they?

She looked back at Rod and lowered her weapon to ease it into the back of her pants.

"This doesn't end here," she said. "I will find out who you are and what you're up to. I'm not the hunted, I'm the hunter."

"You're wrong Sarah."

She touched the door handle and cracked the door a little.

"How's that?" she asked.

"We are coming for you. You cannot hide from us. I was supposed to try to convince you to come willingly but now I can see that that will never happen. Our next directive was to take you by force. But not now. We'll wait. We'll watch. And when you're not expecting it, we'll be there. And we will take you Sarah Roberts. There is nothing you can do about it. You are now property of the United States government."

She almost pulled her gun out and shot him in the face for that last bit. Instead she lowered her head and said, loud enough for all the hired gorillas to hear:

"I will bury you first."

She eased the door open, slipped through and walked past the man holding people back. To make sure she wasn't being followed, she kept looking over her shoulder.

Rod stepped out onto the pavement and watched her go.

She turned a corner and walked out of sight.

A small park came up on the right. She walked to the open gates, stepped in and sat on one of the benches where she put her face in her palms and wept.

Fear motivated her. Threats inspired her to action. But this was different. Those men meant what they said. She was in real danger.

Real danger scared her.

For one of the first times in her life, Sarah was seriously afraid.

She wept as if her emotional side opened a dam and released all the pent up sadness at what her life had become.

She needed to be held. Her mother would be good, but maybe it was time for a man. Someone strong who could take care of her in her weaker moments.

Sarah hugged herself and shuddered under the pressure of her tears.

THE CRYPT

JONAS SAUL

Chapter 6

At nine in the morning Sarah entered a pharmacy that was just opening its doors. In less than ten minutes she'd accumulated everything she needed.

By nine-thirty she had found a hostel-like hotel that would allow her to rent a room for the night. The room was ready so she settled in right away. In the bathroom she applied the brown hair color she'd bought and began the grueling task of dying her blond hair.

After rinsing it all out in the shower she tied her hair into two braids that hung over each shoulder.

She studied her new look in the mirror. With the hair so vastly changed from the old layered blond that fell past her shoulders to two brown braids that resembled a young Laura Ingalls from Little House on the Prairie, Sarah was confident that no one would recognize her. At least not at first look.

She applied eyeliner and eyeshadow to her eyes, adding a small black line on the outside of each eye to make them appear longer and thinner. After the mascara she stood back and stared again.

Perfect. No one will recognize me.

She stepped back into the room and checked the time. Just after twelve noon. She grabbed her passport and the gun, checked that its safety was on and left the room. A few doors down from her room she stopped at the fire extinguisher that sat embedded in a recess in the wall. With a glance both ways to make sure no one was watching, Sarah reached in behind the extinguisher and set her passport completely out of sight. Unless there was a fire in the building in the next twenty four hours no one would find her passport.

After a lunch of french fries and a Coke, (they'd offered mayonnaise for the fries but she declined), Sarah started for the Great Market Hall to meet Armond Stuart by "the red Ape".

She'd been there before. In the first four weeks of living in downtown Budapest with no contact from Vivian and nothing to do, she had explored the area. She'd been to the castle district, the Citadel, rode their buses and shopped in some of the walking streets. She'd learned that Saint Stephen founded Hungary in the year 1000 AD and that the Parliament buildings were some of the prettiest structures made by mankind.

In that time she had ridden the tram to the Great Market Hall a couple of times. The market held over two hundred stalls - she had ambled through and had lunch there, enjoying goulash the way it was supposed to be prepared.

But today was different.

Today she was armed. Armond Stuart would be there. She would find him by "the red Ape", whatever that meant. No doubt Parkman would show as he'd read the note too. He'd asked what the hell a "red Ape" was but she had no idea. He'd be pissed that she didn't tell him where she was going this morning. She knew it wasn't fair. After all he'd done she should have at least left him a note.

Would the Sophia Project guys be there? Is that where they'd try to apprehend her? Could they really exercise that kind of power? Even in a foreign country?

She shook the thought off, as it only served to unsettle her. She needed to concentrate. She needed to stay focused and not worry about men in business suits, fedora hats and globs of gel in their hair. They'd come when they came and she would deal with it then.

The sun beat down on her as she walked. Another cloudless day in lovely Budapest, Hungary. And another body murdered.

Armond Stuart, I'm coming for you.

But could she do it? Would she do it? Back to that debate. Was it murder when he was just standing there? How about when he was just standing there in the Mormon Temple a few months back? Would it have been murder then? His female victims were being held captive. Armond was waiting for the right price before he'd sell those innocent teenage girls into sex slavery. He shot Sarah that day. Why can't she just shoot him back? Make it even. She'd be the better shot. Once Armond was dead no more little girls could be kidnapped, shipped overseas and sold to horny old men.

Once Armond was dead the world would be a better place.

Besides, it was her duty. If she wasn't supposed to do it then why would Vivian send her to the Great Market Hall? Why tell her where Armond would be in the first place? Why not abandon this and start saving people's lives again? If she wasn't supposed to kill Armond, then why was she here?

She got close to the front doors, looked in the reflection of a large window, saw nothing of interest and then entered the Hall.

For a Thursday the market was busy. She edged to the side of the hall and began walking the length of the tables. People shouted back and forth in Hungarian. Young and old bustled about carrying their items and searching for more, always looking for a better deal. The smell of food assailed her nose.

What a place to hold a murder. There would be too many witnesses. Sarah knew she would have to follow Armond outside and wait for the right opportunity.

In the meantime she had to stay on the lookout for too many things. First she had to find a gorilla. The note said that Armond would be by "the red Ape" at 2:12pm. She also had to watch for Parkman. If he saw her first, he would be the only one who could easily see through her new look. He'd studied her for years. He would know the curve of her face, her gait as she walked. Although he was the only cop she trusted, he was also the one who would try to stop her if she got the chance to execute the vermin. Keeping him at a distance around 2:12pm today was better for the both of them.

The only other people to watch for would be the American government men and the Hungarian police, although no one could predict where she'd be this afternoon. It was unlikely anyone other than Parkman would show.

Unless he woke up, saw she was gone and called in the police to help find her. Or told them where she'd be at 2:12pm today?

He wouldn't do that, she assured herself. *Not Parkman. Not after all they'd been through? Never.*

Sarah had walked to the middle of the Market Hall and seen no Ape of any kind, let alone a red one.

She continued on. Maybe it was at a booth? Or along another section.

Wherever it was, Sarah knew that "the red Ape" was here. Vivian wouldn't send her on a wild goose chase.

A clock on the wall said it was getting close to 2:00pm. She was running out of time.

Another check behind her. No one seemed to be following or monitoring her in any way. Everything was going perfectly. She just had to find the Ape.

In five minutes she'd reached the end of the hall. There had been no ape. She turned around and began half-running up and down the side aisles looking at all the signs on the various shops, searching for anything resembling an ape.

Nothing.

Maybe it was upstairs?

She took the closest staircase and ran up. A quick three minute scan revealed no apes.

She was out of time and out of luck.

She ran back downstairs and looked for a clock. She found one by the exit to Pipa utca.

2:14pm.

He was gone.

I fucked up. Somehow I missed the fucking red Ape.

Nothing pissed her off more than getting a message from Vivian and then not executing it properly. She'd done it before. Four years ago when she started getting the dark visions she'd screwed up a message about the *north face*. It ended up getting her kidnapped and almost killed. Last year she'd gotten a message of exactly where Armond Stuart was. When she nabbed him he identified himself as a retired police officer named Jack Tate. It was true. He used to be a cop. His name was Jack Tate then. She believed him and he led her into his trap and almost killed her again.

And now she had another message and she completely just danced around the Great Market Hall and fucked the goose on it.

"Damn!" she slapped the wall beside the exit door. People had been coming in. Two doors were wide open when she exclaimed. People in the street looked her way. Sarah looked at them.

A red three-wheeled vehicle sat parked at an odd angle on the sidewalk just outside the door. On the side of the vehicle it said in English *Street Coffee*. It looked like a miniature UPS truck but red and the back door lifted straight up above the rear of the small truck displaying the menu and prices of this mobile coffee shop. There was one wheel in the front of the vehicle and two in the rear. It was an Italian model. An automobile they call an *Ape* and it was red.

She couldn't believe it. A vehicle had been the furthest thing from her mind when looking for a red Ape. She had thought gorilla. Couldn't Vivian be more specific?

Four men stood around it with coffee cups in their hands. The seller of the coffee was off to the side wearing an apron and tending to a machine of some kind.

The doors closed in front of her. Three of the men turned away and starting talking again.

Sarah didn't waver. She stared long enough to see that the man who was staring back at her was Armond Stuart.

There could be no doubt. He was the same height, about the same weight and build but his face was slightly different and his hair had been chopped to a military buzz cut. There was a new scar that traversed the side of his jaw. His nose looked different but it was his eyes that told her she'd found the right man.

She'd looked into those eyes before. She'd seen the evil in them and now she watched as they widened. He was just realizing who she was.

The moment had come. Her stomach turned as adrenaline secreted throughout her body. She hadn't moved. Her hand still rested on the wall. She leaned in closer, resting her shoulder against the brick. Her right hand had to remain free and clear. The gun was close. In under two seconds Armond could have a bullet in either eye, his brain nothing but mashed squash.

The three men around him were dressed in suits. Not the American government kind. More of a professional bodyguard kind. Armond wasn't playing games anymore. He was getting more serious about staying alive as probably hundreds of people, including many police forces, were hunting him.

Armond's mouth moved. He whispered something to his men. Just like a slow-motion scene in a movie, all three men turned toward her very slowly.

Hungarians hustled by, bags in their arms, opening and closing the doors as Sarah and the four men watched each other, neither one making a move.

Her hatred for him continually screamed at her to attack. Her rational side explained the futility of it. If she were to draw her weapon and begin shooting, Armond's bodyguards would do the same. Could she survive such an assault? How many witnesses would there be? Was this one man her end goal? Kill him and she could die too? Was that all that mattered? Vivian had said something about seeing his new face. Maybe that was all this was supposed to be?

Maybe, but no, she didn't want to die nor did she want to spend the rest of her life in a Hungarian prison for murder. Armond would have stolen the life of another girl if that happened.

In the half a minute they stared at each other Sarah realized that today was not a good day to kill him.

She eased off the wall and slowly stepped through the door toward them. They all continued to stare at her. Two of the guards reached inside their jackets, no doubt to caress the butts of their weapons.

She stopped about seven feet from the foursome. It felt like the world stopped around them as the tension rose.

She stared at him as hard as she could, memorizing every facial expression, every dimple, every eye movement.

"You're looking good, Sarah," Armond said.

She didn't respond. The two brutes lifted their arms out in unison, both holding a small compact piece.

"Can't fight your own battles?" Sarah asked.

"Sarah, Sarah, Sarah," he said while shaking his head back and forth. "You are one seriously hard person to kill. I swear, if the world experienced nuclear war, you and the cockroaches would survive along with those scorpions and beetles or whatever the fuck. But now things have changed."

"How so?"

She felt her anger rising past controllability. Her mind raced across possible scenarios. *Draw their fire. Shoot in self-defense. Kill Armond and walk away after an investigation. Try to execute the guards too. Vermin needed to die. That's my job.*

"For many reasons. You've seen my face. The time and money I spent on it has now been wasted. Also, you're in Hungary. That tells me that you've traveled a long way to hunt me down. You're becoming a nuisance. You and Vivian have to go. And I've now realized something else."

"What's that?"

She stood in the mid-afternoon sun, listening to her sister's murderer and with the control of a thousand men, refrained from diving for his throat and strangling him to a fucking bloody pulp. She had no idea where her self-control came from, only that she despised rules. The rules that stopped her. Even though she knew he was a psychopath and he was responsible for many ruined lives, she couldn't throttle him to a mass of blood and skin.

"I've realized that nothing I do will ever stop you. I cannot continue my business until you're dead. You're like a fucking Jack-in-the-box. You keep popping up. How did you know where to find me? Vivian? Of course, *how* could you know without her? And since I can't stop her because she's already dead, I have to kill you. Oh, and by the way, I know your sister is dead because I killed her myself. But, we both know that."

She knew he was goading her to make a move. Taunting her like a carrot to a horse. Her fingers twitched. One bullet. It would be done. She was tough. She could handle prison.

One bullet.

In the second she decided to kill him, she reached back for her weapon.

Her hand was behind her back, gripping the butt of the police gun she'd stolen two nights ago. She lifted it out of her pants. In that second, the two guards who already had weapons in their hands lifted theirs up to aim at Sarah.

She didn't care. This was it. The end. This was her mission after all.

She pulled the gun free and went to bring it around.

Then her hand went instantly numb.

A blackout was coming.

"No!" she shouted.

Her arm went numb. The gun fell from her grasp and hit the pavement. She met the concrete a second later.

Then it was over. The blackout lasted two seconds.

She looked up. Both guards had lowered their weapons. Perceiving no threat they had decided to not fire.

"Well done Sarah. You really know how to scare people. What was that? Why did you fall? Got brain cancer or something? Epileptic?"

She grabbed the gun that lay on the ground beside her and stood up, jamming the weapon back in her pants. It was obvious that Vivian didn't want her to shoot anyone today. Vivian had taken control of her body at the exact moment she had planned on using the weapon thereby telling her not to. There was no written message to receive. Only one of body language.

It also told Sarah something else. Vivian had control of her body and could exact that control at any time. That kind of power over her wasn't good for Sarah. Using her for messages was one thing. Taking her body over to stop her from doing something was another thing altogether.

"There will be another day. You and I will have our moment," Sarah said.

"I'm sure we will."

Someone grabbed her arm from behind.

Sarah instantly turned, clamped her left hand on the person's wrist and used her right to grab the elbow. In the second before she rammed the person's elbow straight up, breaking it in half, she realized that the person was Parkman.

"Let's go. We're finished here."

He pulled her away. She went willingly.

"What were you doing? I saw you from thirty feet away. You reached for your gun and then fell down. I thought they'd shot you. What the hell were you doing?"

"Vivian interrupted me."

"What? How is that possible?"

"The same thing happens when she gives me a message. My hands go numb and then I fall. When I reached for my gun, she did that."

"To stop you?"

Sarah nodded her head as she turned around and looked behind her. Armond and his bodyguards had disappeared.

"Who were all those men in suits?" Parkman asked.

"They're his bodyguards."

"No, I didn't mean the three guys standing with Armond. I was talking about the ten men standing beside three black Cadillac Escalades across the street. When you reached for your weapon and then fell, all ten of those men pulled out some kind of weapon of their own and took up position around Armond and his men. Before the bodyguards even lifted their guns, these men had them in their sights. A major gun battle came within one second of happening. The only thing that saved everyone's life was when Armond's guards dropped their weapons. The ten men in suits lowered theirs and stepped back."

Sarah was stunned. She turned around again. No one was in sight. No men in suits. No Armond. No bodyguards. No Escalades. Only regular people shopping for fruit and vegetables.

"Do you know who they were?" Parkman prodded.

"It was weird. They all wore beige fedoras."

"Those men are with the American government. I think you and I need to talk, Parkman. I'm in some kind of trouble."

Chapter 7

Parkman got Sarah back to the Hotel Erzsebet where he'd rented the room for another night. It was already going on 3:15pm.

"We can't stay here," Sarah said.

"Why not?" Parkman asked. He was in the act of unpacking something from his small suitcase, a toothpick in his mouth again. "They think we're leaving today. In the morning we can go to the airport. This evening both of us can give Imre a statement of what happened at the Market Hall. Let him and his men hunt Armond down. He's connected. Imre can get our description out to other agencies."

"You've used a credit card to reserve this room. Everyone will know where we are, including Armond. The Hungarian authorities have asked us to leave the country by today. When we don't leave they will want to know why. Sure we can surrender a statement but they're going to want to know how we knew where Armond was in the first place. They may think it suspicious considering they already think that it's my sole purpose in being here. Therefore, in order to figure this all out and stay under the radar we need to get out of here. No surprises. By staying here we could be the ones surprised and you know I hate that."

"Okay, where do you suggest we go?"

"I've rented a room several blocks from here."

Parkman looked at her. "When did you do that?"

"This morning. So I could do this," she said as she used both hands to wave past her braided hair.

Parkman turned back to his suitcase and started moving things around to pack the rest of his belongings.

"Okay. You're right. We leave in five minutes. We should go out the back door and catch a cab behind the building or on another street. No doubt someone is already watching the front."

Sarah turned away and used the adjoining door to access her room.

"There's something else that disturbs me about this morning," she shouted through the open door.

"What's that?" Parkman replied.

"If those American government men found me so easily that they could position themselves where they did in such an advantageous place, where were the Hungarian authorities? You and I were there because of Vivian's note. Armond and his men were there as Vivian said they would be. But no cops were present. Only the Sophia Project people. Why no cops?"

Parkman stepped into the doorframe. "Sophia Project?"

"We'll talk more about it on the way. But answer me that. Why no cops? You're a cop. Is there an American government agency that could have the kind of power to supersede another country's police force? Or are these government men just that good? Because if they are, and if they followed me to that street behind the Market, then they are *really* good. And I mean really good. That kind of good unsettles me."

Parkman stepped closer. "They scared me too and I've been a cop a long time. But don't worry. We'll look into this and find out what their mandate is. America's a free country. It isn't State run. We never bought into the Communist Manifesto. Karl Marx left his stamp in other parts of the world. Not in America. So you're a free girl right now. You really have nothing to worry about."

Sarah grabbed her bags, set them on the floor by the door and looked up at Parkman.

"I understand what you're saying but I think you're wrong here. These men are powerful. The last thing the guy said to me was that I was now property of the United States Government. That was why they were there this morning. They can't afford to have me killed. They need me for something. I think they want to do tests on me. They're watching. They won't let this go."

Parkman stared at her a moment. "Okay. I trust your instincts. You're rarely wrong on this sort of thing. But tell me, how are you with leaving Armond behind?"

"What are you talking about?"

"Leaving him for the authorities to pick up. Walking away. Going home, back to the States. Are you okay with that?"

Sarah nodded. "Sure. I almost shot him in broad daylight today right beside a shopping area. People were coming and going. If it wasn't for Vivian I would've shot him and he would've killed another girl. Me." She looked away, reached down and grabbed her bags and spoke again. "Yeah, I'm ready to leave it behind. He'll be caught soon enough. My goal is helping people. Not being goaded into murder. If there was provocation I would've killed him, but there wasn't. I'm not like him. I don't want to be. I think…"

"Are you trying to convince me or yourself?"

Sarah opened the door and stepped into the hallway.

Two large men in suits grabbed her and shoved her back into her room with such force she lifted off the ground and landed by the foot of the bed seven feet away.

She heard Parkman yell something. Dazed, she shook her head and tried to stand.

Her vision blurred even as her mind was yelling *get up and fight*. She rested her head back down and tried to take in the room.

Parkman looked unconscious. She saw his shoes as he was being dragged from the room. More men than she could count stood in the doorway.

Then the hotel room door slammed shut.

She was alone.

Her neck ached.

What the hell is wrong with my neck?

She reached up to feel around but her arm felt like a chunk of lead. She finally got it to her neck and felt the end of a needle sticking out.

Drugged!

Her thoughts grew more fuzzy. Her eyes closed.

Her arm dropped at an odd angle as Sarah fell into an anesthetized sleep on the floor of her hotel room.

Chapter 8

Consciousness came back slowly. She wavered in and out and then reality seeped in and she recalled what had happened. She sat up too fast gasping for breath. Her head spun a little, the room tilting.

"Parkman? You here? Parkman?"

She eased up off the floor and sat on the edge of the bed. Aches and pains were evident everywhere. Her right arm was sore as it had been bent back while she slept.

What happened to Parkman? Who were those men?

She couldn't tell. She hadn't gotten a good look at them. They wore suits. Well dressed for sure. Strong, too.

She looked at the door to her room and then where she sat now on the edge of the bed. At least seven feet. Happy that nothing broke, she twisted her upper body back and forth to loosen her cramped muscles.

Needle. Drugged.

Shit.

She reached up and gingerly felt around her neck. The needle was still there. She eased it out slowly. Examining it revealed nothing to her other than it was shaped like a dart. There was no way to discover what had been in it without the aid of a laboratory.

Sarah tossed it into a corner and stood up. Her head was a little woozy, causing her to waver on her feet.

She looked into Parkman's room. His suitcase sat on the end of his bed.

"Parkman?"

The early evening sun beat in through the window. There was still daylight.

She started for the open adjoining door and glanced at the alarm clock on the side of her bed.

7:15pm.

Shit, I've been out for four hours. Anything could've happened. What the fuck did they drug me with? That shit fucking pisses me off.

Parkman was gone. There was no sign that anyone had been there since the kidnapping.

Why take Parkman? He wasn't a threat. If anyone should be prone to kidnappings it was Sarah. She'd been taken twice in the last four to five years. Both times by people determined to kill her. Both times she got away, and her kidnappers were all dead.

Except for Armond Stuart. He was behind everything from the start. So it stood to reason that Parkman was taken by Armond's men. Big strong bodyguards. Strong enough to throw Sarah over seven feet.

Unless it was the Sophia Project men. Although, were they really with the University of Arizona? Could that be possible after what Parkman witnessed yesterday? They had weapons. They were about to attack Armond and his men. Or maybe the Sophia shit was a ruse and they were really just government workers looking for a real psychic to add to some kind of war machine.

Parkman saw them yesterday. Parkman worked with Sarah. He knew Sarah better than even her own parents when it came to the psychic stuff. He'd researched her extensively and worked with her over a month ago, following her clues from Vivian to save Sarah's life. Parkman was the only cop she trusted.

That's why they took him. He added himself to the mix when he came for me and the agency men want to learn more about his motives. Parkman could be in some real trouble.

She turned away from his room and spoke out loud. "Vivian. You gotta help me here. This is getting scary and you know it takes a lot to get me scared. What's happened to Parkman? What's my next step? Where do we go from here?"

Nothing.

Her arm didn't go numb. She received no response.

Maybe someone was already bugging the room?

She had to get to the hostel. There she was sure Vivian would talk to her.

Sarah grabbed her gun, slid it into the back of her jeans and headed for the door. She decided to leave everything behind as Parkman had said the room was paid for another night.

She eased the door open slowly. No one was in the hallway. She stepped out and walked past the elevators to the stairwell.

Sarah got downstairs and out the side door without trouble. She skipped around the building and started for the hostel. As often as she could she would stop and look in the windows of stores looking for a follower in the reflection. After all she had learned, and the skills she had acquired over the last five years, she could tell no one was following her. If anyone was, then they were either the best in the business or they had bugged her person somehow.

Her muscles felt better. Everything was acting normal again and her head had cleared. She kept walking as her stomach growled.

When was the last time I ate anything?

She couldn't recall. She stopped at a street vendor and bought a small container of french fries and a Coke for energy. She ate them dry as she didn't want any mayonnaise.

The fifteen minutes it took to order the fries and eat them gave her another chance to watch everyone passing by. No one appeared interested in her whatsoever.

Yet she still felt watched.

Twenty minutes later she walked into her rented room at the hostel and lay out on the bed. In the night table beside the bed she found a pen and paper. Sarah pulled them out and placed them by her hand.

"Come on Vivian. Give me something."

It was around eight in the evening. As far as she could tell, no one knew where she was or where she would turn up next. This was a great opportunity for Vivian to work her magic.

As if on cue her hand grew numb.

Sarah closed her eyes and rested, waiting to wake and have Vivian tell her exactly what to do.

The sun was lower when she woke. She could tell by the amount of light in her room.

Vivian, she thought.

Sarah sat up fast and grabbed the piece of paper. It was riddled with her handwriting this time. The message was scrolled across two full pages.

Nothing about Parkman. Most of the note was about the immigration officer that worked with Imre. She'd never forget his knowing smile. Now she knew what he knew and who he was. Vivian's note went on to say that the immigration officer was the one who ordered her jailed. He was the smug bastard who thought he had the upper hand.

According to Vivian he was also the one who facilitated Armond's entry into Hungary without a problem. Vivian explained how much of a crook the immigration officer was and how to deal with him if she was going to get to Armond.

The note also went into detail about one of the immigration officer's neighbors. Sarah had to read that part twice.

The bastard. The neighbor should die for that too, she thought. *In a few hours I'll make sure both of these men pay a dear price for what they've done.*

At the bottom of the second page the note talked about a final date for Sarah.

The crypt. Eight days left. I'm sorry but there's nothing we can do to avoid it. You only have eight days left.

It has to do with vampires.

What the hell was that? Is this some kind of fiction story now? Her life wasn't a book or a movie. This was real. Vampires weren't.

The "eight days" thing scared her. Was Vivian telling her that she was going to die?

Vivian had been right all along. She also said that dealing with the immigration officer would get her one step closer to Armond. If that was the case, then she would get her vengeance and if there was nothing she could do to avoid this crypt thing, then so be it. Armond Stuart was her priority.

If only she could handle that without being killed.

And what the hell is this "vampire" business?

Chapter 9

Sarah stood outside the immigration officer's apartment building in the fifth district. It was close to midnight. At the late hour the streets were pretty empty. She was well rested as she'd spent four hours sleeping a drugged sleep and about a half hour at the hostel knocked out while writing the note.

Now, with real purpose again, something to do, she walked around the building twice, looking for a way in and attempting to see if anyone had been following her.

Surely she was being paranoid. But with so many new people in the mix lately, things could get out of hand rather quickly.

The front door was like any American building with a buzzer and locked access. With no way to get in she sat back and waited for someone to walk out of the building.

For tonight she had tied her hair into a pony tail to keep it out of the way. Things were going to get serious and she didn't want to have to think about it.

A man, she guessed he was in his forties, approached the door wobbling along. He appeared from the distance to be quite intoxicated. Sarah was surprised he could even stay on his feet.

"How was your evening?" she asked as he drew near.

He stopped and looked at her. "Who wants to know?"

"You look like you had a great time." She was grateful he knew English. While she had expected *some* people in Hungary to speak it, her experience so far in Budapest was that almost everyone she encountered spoke passable to great English.

"*Kurva eletbe.* A fine night."

Sarah had been there long enough to know that he said something like *fucking good* or *bitching good* in Hungarian.

The man passed her and took out his keys. He looked over his shoulder and then opened the door.

"You want in?" he asked.

Sarah stood up. "Yeah, forgot my key."

"Bullshit. You don't live here." He looked her up and down. Then he smiled a crooked smile and said. "Gonna cost you."

It would be nice if some things in life were easy, Sarah thought.

"What do you want? Money? Booze?"

"No. Half hour of your time in my apartment." He stepped into the lobby and held the door for her. "How about it, Miss America?"

"I don't think so."

Sarah stepped forward and made to enter the building. The drunkard pulled on the door at the same time. With the alcohol working in his system he didn't have his normal strength. Sarah easily stopped the door from closing and stepped inside.

"Hey!" he shouted.

She pulled out her gun and held it up under his chin.

"Stay quiet or die."

The threat worked. He stumbled back and leaned against the wall. Instantly a wet spot began forming on the front of his jeans.

"I was only kidding."

"Me too. But now you can do me a favor."

She lowered the weapon and gently eased it back into her pants at the back.

"Anything," he said, suddenly a lot more sober.

"Call the police. Tell them you were threatened by a girl with a gun in the lobby. Also tell them that I will be on the third floor."

"What? You want me to *call* the police on you? Why should I do that?"

"Because I need you to. Will you do it?"

The light was dim in the lobby. She could tell he was thinking it over. He stared at her a moment longer. Time was running out. She needed to get this done.

"Well?" She asked.

"Should I let them know what apartment?"

"By the time they get here they'll know."

"How?" he asked.

"There'll be gunfire by then." She turned and ran for the stairs. "The whole building will know soon enough."

Sarah reached the third floor and scouted out apartment 303. She wanted to know where the neighbor's apartment was before knocking on the immigration guy's door. She continued down to 306 and stopped in front.

Gently she placed an ear against the door to listen. She heard nothing but that didn't matter. According to Vivian, he would be home.

Her stomach didn't protest. Her nerves were firing in time. She marveled at how acclimated her body had grown over the years after having dealt with so much. Maybe she had finally become desensitized to conflict? If that was the case, then she could approach fights and battles like the one she was about to have with wit and thought, not actions based on fear.

She tried the door knob. Locked.

Of course.

After a look both ways Sarah knocked on the door and waited off to the side.

After about ten seconds she knocked again, this time harder.

A soft, subtle sound came to her from behind the door. Then a voice asked, "Ki az?"

Who is it?

Your judge and jury, motherfucker.

She knocked again, hoping this time he would crack the door a little to see who was bothering him at this late hour.

As soon as she heard the bolt click open and saw the knob turn, Sarah jumped in front of the door and charged as hard as she could. Her shoulder hit it the second it moved inward an inch.

The door shot open hard, breaking the cheap chain it was connected to and smacking into the immigration officer's shoulder. He stumbled back, hit the wall and slumped to the floor as the door finished its arc.

Sarah maintained her balance and pulled her weapon out. She aimed it at the corrupt officer and motioned for him to get up.

He looked up at her from the floor while reaching to rub his shoulder. The look on his face told her everything. He'd moved beyond anger and into rage but he was also seriously surprised to see her.

"What are you doing here?" he asked.

"Get on your feet. If you don't listen to me you will have to answer to my little friend here." She turned the gun sideways to show him her friend. "What is your name?" she asked.

"István."

He rolled to his side and got up using the wall for support.

"Take a seat at the kitchen table."

He followed her instructions and moved deeper into his apartment. The whole while Sarah kept her weapon trained on his midsection.

"What is this all about?" he asked.

Sarah didn't respond. She was trying to assess how much time she would have. Would the drunk call the police? If he did, how much longer before they arrived?

István sat down and looked up at her.

"I asked you a question."

His voice was more adamant. If he'd been sleeping he was awake now and assuming his role as interrogator. He expected an answer. He was used to this kind of exchange as this was a part of his job.

It was time to unsettle him and in doing so she would effectively get the police called for sure.

Sarah lifted her gun a little higher and flicked off the safety.

István leaned back and raised his hands in protest. She knew what would be racing through his mind. She was here to kill him. Break in, use a cop's gun, wipe it clean and run off into the dark Budapest night without a trace. He was scared and how he showed it was by being authoritative.

I've got authority too, assfuck.

She fired her weapon. The recoil was minimal but the sound was quite loud in the small apartment. The bullet flew by István's head missing him by a foot and imbedded itself into his microwave oven on the counter behind him.

He jumped in his chair, held his ears with both hands and instantly began breathing rapidly.

"Are you fucking crazy? Someone will hear that. The police will be called. Is that what you want?" he shouted, his hands still over his ears.

For the second time in an hour she had made two grown men soil themselves. István urinated where he sat, a small puddle forming near his feet.

"Now that you can see how serious I am, we need to talk and we don't have a lot of time. I will be the one asking questions. You will not ask anything. If you do, there will be pain." She lowered her gaze. "I don't bluff. Are we clear?"

He dropped his hands from the side of his head and set them on the table. "Clear."

"Where is Parkman? Is it your people who have him?"

"No. What happened to Park—"

Sarah shot forward, flipped the gun in her hand so the butt end aimed outward and swatted at his face like she was trying to smack an errant fly. The handle of the gun connected perfectly with his left cheek. He dropped his head to the table and held his face.

"What did you do that for?"

This time she lifted her right leg and kicked into the side of his knee. She hit him so hard that he came off the chair sideways and hit the floor.

"I told you no questions. Not even one," she said through clenched teeth. She leaned down closer to him. "I said, *are we clear*, and you said *clear*. But obviously we weren't."

He lay moaning on the floor, holding his face and his leg simultaneously.

"I also recall telling you that I don't bluff. Ask me another question you piece of shit and I will make sure you don't walk right for a year." Calming a little, she unclenched her teeth, took a deep breath and said, "Are we clear?"

He nodded his head.

"Good. So it wasn't your people who took Parkman?"

He shook his head back and forth.

"That was the last answer I get from your head. Every answer after this will be spoken. Understood?"

He went to nod again and then thought better of it. He looked up at her from the floor and said, "Yes."

"Good. Now we're getting somewhere. Do you know a man named Armond Stuart?"

He lifted one finger in a gesture to ask her to wait for a second. Then he leaned on his good leg and got up back onto the chair. He angled over close to her and whispered, "Not here. These walls have ears."

Sarah nodded. "I was waiting for you to say that."

She grabbed his lapel and helped him to his feet. Time was running out. No doubt the police were coming now. She guessed that she only had five minutes or maybe ten left.

With the gun firmly planted in his side, she half shoved, half guided István to his apartment door.

"Where are we going?" he asked.

"Don't speak," she said. "The walls have ears. And that was another question. Oh how you forget so easily. That's one in the bank. I owe you for that question."

They hit István's apartment door and entered the hallway. The corridor was deserted. She looked left and then right and made it look like she was being indecisive. Then she turned for apartment 303.

When got to the door, Sarah knocked. After a moment someone asked who it was.

"Tell him it's you from apartment 306," she whispered.

"It's me, István from 306. I need to borrow some sugar."

That was so fucking lame, Sarah thought.

"Couldn't you have thought of something better?" she asked. "Sugar? At this hour? Bit late to be knocking on doors isn't it István?"

István looked at Sarah with a *what do you want me to do* expression.

Smart of him. He didn't ask.

"Think of something," she said and pushed the gun into his side a little deeper.

"I ahh...I'm in a little trouble. Got this little lady coming over in twenty minutes and I don't have any sugar. You see, her favorite drink is a Margarita and I have to dip the glass. There's no way around it." István leaned in closer to apartment 303's door. "Many times when I come home late I often hear that you're up so I thought I could call on you."

He stepped back and waited. Sarah thought what he said was pretty good. She hoped it worked. They were running out of time.

A distant police siren wailed in the night. If they were coming to this building then she was down to five minutes or less. The waiting was taking too long. She stepped away from István and raised her gun to blast the door knob. As she did a lock clicked.

The gun still raised, Sarah stayed in position.

The door opened slowly. "Come on in," a heavy-set man said.

Then he laid eyes upon Sarah and they widened.

"What's this?" he asked.

"Step away from the door or die. Your choice."

This guy was smart. He stepped back.

Sarah pushed István inside and followed close behind. Living room lights illuminated the area. The television was on but no sound emitted from it. The guy appeared to have some kind of pajama bottoms on and a T-shirt.

"Step away from us," Sarah said to the tenant of apartment 303.

He moved back.

"Pick up the phone," Sarah instructed.

István stood beside her at an angle, favoring his injured knee. He remained still while Sarah set the scene.

"Now, I want you to call the police and have them come to this apartment."

"What do I tell them?"

"Just tell them that you've been shot."

"What? I haven't been..." he paused.

Sarah lowered her outstretched arm and aimed her weapon at his lower leg.

"Wait. What is this about?"

Sarah fired two rapid shots. Perfect aim. Two holes formed in each foot.

The man screamed and stumbled away. He fell to the floor as his feet weren't responding quite well anymore.

"What the hell are you doing?" István asked.

"You're not supposed to be asking questions," she reminded him.

Sarah reached up, grabbed a clump of his hair and placed the gun at the base of his neck.

"Walk."

He started moving. She guided him down a small hallway and into the apartment's main bathroom. After letting go of his hair, she turned him around and shoved him down on the closed toilet seat.

The bathroom had a mirror that ran the length of the wall beside her. She almost caught a glimpse of herself but kept her eyes on István. The rest of the room was decorated by a female. Flowers sat on the back of the toilet. The shower curtain had a floral pattern and the counter contained feminine sprays and soaps.

She refocused and turned to István.

"Now, talk. Answer my questions and do it fast or I will shoot you in the forehead."

"I know of no one who has kidnapped officer Parkman. That would be bad policy of the Hungarian Government to grab an American police officer. We are part of NATO after all. The Americans are our allies. About that name you mentioned earlier, of course I've heard of Armond. As far as we know that's why you're here. To execute him."

"Tell me more. What are you hiding?"

"I have no idea what you're talking about. I'm an immigration officer with the Hungarian Government. I'm not hiding anything from you."

"You lie to me. I could detect more anger oozing off you when I was in your interrogation room than was normal. The only conclusion I have is that you're protecting Armond and after what my sister told me, I know you are. The crazy thing is, you can't lie to me. And you asked a question earlier. You raised the stakes."

Sarah raised her weapon and shot a bullet into his right thigh. Almost instantly his leg started bleeding. The surprised look on his face was priceless.

"You're crazy," he shouted.

His eyes watered. He grabbed at his leg and pushed in a feeble attempt to keep the blood in.

Sarah grabbed a towel from the rack beside her and tossed it at him.

"Tell me more or get another bullet. It matters little to me. Actually, I prefer that you're dead. So save your own life and tell me everything you know. No one can hear you in here. Give it up."

He raised his right hand. "Okay, okay, no more shooting. Please, I'll tell you."

His eyes bulged. His face was red and covered in sweat. Sarah watched him a moment and then nodded.

"You've got maybe two or three minutes before the police come, so hurry up."

He had wrapped his thigh pretty good but blood was now soaking through the towel and dripping to the floor.

He looked up at her. "You are one sick woman."

"No. I get results. Talk now or forever hold your peace."

Sarah felt so at home. This was what she was good at. Bringing down the criminal element in society with massive and intimidating force.

"It all started in the 1950's. During the Russian Revolution some of the Hungarian officials in the Immigration Department set up a ghost branch that helped people to move in and out of the country without official papers. These documents looked official enough and if they were questioned, our group could back up their authenticity." He stopped to adjust the towel on his leg. Within seconds he looked back up at her, his face pale. "When the individual got to their final destination, all papers were to be burned. At our end we'd monitor their progress and burn ours too. Many thousands of people benefitted from this as they left the country instead of being killed. Now the organization has turned into a profitable group. People like Armond Stuart pay us the right amount of money and he gets a free pass to Hungary. From here he can travel to any other Schengen Area country without a stamp on his passport."

"So you admit to helping Armond get into Hungary?"

"Of course. How else could he get here undetected? We're the best at what we do. Only a few problems ever arise."

"Like what? Give me an example of a problem."

"A few months back in Toronto, Canada, a Hungarian woman and her brothers tried to kill a bunch of people because of some of the documents that my group had prepared for her family. These documents said something that riled her. She went on a rampage. Her name was Monika. She's dead now and so are other innocent people because of her. But the guy she was after, a Drake Bellamy, is still alive. What she didn't know was that all our documents are fakes. They're designed to move people from country to country without a problem. Once in Canada those travelers were supposed to burn their documents. They didn't and now there's some kind of stupid investigation. That's the kind of bullshit we don't need."

"Tell me about Armond. Where is he now? And who heads this group?"

Sarah could hear sirens pulling up outside. They were seriously close now. She was out of time.

"I personally helped him and received a large sum of money for that help. What does it matter now? You're going to burn for this. You can't walk around Budapest shooting people at will."

"Is that what you think I'm doing? You have no idea what I'm doing. I just finished you and your career. It's over." It was time to leave. "Who heads this group?"

"You think I'm going to tell you that?"

"You are such a stupid man."

Sarah raised her weapon and emptied the bullets into the wall behind the toilet in a triangle formation. The gun was so loud she couldn't hear István's screams as he ducked thinking she was trying to shoot him.

She reached past his head and punched a piece of drywall away. Behind it was a camera, exactly as Vivian had told her it would be. A motion detection camera set up by the pervert who rented this apartment and opened the door to them minutes earlier. It was set up to videotape his teenage daughter's girlfriends when they came over to use the bathroom or change in it before going for a swim in the building's pool.

Now the perverted pig lay half in and half out of his kitchen entrance with a bullet in each foot. This way he wouldn't leave the apartment when Sarah interrogated István on camera. The police get two idiots with one camera.

"Your confession is here." Sarah held the camera up for István to see. "I will give you this camera if you tell me who runs everything."

István was panting nearing hyperventilation. He was shaking his head back and forth.

"Tell me!" Sarah screamed.

"A guy named Tony Soprano."

"Come on, like the television show? No way."

"He uses that name. We all know him by that name. No one knows the boss's real name."

Only seconds left. "Where can I find him?"

"Montone, Italy. That's all I know."

He slumped on the seat and slipped off, hitting the floor beside the bathtub. The loss of blood and gunfire had been enough for him.

István's confession about being part of a group inside the government, that helped known criminals enter and exit the country if the price was right, would finish him and his little profitable group. A group that started with the right intentions but ended up helping criminals traffic human beings like they were cattle.

Sarah wasn't just walking around Budapest shooting random people. She was shooting criminals and gathering the evidence needed to have them placed in jail for a long time. She was also learning that this organization was an international one, headed by some tough guy in Italy. A different kind of human trafficking. One that didn't involve prostitution.

She turned and ran for the hallway.

"Wait! You said you'd give me the camera," István said, pointing at her, his eyes wider than she'd ever seen. He lay on the floor looking like he was going into shock.

"You just confessed on camera your role in aiding Armond Stuart entry to this country. It's everything I need for that pig lying out in the hallway bleeding from both feet."

"But you said you don't bluff."

István was shaking all over but trying to compose himself as best as he could and failing miserably.

"I don't bluff. But sometimes I lie. This little device will go to the proper authorities of course. And since I'm out of bullets this'll have to do."

She stepped forward and dropped the butt of the weapon onto the top of his thigh where the bullet had entered moments before.

He screamed and wailed, writhing on the floor.

"I said no questions. That's for testing me. Our chat is over now. Goodbye."

Sarah turned and ran from the bathroom. The tenant/pervert of apartment 303 still lay on the floor, the phone near his ear.

"That's right. Good boy. Talk to the police. I'm so happy you called them."

She held up the camera. His expression changed and his eyes widened. He knew he was caught.

She watched as he hit a button on the phone and set it down.

Too late, she thought. *The police are already here.*

Before stepping from the apartment she checked the hallway. No one in sight yet.

She edged out and down to István's apartment 306. She eased in and closed the door, locking it behind her.

In under a minute she had the camera hooked up to his DVD player. She turned the television on, rewound the recorder and then pressed play.

Young girls showed up on the screen in various states of undress.

Sarah turned up the volume and looked away.

She walked back out to the apartment door and opened it wide. Someone ran by but they didn't look in.

Leaving the door open, she turned and walked back into the apartment, heading for the small balcony.

Someone shouted from the hallway.

"In here."

She opened the balcony door and stepped out, closing it behind her.

Third floor. Couldn't be more than thirty feet down.

She jumped onto the other side of the balcony and slowly slid down a side bar until she was dangling above the balcony of the second floor.

She calculated the distance and waited for the right moment. After her body swung enough to the inside she let both hands go and dropped a foot to the top of the railing on the second floor. Balancing perfectly for a brief second she hopped off and into the balcony area.

Then she jumped over its edge and did the same procedure to get to the first floor balcony. The only difference was instead of jumping onto the first floor balcony she jumped the other way and landed on a bed of grass.

Luckily István's apartment faced the rear of the building. All the police showing up were at the front.

Sarah released her hair out of the bun and shook it back and forth to loosen it.

When she turned to start walking two guns came up to meet her. One was placed against her forehead and the other was leveled at her chest area. She stopped instantly and stared down at the one over her heart.

"We need to talk," the gun holder said.

Chapter 10

She froze in the dark and tried to see the face of her would-be shooter. His voice was familiar but his face was hidden enough in the gloom that she couldn't make it out.

"If I pull back my weapons can I trust that you won't attack me?"

"That depends on who you are."

"Imre Mátyás. I was the officer who met you in the Best Western and detained you regarding the incident with the stolen gun."

Sarah nodded. "I won't attack."

Both guns retreated from her person.

"We need to move. We're not safe here."

They started walking away from the apartment building. Sirens could still be heard pulling up to the front.

"Sorry about the guns, but I thought if I just showed up you might shoot me or something."

"What would make you say that?"

"I've read your file or at least what the Americans would release to me. And I heard what happened upstairs."

Sarah slowed a little. "How did you hear that?"

Imre slowed too and looked back at her. "Come on. We can't stop. We're probably being watched right now." He turned and kept up the pace. Sarah followed as he began speaking again. "István has been under investigation for some time. He knew it and we knew that he was aware of us. I'm one of the officers that work with him so I listen into the recordings. I was in a van across the street. I heard you when you first entered his apartment."

"Why were *you* in the van listening in? That's quite a coincidence. And since you were there and you're a police officer, why did outside police come when called? Is there a reason you guys didn't storm the apartment?"

Imre ran a hand through his hair. He kept looking left and right and a few times behind him.

"I was in the van because of an anonymous tip. We were told you'd be there with the evidence we needed to lock you up. The police were called by a tenant. We waited in case you actually got a confession out of István. That's why we didn't storm the apartment. Our instructions were to get both of you."

"Then what are you doing now? Letting me go? If so, why?"

"Yes and no. Look, I know that the police want you but other than stealing the gun we have nothing on you. And from what I just heard you do in that apartment I'm happy you had the gun."

"Did you listen to all of it?"

"We heard you enter his apartment. You told him *no questions*, hit him after he asked one and then you both got quiet. We waited. We couldn't tell what you were doing. We still had nothing on you or István. Then, we heard movement again and now there's some kind of recording playing back in István's apartment. Once the confession part started all our officers were dispatched upstairs to apprehend all parties involved. We were also supposed to nab you so I went around to the back of the building to watch for you."

This was getting confusing. "Okay. You got me. So what are we doing running away?"

"Because I need information. I thought we could talk. Do a little exchange."

"What kind of exchange?"

They were at least a block away now. Imre turned right on a long street and headed for a small park coming up on the left. Sarah followed. He kept a watchful eye on their backsides.

"And why do you look so paranoid?"

"Because they're everywhere."

"Who's everywhere?"

"The American government guys."

"You're not making much sense," Sarah said even though she suspected who he was talking about.

"Follow me," Imre said as he crossed the empty street.

Sarah followed him as they entered the darkened park and found a bench to sit on. A small line of bushes covered their back and the front looked on toward the park. Unless someone saw them enter, there was no way anyone would know where they were.

"All I know," Imre started in a whisper, "is that these American guys showed up about three weeks ago. They come with a lot of clout. I have a friend at the FBI. I asked him who they were and he didn't know. Never heard of them. After he looked into it, he found out that they're run inside the United States Department of Defense under the National Security Agency in an unknown branch that handles something of an interpretation of messages from the Other Side. After he had asked a few questions he was warned to watch himself. These weren't people that you piss off, apparently."

Sarah looked around now that her eyes had adjusted better. "Are you being serious with me? I mean, how powerful are they?"

"A dozen men came to Hungary in their group. They operate like a military unit. They come with full diplomatic immunity. Our government isn't allowed to touch them and that comes from the higher ups. Actually, we're supposed to cooperate fully in the event that they need our assistance. They have only one task and that is you."

She felt as if she'd been punched in the gut. How could she be of interest to the NSA? What could she have done to spur their interest? She understood if they were a paranormal group, but not the NSA.

"I'm not following."

In the dark she could tell he turned to face her.

"Come on, Sarah. I told you, I read the file they gave me. Even in that small file I know that you have some ESP thing going on. It tells you when people are in trouble or going to die and you save them. The government wants people like you. Are you even aware of your potential?"

"They'd get really tired of me quick," Sarah said knowing that Vivian wouldn't send her a message if someone was watching as evidenced from the day she got to Hungary until Parkman checked them into a new hotel where she wasn't being monitored. "How do I know you're not one of them?"

"You don't. But if I was wouldn't they just grab you right now?"

Sarah considered that and then asked another question. "Where's Parkman? Do your people have him?"

She could tell that Imre had looked away again. His head was roving, watching the grounds for movement.

"We don't have him. They do."

"What do they want with Parkman?"

"I don't know but it makes me think they want to sweat him for intimate details about you. It sounds like he would have a wealth of knowledge the way he talked about you when he sprang you from jail."

"Are they human?"

His head shot around at her. "What kind of question is that? Of course they're human."

"Then they bleed and if they bleed then they die like anyone else. They only think they're powerful because of the agency they're assigned to."

"Sure, you keep telling yourself that but I've heard these guys are the best of the best."

"Are you trying to sell me on them?"

"No Sarah. They scare me. I haven't seen men with this kind of power since the KGB and even those guys wear tutus and do pirouettes compared to these black operation men. I'm telling you this too so you'll be careful. Maybe you should silently leave Hungary. Get out while you're still a free person."

"When you first started talking you said something about an information exchange. I've heard what you've had to say. What do you want from me?"

Her hand started going numb in that second. *No,* she screamed in her head. *Not here, not now.*

Her arm followed and a second later she slumped to the ground.

The blackout lasted all of one second. Another time Vivian had taken over her body and it had nothing to do with giving her a message. This was starting to get annoying.

She opened her eyes and looked straight ahead along the cement floor. Imre was also on the ground in front of her.

What the fuck?

She reached forward and touched his shoulder.

"Imre?" she whispered.

He didn't respond. She moved her hand to slap his face but it brushed against something like a feather around his neck area. She reached back and felt the feather. It was attached to a steel pin that protruded from Imre's neck.

A tranquilizer dart. Like the one I got in the hotel. Rod's here.

Panic set in. She heard rustling, footsteps running. A light came on. Someone was coming toward her with a flashlight.

"I got both of them. They both went down, sir."

Someone about twenty feet away was reporting in. Sarah looked up and saw another tranquilizer dart in the bush about where her head had been. Vivian had saved her by knocking her out for that brief second.

Thank you.

She leaned forward and reached inside Imre's jacket. Feeling her way around as fast as she could Sarah grabbed both guns and yanked them out of their holsters.

With two new weapons, she rolled away and under the bench. As the shooter stepped closer he lowered his flashlight. Sarah had moved enough to avoid being caught in its beam. She was behind a small set of bushes. The shooter turned away and scanned the area while reaching for a radio clipped to his belt. While his back was to her, Sarah stood up quietly and tiptoed to stand behind a tree seven feet from the bench.

"Come in sir."

She could hear the shooter talking. With the stealth of a predator she leaned around to get a glimpse of his face. He was hard to see in the dark as his flashlight cast him in silhouette. She assumed he was listening to another party through the use of an earpiece as he started talking again.

"Yes sir, I understand. I shot two darts. Both parties went down. The girl first. These darts would take down a horse. There's no way she's awake."

There was a few second pause.

"Yes sir, copy that. But I saw what I saw. When the girl...wait, sir, I see the problem. There's a dart in the bush behind where Sarah was sitting. She must've ducked down for some reason at the exact moment I fired. In the dark I must've missed her dropping and thought it was because of the dart."

"Yes sir. Copy that. The girl's the priorty. Yes sir. I'll have my team scour the area. We'll get her, sir. We'll get her."

Sarah placed both guns in her belt line and moved away from him as quietly as she could. She got twenty feet and then climbed a small fence to exit the park area.

After clearing a full city block, with no more concern for noise, she ran for her life.

Chapter 11

She made it to the block where her hotel was without being stopped. It had to be at least two in the morning. The neighborhood was quiet. She knew they would be watching the building by now. They had to have an operative staking out everywhere she went. Even if she was wrong, she had to assume the building was being watched.

Before getting any closer Sarah eased up and jumped into the darkness of an alley that cut between two buildings. She needed her passport from behind the fire extinguisher in the hall on her floor if she wanted to travel anywhere but she couldn't just walk in and grab it. A tranquilizer dart may be waiting for her and then who knows what after that.

She would wait and watch. Eventually they would give themselves away. The building she leaned against was as old as the rest in the area but this one had cobwebs on it and garbage strewn about the alleyway.

Her hair had come loose with all the activity in the last couple hours. She tied it back into a bun again. It was a lot easier years before. She didn't have as much hair and what she did have she used a red bandanna to cover it up and keep it out of the way. Come to think of it, everything was easier then. She didn't have an NSA organization trailing her while wearing fedoras and she wasn't after an international human trafficker. In those days she would get a message and save a stranger from some accident or something less challenging. Mostly anonymous stuff.

But it wasn't so anymore. She had risen in the ranks from an unknown to one sought after. The American government wanted her and she didn't want them. Even if she stopped listening to the messages they wouldn't stop coming after her. This was a new problem, one that didn't seem to have an easy solution.

And now they had Parkman.

She leaned out and scanned the street. Nothing moved. Wherever they were she couldn't tell. This could take hours. How long could she wait? These were trained professionals. They could probably stake her place out all night in the comfort of some vehicle with a nice cup of coffee and something to read, while she stood a block away fighting off spiders and the horrid smell that was really starting to assault her nose.

She scanned around again, trying to assess the best places from which to watch the hotel. Buildings rose on either side. Maybe they were watching the front of her building from a room across the street? But if they had grabbed a room on the other side of the street they would've had to work quickly. Did things like that happen so fast that they could be all set up within a day? She thought not. Especially with how transient a hotel room could be. Would they go to all that trouble just to have her check out in the morning and never come to this area again?

No, they would watch the building with something more transient themselves. Like in a car or maybe they'd be in the hotel itself. They could probably rent the room across from hers. Or could they have replaced the clerk from behind the counter with one of their men?

She was starting to think of too many conspiracy theories. These were just men. They didn't own the planet. They couldn't just go around taking over anything and everything they wanted.

With not much else to go on and knowing she couldn't stand there all night coming up with ways in which they perform stakeouts, Sarah stepped from the safety of the shadows and started up the block. With each step she expected a dart in the neck, but none came. She looked up at the windows of the buildings around her. Only a random light or two shone through.

The front doors to the little hotel were propped open. Light came out and lit up the sidewalk in front.

Halfway there and no one had shot her yet. Things were looking up.

A lone car turned onto the street up ahead. Sarah slowed and stepped into a recessed doorway. The car approached and then shot past her without pause.

She waited for a breath and then stepped back out onto the sidewalk. It had been a long time since she was this spooked. These guys were really getting under her skin. They were just so damn good. Her opponents in the past were often amateurs or well trained criminals. They'd never been American military types. Trained operatives.

This was out of her league.

"Come on Vivian. Where are you when I need you?" she whispered.

Sarah stepped off the sidewalk, out into the street and crossed it. When she got to the other side she leaned up against a wall and stared at the windows on the side she was just on. She could find no movement at all. Nothing untoward.

This was taking too long. What if they weren't watching the hotel? She was wasting her time.

What was the worst they would do to her anyway? Tranquilize her, take her to their lab and wait for a message from Vivian which wouldn't come. After a few months of tests and an exercise in patience they would release her because she wasn't psychic.

Yeah right. They'd find something and keep her for years against her will.

Now was the time to get proactive.

She was feeling threatened. Sure fear took over, but so did action.

Entering the building was more than grabbing her passport.

She needed to make a statement.

She eased off the wall of the building and walked with purpose to the front doors of the hostel.

When she entered, she saw that the guy behind the counter was the same one she had rented her room from the morning before.

She nodded his way and he nodded back. He looked down and continued to shuffle a stack of papers on his desk.

Sarah walked through the lobby looking everywhere, taking it all in. It was a small lobby with just a couple of seats. A janitor working the night shift was moving his mop back and forth across the tile floor in the side corner. He had placed a *caution: wet floor* sign out in Hungarian, English and German.

Since when do janitors work this late? Don't night auditors handle the lobbies of smaller hotels on their own?

Sarah headed for the stairs and hopped up the first two as fast as she could. There she stopped but continued slapping the steps with her feet as if she continued higher, each step hitting softer as she wanted to make the sounds of her ascending.

With the skill of a professional and her wits about her she waited.

She didn't have to wait long. What a great spot for him to be. He could clean everything over and over, waiting for his prey to enter the lobby and then radio in where she was.

But Sarah refused to be taken.

It was her turn to push back. It was time to get serious.

She could hear the mop as it hit the floor. He was whispering something. From where she stood she couldn't see him, only a corner of the front counter. She leaned out enough to watch the guy behind the counter. He'd looked up and was staring at the janitor. Sarah watched as his head turned slowly as he tracked the janitor toward the staircase.

The seconds ticked by. In absolute silence she eased one of Imre's guns out of the back of her pants and placed it in her left hand. That wasn't her shooting hand but she needed her right available.

The guy behind the counter was still following the janitor. His head was just about at the stairwell.

Game on.

The janitor stepped into view and half ran, half jumped up the first two stairs, almost colliding with Sarah.

Just as he appeared his whispering became coherent. The last thing Sarah heard was, "I've got her".

She set the gun tip on his right eye and reached down to his crotch. Caught by surprise his eyes widened and he almost fell back down the stairs but her right hand was in place.

She clamped onto his scrotum and squeezed enough to get his attention.

Sarah leaned in close and whispered in the ear that didn't have a wire extending from it, "No, I think I've got you."

He nodded vigorously, a vein bulging on his forehead.

Barely audible, she whispered, "Kill the connection to the outside or I kill you. Your choice."

Both his hands had already raised above his head. He slowly brought his left hand to his ear and yanked the wire out. Then he reached down and pushed a button on a small device clipped to his breast pocket. A red light blinked out.

"There. Done," he managed through clenched teeth. "We're alone."

"Great," Sarah said. "Since we're alone, let's head up to my room. Try anything and you know what happens. You're a smart man. I don't have to threaten you. No hero shit. Are we clear?"

He nodded.

"No, I need to hear it. Are we clear?"

She emphasized the last three words with a violent squeeze. His head lifted as he almost fell to his knees. To his credit the man stayed standing.

"Yes," was the only word he said, the pitch of his voice higher then she expected.

A side of her anger made her want to just squeeze until something in her hand popped, but she controlled it. She needed to see what he knew.

Slowly, staring into his eyes, she released his sack and stepped back, Imre's gun about an inch from his eye the whole time.

"Move."

He started up the stairs on wobbly knees. Good to his word, they made it to the third floor without him trying to be a hero.

Sarah saw that the fire extinguisher was exactly where it sat earlier. She reached behind it and snatched her passport back placing it in her front pocket. It might get bent in there but at least she knew she'd never lose it.

The man was informed. He knew what room was hers. He'd walked to the door and stopped in front.

"We going in?" he asked.

"Open the door."

He didn't ask for the key nor did he use one. Even though when Sarah left last she'd locked it, her door was unlocked now.

From what she could see the room was a mess. They stepped in and Sarah ordered him to go stand in the corner.

Never taking her eyes off him in case he pulled a weapon, she took quick glances around. The room had been ransacked. They'd been looking for something. Maybe notes from Vivian. Or her passport so she'd be stuck here and then the only option would be to go to the American embassy for help. That must've been their plan as they could easily snatch her there.

Sarah knew that asking what they had been looking for would be pointless. But she couldn't help herself.

"What happened here?"

He stood five feet away from her. His breathing was more under control, the veins in his forehead gone back down. He smiled and shrugged his shoulders.

"Well now, that's no kind of answer."

Sarah flipped the gun to her right hand and clicked off the safety. Then she aimed the weapon down to his right leg below the knee and fired.

His leg shot back with the impact of the bullet and smacked into the wall behind him. He instantly fell to the floor and curled up in the fetal position trying to grab at his wound.

Sarah stepped forward and with both hands on the weapon leaned over him.

"Hands up or the next bullet is between the eyes," she ordered.

He complied. She couldn't take the risk he would pull a weapon out of some hidden place.

"Where is Parkman?" she asked.

He lay on the floor, bleeding from the hole in his leg and panting in and out in a rapid gesture, yet defiance was written all over his face.

"You know, I don't want to do this. But you leave me no option. What you ass whores don't get is that loyalty is stronger than a paycheck. You do this for a living. I do this to live. Parkman saved my neck more than once. I intend on saving his and I will do it at any cost, making me loyal to him as he was to me. I owe him." She stopped and leaned down on one knee, placing the end of the gun on the bridge of the guy's nose. "Think of me as a psychopath. You're nothing to me other than an obstacle. I don't even see a human before me. After I kill you I will feel no guilt. Actually there's something oddly pleasurable about that. Your side will have one less fighter thereby evening the odds for me a little more. Killing you makes it a point for my side. One to nothing."

He shook his hands back and forth. She was getting through to him. "Wait, wait. We have Parkman."

"I know that. Tell me something I don't know, like a location."

"There is no location."

"Talking in riddles doesn't make you any less dead."

"We don't have offices here in Hungary. All we use are three Escalades. Anyone we take in to question is usually placed in the middle Escalade. Find the vehicles and you find Parkman."

"Why did you take him in the first place and not me? When I was with Imre your team decided to tranquilize me. I mean, when is the best time to kidnap someone?"

"Parkman was forced to talk. He told us what we needed to know about you. Kill me if you want, but they will never stop. Now that we have proof of your abilities, you are property of the United States government and you will be treated as such."

She pushed on the barrel of the gun, ramming it into the guy's nose. His head leaned back to avoid the pressure. She couldn't think of anything else to do. Her anger was really starting to burst through the dam she had walled it in.

"I'm seriously getting sick and tired of people saying that I am property of the American government. I'm not and never will be. What did your people do to get Parkman to talk?"

"That wasn't my doing. I'm part of the surveillance team, that's it."

Her legs were starting to cramp. Sarah stood back up. In the time she had been down talking to the guy she hadn't noticed how white his face had gotten. A glance to the side showed his leg wound was bleeding profusely.

"Before you lose too much blood and die in this dirty hostel, tell me one last thing. Where will I find these Escalades?"

"I never know. They're always on the move. We're a roving force. We monitor through the use of electronics and continuously drive to the next target. It makes less of a target of us too."

Sarah leaned back down and snatched the device out of his breast pocket, the earpiece cord coming with it.

"Not anymore. You're in my sights now." She took a step back toward the door. "You guys made a mistake."

She paused at the door and looked into the hallway. Luckily no one was around. Maybe the gun going off sounded like a firecracker to the hotel's tenants or maybe it was just filled with heavy sleepers.

"Your mistake was coming after me," Sarah said and slipped out of the room. She ran down the hallway and down the stairs as fast as she could, the gun still in her hand.

She reached the lobby without incident. The front desk guy wasn't there. The area was too quiet.

She guessed the only reason the hotel wasn't being stormed was because the janitor had radioed in that he had her and was following her up to her room. After the gun shot, if anyone had called the local police, the fedora wearing government men would have told them they were on the scene and to not respond to that call. Which meant that the government men would be attempting to get in touch with their guy who was without a radio, lying upstairs bleeding.

That gave her no more than a few moments time to clear the area before they stormed the hostel wondering what happened to their man. But since no one could've predicted where she would turn up, the roving Escalades could be anywhere. Either way she looked at it, they weren't there right at that moment but they would be seriously soon.

She ran up and jumped over the front counter, landing on the other side easily.

She lifted her weapon and opened the door to the back room.

The night auditor guy was sitting in a chair with a coffee in his hand, a television on in front of him.

"Why did you have the janitor doing the floors? That wasn't cool."

The clerk raised his hands at the sight of the gun, the coffee cup balanced perfectly. "Bocsánat, I'm sorry, I'm sorry. The guy came in earlier and paid *me* to do the floors. I was told that when he leaves the lobby I was to spend the next half an hour in here on a break. That's it."

"How much did they pay you?"

"Five hundred American dollars. That's good money."

"Okay, not your fault. But I need something and I'm not going to pay for it."

His hands still raised, no coffee spilling yet, he said, "Take what you want."

"I need a knife. A good knife, nothing dull."

He pointed to the side bureau. "In the drawer over there. I have fork and knife for when I eat on duty."

Sarah moved a few steps to the side and pulled open the top drawer. All she saw were papers and notepads.

"The other one to the right."

She shut the drawer and moved to the right. This one held eating utensils, napkins and paper plates.

She grabbed the steak knife and stepped back to the door.

"I'm checking out now. You won't see me again. Actually it would be better for you if you didn't see me at all. Do you understand? All you did was take the money and let a stranger mop your floor."

He was nodding his head. "I understand." A little coffee slipped over the edge of the raised cup as his hands began shaking.

Sarah turned, walked out of the back room, hopped over the counter again and then hustled over to the front windows. Nothing was happening out front yet. The Escalades hadn't shown up to rescue their man.

Won't they be surprised when they see what I've got planned for them?

Sarah ran from the front and headed to find another exit in the back. She wanted to be ready when the cavalry showed up. She had two guns on her now and a steak knife and she knew exactly what she was going to do.

Chapter 12

Sarah exited the side door and stepped out into the warm Budapest night. It was around three in the morning, which left only six days until "the crypt".

She silently wished she could talk to Vivian about these things in a more detailed manner. Knowing that something ends at the crypt in so many days doesn't give her a lot of details to work with. What ends, and why is Vivian sorry about it? Where is this crypt and how will she get there? Vivian had said it had something to do with "vampires". How could that be? She would have to do some research on the Internet if she could ever find the time.

Vivian's messages always seemed to be a riddle when they involved Sarah personally. But the *go here and save someone's life, or run there and stop a kidnapping* were messages with clear details. When the message was regarding Sarah, Vivian never gave specifics, just cryptic notes. Maybe she wasn't allowed to offer Sarah too much of a glimpse into her future. Maybe there were rules about this kind of exchange after all.

Focus Sarah. Come back to the here and now. They could arrive at any moment.

Sarah headed around the side of the building until she had a clear view of the front. She hung back in the shadows and waited for the three SUVs to arrive as she knew they would.

And they didn't disappoint her. Not two minutes after being in place three Cadillac Escalades pulled up about half a block down from the hostel. Sarah leaned out of the shadows and watched as the passenger doors of the first and third Escalade opened and two men got out. No one moved from the center vehicle.

The two men dressed in suits and wearing fedora hats walked with purpose to the front of the hostel and stepped inside.

Sarah edged along the building. Staying as close to the wall as possible, she made her way toward the three parked vehicles. If anyone inside either vehicle saw her she was sure they'd recognize her for who she was, even with her new hair color, and the problems would escalate quickly.

Five feet from the SUVs she could make out a little of the interior of the first vehicle. A lone driver sat staring at the hotel his passenger had just entered.

She was as close as she needed to be to the lead vehicle. With the stealth of a cat, Sarah hopped across the sidewalk and dropped down below the hood. If she'd been seen the driver would exit his vehicle so she waited to a count of three.

Nothing. No noise of any kind.

The three vehicles were parked one after another. The way she had approached them kept her out of view of the other two. Since no one had exited the center SUV to go into the hotel Sarah assumed Parkman was in that one.

She crawled along the baseboards of the lead vehicle until she reached its back bumper. A quick peek around the bumper revealed two men in the front of the second SUV.

Her time limited, knowing that the two men who entered the hotel were going to be coming out soon, or radioing down the condition of their colleague, Sarah had to act and she had to do it fast.

She lunged out from behind the lead vehicle, staying low, and reached the front tire of the second SUV undetected. The steak knife sat firmly in her grip as she lay down on her back and slid along in the dark feeling for the brake fluid line. It was all she could think of on such short notice.

Or maybe she should puncture the gas tank? What kind of damage could she do that would slow them down or stop them? They'd only jump into the other vehicles.

She lay there in the dark, going through scenarios knowing that time was running out and she was in a precarious spot.

She realized that she needed to steal one of the SUVs. Preferably the one with Parkman in it. She set the knife down gently and rolled away from the underside of the vehicle. She continued to roll across the sidewalk until she hit the side of the building and was covered in another shadow. This low on the ground, someone would have to be looking right at her to have seen the movement.

She got to her feet, careful to do it slowly and remain covered by the shadows. Then she removed one of her weapons and clicked off the safety. As fast as she could, Sarah fired with precision and care into the front tires of the lead and rear SUV. Instantly doors opened on both vehicles. The drivers walked around, a gun in hand, to inspect the damage. Unless they changed the tires themselves or called a tow truck, both SUVs weren't going anywhere anytime soon.

Both men stood armed about ten feet on either side of her.

"Drop the weapons," Sarah said.

She watched as they both looked her way and tried to find her in the shadows.

"Who are you?" one of the men asked.

"Your first mistake," Sarah said. She fired in his direction aiming a little left. The bullet hit the passenger side window and ricocheted off in the distance.

Of course, bullet-proof glass.

It startled the guy enough for him to set his weapon on the pavement and raise his hands as he stepped back.

"Take it easy," he said.

"You too," Sarah aimed her weapon just enough out of the shadow for the other guy to see the barrel.

He lowered his gun and stepped back. She was amazed that neither one had tried to shoot at her, but then she remembered that this group of men couldn't kill her. She was too valuable. How would they explain that to their bosses? Oh, sorry, your United States government property has been terminated by accident. Might piss people off.

Movement caught her eye. The two men who had entered the hotel were back. They had just walked out the front door holding their injured friend between them.

Time was against her and so was the manpower. Run away or act now and act violently.

She stepped from hiding and fired her weapon openly toward the three men in front of the hostel. The two guys dropped their friend and ran for cover. She turned toward the man by the SUV on her right and fired at him. Each bullet was not meant to hit her targets, only scare them. Before anyone returned fire she made it around to the driver's side door of the middle vehicle and pulled on the handle. The driver shook his head and smiled.

He mouthed the words, *no way*.

"Are the gas tanks bullet-proof too?" Sarah asked as she turned and emptied her gun into the rear of the lead SUV. When that weapon clicked empty, she tossed it into the street, removed her other gun and aimed it. Things were going downhill fast. If she ran out of bullets in this weapon, she'd have no way to defend herself. If she actually hit the gas tank and succeeded in blowing the SUV up, how much damage would take place? Could innocents get hurt? How exposed was she right now? Amid all the questions another thought struck her. If this was the end wouldn't Vivian have warned her?

She didn't have to wait long. The SUV's driver side door clicked as the driver opened it a crack.

"Okay, I'm getting out. Stop shooting."

Lucky for Sarah she hadn't used a single bullet from the second gun yet. She stepped back and gave him room.

"Step aside and go join the others." She leaned into the vehicle a little and said to the guy still sitting in the passenger seat, "You too."

When the two front seats had been emptied she jumped up behind the wheel, closed the door and leaned across to close the passenger door. Now fully secure in an armored vehicle Sarah looked into the back of the SUV and saw Parkman. Sitting beside him was the man who had approached her in the Best Western hotel lobby.

Rod Howley.

"Good to see you Sarah. I wasn't sure we'd meet again so soon. Parkman here and I have been enjoying a little chat. We're glad you could join us."

"There's no more chat. Get out."

"I don't think so."

Sarah turned enough in her seat to show him her weapon.

"Go ahead Sarah," he said with a smile. "Shoot me. Get it over with. More will come for you when I die."

Sarah held the weapon tight, aiming it at his face.

"I know who you are, Sarah. You help people, you don't kill them. You and I both know that you won't shoot to kill me so let's be done with the bravado and have a little chat."

"There'll be no talking," Sarah said as she shifted in her seat, dropped the SUV into drive and hit the gas. She spun the wheel around to clear the lead Escalade and bolted down the street. With a look in the rear-view mirror she could see Rod's men step into the street to watch her leave. Then her eyes met the fedora wearing American in the back.

"If Parkman has any restraints on remove them."

"He's unrestrained."

"Good. If there are any restraints back there Parkman, use them on this guy."

In the mirror she saw Parkman shrug his shoulders and shake his head.

"Where are you taking us?" Rod asked.

"To the airport."

"And why's that?"

"So Parkman and I can leave this country."

"Where will you go? Do you really think you can get through customs without me knowing about it?"

"I'm going home to the States," Sarah said, trying to be as convincing as she could be. "I haven't done anything wrong. I didn't kill anyone or break any laws and yet my life is in danger. I'm being followed by you guys, my own countrymen. And my friend Parkman, who has been there for me countless times, was kidnapped by you. If anyone is breaking any laws it's you people. Parkman and I are buying two tickets back to the States and we're leaving and there's nothing you can do about it."

"Good. It'll be easier to deal with you on home soil."

Sarah looked back at him in the mirror. Parkman was being strangely quiet. Something was wrong. He looked outside and then back at her.

Five blocks from the airport Sarah pulled the SUV over into a large economy parking area for long term travelers. She drove to the back corner and turned the SUV off.

"What now?" Fedora Man asked.

"Parkman and I are going to leave. That's what now," Sarah responded as she swiveled in her seat to look at the two of them, her gun hand loosely aimed at Rod.

"I don't think so," Rod said.

Then Sarah saw why Parkman had been so quiet. The American Government man was holding a syringe against Parkman's leg.

"If you shoot me, I will plunge this into his leg. If your bullet is a perfect shot and I die instantly my nervous system will contract my hands enough to plunge this baby into Parkman's leg and my thumb will depress the snake venom."

"Snake venom? Are you kidding me?" Sarah asked. "You couldn't think of something better? Fucking amateur."

"Well it's not actually snake venom but the juice in this needle will act the same way on the human body. Death takes place in less than five minutes. Pretty potent shit."

Sarah had had enough. Rod needed a bullet for being such an asshole but her finger stopped short of pulling the trigger as she ran through the options.

"What do you want?" she asked.

"You."

"You can't have me. Next demand."

"There are no other demands. We need you. Come back to the States with us. I will personally escort you to America and make sure your stay there is quite comfortable. After a few months of tests and experiments you can go home. It'll be like nothing had ever happened."

"Yeah right. You sound like you're a member of the Flat Earth Society or those people that run around saying we never put anyone on the moon. Even though there's scientific proof, you're the kind of guy to debunk reality."

"What are you talking about?"

"You'd do your tests and experiments and realize that I'm the real thing and never let me go. There'll be no going home and none of the *like nothing had ever happened* shit. So drop the syringe and ease back in your seat, or die with Parkman when I shoot you. Whatever decision you make, I'm leaving this vehicle in one piece."

She moved her hand to make sure the weapon was aimed at Rod's face. Was he bluffing or not? No way was he going to kill a decorated American police officer. He didn't have that kind of power. Or did he? Sarah was sure he was the one bluffing. At least he'd better be because she wasn't.

"We're running out of time. I'm not good with patience. Make a decision or you force me to."

He held the needle firm, his gaze never wavering. During the standoff she forgot to check on Parkman. He seemed tense like he actually believed the guy would inject him. Time was wasting away. Now or never.

"Okay, time's up."

Sarah closed one eye, aimed from a few feet away and began to depress the trigger. With only a couple pounds per square inch to spare, Fedora Man moved the needle away from Parkman and held his hands in the air. Parkman breathed an audible sigh of relief.

"Okay, okay, you win." He tossed the needle into the back of the vehicle and addressed Sarah. "What now?"

"Get out Parkman," Sarah said.

The side door opened and he hopped out. Alone with Fedora Man, Sarah asked, "Are you wearing a belt?"

He cocked his head sideways. "Why do you ask?"

"Don't toy with me or I'll shoot you on principle. Are you wearing a belt? I won't ask again."

"Yes."

"Good. Pull it off."

Parkman knocked on the driver's side window and said *let's go* through the door. Sarah held up a finger to motion for him to give her a second. Fedora Man pulled his belt through all the loops and held it up for her to see.

"Okay, you'll need your belt as a tourniquet for your wound."

"What wound?" he asked, a look of bewilderment on his face.

"This one," Sarah replied as she lowered her weapon and shot him in the right shin. The bullet entered a little to the right of center. He gasped more out of surprise at the loud report in the closed vehicle than the pain. That would come in a few moments.

Knowing she couldn't take a gun into the airport she had to get rid of it here. Fedora Man was furiously tying his leg off below the knee and reaching for a cell phone.

Sarah jumped out of the SUV and opened the door Parkman had just left. She grabbed the cell phone before he could dial out. After that she turned toward the front of the Escalade and emptied the rest of her bullets into the dash making the vehicle useless. Fedora Man and his SUV were now immobile. There was no way he could follow her or contact his friends.

"Ciao," Sarah said as she closed the vehicle's door.

She leaned down and placed the empty gun under the SUV behind the back tire, grabbed Parkman's hand and ran for the airport terminal.

Chapter 13

"They will catch up to us before we land and have an even larger team waiting for our plane. And that's even if we can board without being stopped. This plan isn't very good," Parkman said.

"We aren't flying anywhere."

They entered the sliding doors to the main terminal. Sarah started looking for a ticket booth and found one off to the right.

"Then what are we doing at the airport if we aren't flying anywhere?"

"We're buying two tickets to the cheapest American city with a plane leaving as soon as possible and then leaving the airport on foot before the cavalry arrives."

Parkman followed alongside her. She could tell he was enjoying how she thought everything out.

"Then where are we going?"

"Montone, Italy."

"Italy!" he stopped and stared at her. "Why are we going to Italy?"

Sarah turned around. "Come on, let's buy the tickets and I'll bring you up to speed after that."

Within twenty minutes they had two tickets to New York flying Hungarian Malév Airlines, leaving in forty-five minutes. The two of them headed for the security gates and once they were out of sight of the ticket booth they turned and headed for the exit doors. The airport was getting busier as the early morning rush was starting up.

Once outside Parkman grabbed her arm and spun her around.

"Bring me up to speed. We're in a lot of trouble and I'm sure my career is over when I get back home. Those Sophia Project guys are serious assholes."

Sarah pulled her arm out of his grasp. "Yeah well, we're more serious. There's a human trafficking ring that we are going to bring down. These are the people that let Armond go from country to country without being detected. My suspicion is that it's the same group he uses to locate any girl he needs and then brings them to America for the highest bidder. The way to Armond Stuart is through these people in Italy."

"Where in Italy? Do you have a destination? A name?"

"Sure. I told you. Montone. A guy named Tony Soprano."

"Oh and we're the serious ones. Get real here," Parkman said, looking even more exasperated.

Sarah walked away. Parkman followed.

"We need a car," she said. "We have to get into Germany or the Czech Republic and then use the train from there to get to Rome. After that we can catch a train to Montone, wherever that is."

"So you weren't fucking around? We're really going to this Montone city to look for a guy named Tony Soprano?"

"When do you know me to fuck around? Now focus, we need a car."

Parkman gestured toward the terminal. "Let's just go in and rent one."

"We can't because your name would be on it. We need them to think we're on our way to New York."

Sarah headed for the parking area of the terminal. It was after five in the morning. The sun had risen enough to cover the area in sharp reflections off the roofs of the parked cars, causing her to squint her eyes.

Doubt entered her thoughts as she walked. Could she steal a car and cross international borders? The owner of the vehicle could arrive back on any flight, report the vehicle stolen and once the plate numbers were sent out to all police agencies Sarah and Parkman would be on the run for entirely different reasons. And would Parkman take part in such a crime?

"Sarah?"

She kept walking.

"Sarah?" Parkman said louder.

Frustrated by how everything was so fucked up she turned to Parkman and almost opened her mouth to shout. Instead she just stared at him and waited.

"We can't steal a car."

She waited some more, afraid of where this was heading. Something else was bothering her. She always worked alone. Or with Vivian. Teaming up with a cop was never her plan. Having him around couldn't really hurt but she couldn't think straight with him schooling her on what she can and cannot do.

"We can't fly either," Parkman added.

"Are you done telling us what we can't do? I already know this shit."

Parkman turned a little to avoid the direct rays of the sun. "But we *can* take the train."

"The train?"

Parkman nodded. "Yes, the train."

Sarah crossed her arms. "What about border crossings? Italy is through Germany and possibly another country. Passports too. They will record our names and everyone hunting us will see the bullseye we just placed on our train car."

Parkman was shaking his head *no*. "Follow me," he said and turned to walk toward a taxi. "At the train station you buy a ticket and validate that ticket and then get on your train. The trains take you where you want to go and you get off whenever. No one checks."

"Border crossings?"

"That's old Europe. They have the Schengen Agreement now. You had your passport checked and stamped when you landed in Budapest. You have three months in the Schengen area which includes Germany and Italy."

"Hold up," Sarah said. "Are you saying that we can go to any other country in the Schengen area and no one would know?"

"Precisely."

"Then what stops people like Armond? He could land in Prague and have a car waiting to drive him to anywhere else in Europe and no one would ever know where he was."

"This is a problem. One that recently has sparked debate among countries like Denmark who want to go back to border guards so they can at least see who is entering their country. Germany is one of the loudest dissenters of this idea."

***

The train company was called Rail Europe. Parkman paid cash for two tickets to Bologna, Italy. There was a brief stopover in Germany, but they'd be in Bologna in fourteen hours. They bought a quick breakfast and jumped on the train an hour after buying the tickets. Neither one talked about how every second counted. They were both being hunted by numerous organizations with vast resources. The airport would be scoured and teams would be sent to the bus and train stations. Every second counted but there was really nothing they could do but sit and wait for the train to leave.

Sarah tied her hair up and leaned back in her seat, watching the train station's platform for anyone acting suspicious. Parkman sat beside her, watching the interior of the train.

Eventually the train started crawling down the track.

In fairness, Sarah thought, *no one would expect them to be traveling by train to Italy.*

The only way their pursuers could be onto them is if the crooked immigration officer told someone what he said to Sarah but she didn't think he would as that would incriminate him.

Ten minutes into the trip exhaustion came over her. Sarah fell asleep and only woke at Parkman's insistence when the train was forty-five minutes out of the city where they would change trains.

Sarah used the bathroom and splashed water on her face.

They talked further. Sarah told him about the immigration guy's confession and what happened to Imre. She told him what she did in the hostel and how she found him, knowing he'd be in the SUV. After a while their conversation was nothing more than idle chat.

Changing trains was easier than expected and after another seven and a half hours they exited the train in Bologna just after ten in the evening.

Parkman checked the train schedule and determined they would take a morning train leaving at 8:47am and arrive in Umbertide just over five hours later, after a couple stops where they would need to change trains again. Sarah watched him handle all the details with a sense of peace. It was good to have someone take care of things for her. It had been a long time since she let anyone do anything for her like this. The last time was her parents when she was a teenager.

It was just as Parkman had said, no one had asked to see their passports and there had been no customs or border control to deal with the whole way. It was nothing like home. To get into Canada or Mexico you needed to clear customs every time. In many cases Sarah had heard people were randomly selected to be pulled over and searched or groped at airports. North America could learn a thing or two from the Europeans.

In minutes Parkman had read a couple of brochures and had located a hotel for them for the night. He hailed a taxi and got them to *Pensione Marconi* hotel. On the way Sarah marveled at all the stone architecture. She had never seen so much stone in one place. Ever since they'd entered Italy she'd seen hilltop houses and buildings that had turrets and large walls built into the side of hills. Italy was stunning but she wasn't here to sight see. Maybe one day if she ever got married she'd come back with her husband to enjoy the sights.

Marriage? Why am I thinking about that? Because I like when a man takes care of things for me? I've never even had a boyfriend.

She smiled to herself. *One day. Maybe one day.*

They stepped into the hotel room. It was basic with two small beds that almost looked like two singles. The room was at the rear of the hotel. She had heard Parkman ask for the rear because of something to do with the street named *Via Marconi* and how busy it could get.

Even though she'd slept on the first train, the whole day of traveling had kept her exhausted. She flopped on her bed and closed her eyes.

"What are we going to do once we get to Montone?" Parkman asked.

"Find Tony Soprano."

"Any plan on how to do that?"

"Nope."

"Sarah, look I'm tired too but we need a plan. We can talk about it in the morning if you want, but I don't want to show up in Montone and just walk around asking for Tony Soprano."

"They'll know we're there."

She felt Parkman staring at her. After a few moments, he asked, "And how's that?"

"Someone as big and powerful as this Soprano guy will have sentries posted. They'll know the difference between idle tourists and people like us. For all we know they'll be waiting for us at the front doors of the city. This guy is the ringleader. He's the money man. The boss. That's why he uses the Soprano name. He's the boss. No one gets close to the boss, but we will."

"And how's that? We don't have any weapons. We don't have any backup. No disguise and no plan. I'm willing to go along with you here but we really have nothing to go on."

"Then the only thing we have left is to be taken by his men and led right to him."

"What?"

She heard Parkman stand up but kept her eyes closed.

"Unless we're going in with an army we'll never get close to this guy," she said. "We need his own men to lead us to him. Then we make our move."

"And what move would that be?"

"We'll know it when we see it."

"Great." She heard Parkman sitting down again.

"Oh, and I need an Internet Cafe tomorrow sometime."

"Why?"

"To do a few minutes of research."

"Do I have to pry everything out of you? Research on what?"

"Vampires."

"Vampires?" Parkman said, his voice raised a notch.

"Vivian sent me a message saying that it all ends in "the crypt" in a few days and that it had to do with "Vampires". That's all I know for now."

She heard Parkman get up and walk to the door.

"I'm going to find some food. We haven't eaten right all day. Do you want anything?"

"I'll have whatever you're having, and get me some panties too."

"Panties?"

Sarah sat up on her elbows and opened her eyes to look at him. "We traveled all day with the same clothes and we didn't bring our luggage. I will need a change of undies after my shower in the morning before we travel anymore tomorrow."

Parkman nodded his head and stepped from the room, closing the door softly behind him.

Sarah lay back down on the hard Italian mattress and stared at the ceiling. "Vivian, I need you more than ever. Am I on the right path here? How's everything going to work out? Can you help me with anything for tomorrow?"

She waited but it didn't take long. Her arm started to go numb in the same second she reached for the hotel pen and paper on the desk.

Then she blacked out.

Chapter 14

Sarah held the note in her hand with a bewildered look on her face. Who was Drake Bellamy? And where did she hear that name before?

She reread the note,

Tell them that Drake Bellamy has retrieved the original documents and you have a copy because you know they are about to silence him at the baseball game in two weeks. You also know about Armond and how he gets his girls through customs. And Sarah, use the fire. Remember to use the fire. The Crypt: less than six days left.

Drake Bellamy? Baseball game? Fire?

Not too clear Vivian, Sarah thought. *Use what fire? Why is Drake important? And how do I know that name?*

She snapped her fingers when she remembered. While István sat on his neighbor's toilet he told Sarah that recently their organization had been having problems with some guy in Toronto named Drake Bellamy. Something about a woman killing a bunch of people because the falsified documents this group had produced years ago fell into the wrong hands. That was a threat to a group like this. They couldn't have a light cast on them. The truth would be hard on the public. To learn that trusted public officials were engaging in importing and exporting people illegally for the right price would shatter the system for years to come.

Not that humans haven't done worse things for a dollar. The important fact here was that these were public servants providing a service for a kickback.

She walked over to the little window and looked across at the other building. Fatigue was setting in. Even her shoulders felt heavy. She leaned against the window frame and wondered what would happen tomorrow. One thing she consoled herself with was Vivian had said things would end in the crypt, which meant it wouldn't end tomorrow.

Although there are worse things than dying to consider.

She turned from the window and lay back on the bed. The whatever it was involving the crypt was supposed to happen in about five days now, putting it on Friday. Where in Europe was she supposed to be for Friday? There were crypts all over the continent. Was it a specific one?

Oh yeah, one that had a tie-in to vampires somehow. Great.

With the little knowledge she had of vampires, that would mean Hungary or Romania. After she finished in Italy she would deal with all that. Until then, she needed sleep.

She was out before Parkman got back with food.

***

Light from the open window, and the sound of Parkman in the shower, woke her. Sarah leaned up and brushed her eyes. The water turned off.

"Good morning," she called out.

"Morning. Coffee's on the bureau and there's some leftovers of last night's pizza if you want some."

"Thanks," Sarah said as she turned, got up and sat on the edge of her bed. She waited a minute and then poured herself a black coffee. It was half gone before Parkman came out of the bathroom. He was already dressed and using his hands to mess with his hair.

"Did you get me underwear?"

"Yeah. In that bag. There was nothing available last night but I ran down this morning and found a market two blocks up. I hope the size is right."

Sarah reached in the bag and pulled out a small, pink piece of cloth. There was a triangle in the front and a tiny strip of material for the back.

"You have got to be kidding me?"

"What?"

He stopped playing with his hair. She could tell that he actually didn't get it by the look on his face.

"This is a thong. I don't wear thongs."

"All the kids wear thongs now. You see it every day when they bend over. It rides up above their pants."

"I'm not a kid and I don't wear thongs. This is pink too. What do you think I am? A little girl?"

"Sarah," he reached out, almost pleading. "You should consider being more feminine. Sure it's pink, but no one will see it unless you let them. If you're letting them see your underwear, then pink is a good color."

"Because I have no other option, I will wear these. But after we leave this place I am going shopping for real clothes."

She walked into the bathroom without another word and started the shower.

In forty five minutes they were back at the train station, sitting on their train heading to Umbertide, Italy. After a large number of stops and a few train changes, they got off the train in Umbertide and started walking toward the piazza, the center of town. The signs said Montone was on the other side of Umbertide.

Conversation between them was light as they walked past Umbertide and out into the open countryside. It was seriously hot as the Italian sun beat down on them while they walked in the open. Sarah pegged it for about three in the afternoon.

Too bad she hadn't considered wearing a hat, she thought.

"So what's the plan?" Parkman asked.

"I don't have one. I know that sounds risky and stupid but I really don't know what we're walking into."

"Have you heard from Vivian?"

She looked over at him. "Yes. Last night."

"You going to tell me about it?"

"She said to use the fire, but I don't know what that means yet."

"Anything else?"

They hit a round-about and crossed when no one was coming. The road angled out of the fields and started on a slight incline as it rose to the hilltop town.

"She said to tell these people that Drake Bellamy has the original documents and that I do too. If anything happens to me these documents go public. I'm also supposed to say that I know about their attempted hit on Drake at some baseball game coming up in two weeks. Something like that."

"Who is this Drake? Do you know anything else?"

"That immigration officer, István, in Budapest who I got to confess on tape, he said something about Drake being in Toronto and how people died because of what these immigration people do."

"Maybe this Drake guy is important in some way?"

"He is. Knowing what we know may save our lives today."

They hit a switchback in the road and continued climbing. For all their effort in the heat Sarah was starting to feel seriously drained. Her breathing was rapid and her mouth was dry. As soon as they got to Montone a large bottle of water was on the menu. No way could she deal with aggressors while she was this thirsty.

"Well, Sarah, I do have a plan."

She could hear him panting a little harder than she was. "What's your plan, Parkman?"

"We separate and scout out the area alone. If one of us gets into trouble then we'll have the other for backup. And now that I know what Vivian said to you, if I'm the one in trouble I'll know what to say and do. Does that work for you?"

"Yes. I usually work alone anyway. I don't want to have to watch your back too."

He looked at her. She smiled at him.

They walked on in silence until the walled city of Montone came into view. A few buildings had been built on the outside of the walls in the last hundred years or so. A pizzeria was open on the right. Sarah ran in to locate two bottles of water.

She had spent the last few days traveling and not having to look over her shoulder as they stayed on the move. Now, as she walked into the little restaurant she immediately felt herself become wary. She was back on the clock. *Do I ever go off the clock,* she asked herself.

Parkman waited outside as they had decided that they'd never do anything together while in Montone.

Two customers sat eating at a table in the corner and a lone man dressed all in black stood at the counter sipping from a very small cup. The man behind the counter was overweight and wearing a large white apron with stains on it. Sarah scanned the small pizzeria and saw what she was looking for. A Coca-Cola cooler stood in the corner. She walked over to it, keeping a peripheral eye on everyone, and grabbed two bottles of water. She turned back to the counter and pulled out a couple American dollars. They didn't plan on staying in Italy for long so they hadn't changed any money over to Euros yet.

Sarah had no idea what to say in Italian.

The heavy owner came over to her and said, "Buongiorno."

She handed him a couple American one dollar bills. He accepted them with a smile.

Sarah headed for the door but not before looking back at the man dressed in black. He'd been watching her the whole time she was in the pizzeria.

Parkman was waiting across the street, surveying the hills beyond.

"Parkman, here's your water."

She opened hers and chugged half of it back before Parkman even started on his.

"Any problems in there?"

"There was a guy all dressed in black that stared at me the whole time. I didn't engage him as I would have no idea what to say in Italian so I let him stare and here I am."

"It's probably nothing. If it was one of Soprano's men he wouldn't have made it so obvious."

They turned and headed up the cobblestoned ramp that led into Montone, passing through where a gate had once kept invaders out.

The town was vast, the walls high and made of fieldstone. Sarah was in awe at the immense walls and sheer height of the buildings from an era gone by. A couple of tourists walked by speaking English in a distinctive British accent.

Parkman lightly touched Sarah's arm and pulled her to the side. "Okay, Sarah, here's where I go my way and you yours."

"Where do we meet?"

"No idea. Look, if you're supposed to be here and there's some leader of an immigration scam group here, as per Vivian who seems to always be right, then my guess is you will be meeting them soon. I'm going to go my way, but I'll be watching for you too. Worst case, we meet at sundown out here at the gates and walk back to Umbertide. When we came in on the train I saw a hotel called Hotel Rio. We'll stay there the night. Deal?"

"Sure. Just be careful. And watch out for guys dressed all in black. I don't know why but that guy got under my skin."

Parkman nodded and walked away, heading up a ramp to another part of the town. Sarah continued straight which led her to an open square.

Does every town have a piazza? she asked herself.

Two different restaurants served meals and wine to the patrons seated outside under umbrellas. One of them served gelato. She scanned the people and watched the buildings about her but found nothing untoward.

Four or five cobblestone paths led away from the piazza in multiple directions. She had no idea which one to take or where any of them would lead.

She decided on the one on the right just past the gelateria. As she turned up it and started her ascent, she realized that she was being watched. There was no way she would be able to enter Montone and not be watched. Not if the boss was here. No way.

But where were they watching her from?

She climbed the narrow road that almost looked like a wide path. When she turned a corner she saw two men sitting on a bench. Neither one was dressed in black. They appeared to be in their fifties or sixties, idly watching as people walked by.

It must be an Italian thing. She'd seen it before in Bologna and Umbertide.

When she passed she kept them in her peripheral. They had looked at her but paid her no special attention.

She wondered how Parkman was getting along. Maybe they should have had cell phones or some other form of communication in case either one of them required help. Although, since this working together thing was new to Sarah, it wouldn't have been something she would've thought of.

When she reached the top of the little road she saw a group of seven men setting up some kind of concert apparatus. Maybe they were going to have a show or a festival event of some kind. Lights and a stage were being fixed up. Two black vans were parked with their back doors open as everyone worked away at getting things ready for whatever was coming.

An old man with a cane was coming toward her. She smiled and moved to step past him.

"Another funeral," he said.

Sarah was surprised and elated to hear English. "You speak English. That's great."

The old man stopped walking and leaned heavily on his cane. He had to look up at her as he was about five feet tall.

"My son went to school in America. I learned English many years ago."

He had an accent but Sarah couldn't place it.

"What's your accent? It doesn't sound Italian."

"That's what happens when you have an American educated son and a British wife. My Italian is fine but my English has been confused."

Sarah smiled. Cute old man. She looked around to make sure he wasn't a decoy, trying to avert her attention to a possible attack. The men setting up the stage were all acting normal. There were no furtive glances or hushed words. None of them even noticed her standing and talking to the old man.

Maybe there was nothing in Montone after all? But then why would Vivian say she should use the fire?

"Well, your English sounds great to me. I don't know any Italian so it's a pleasure to talk to you. What was that you said about another funeral?"

"They're setting up for a funeral. Similar to a eulogy in your country. The mayor does this big speech and everyone comes to pay their respects."

"Who died? Was it someone important? Did you know the person?"

A soft breeze wafted past Sarah, cooling the sweat on her forehead. She lifted the water bottle and drained the rest of it.

The area was quiet other than the men who continued their work. Everything felt right in the world.

"A Hungarian man died."

Alarm bells started ringing. "Hungarian? Why is there a funeral all the way out here in Montone?"

"The man's body won't be here. This is more of a ceremonial funeral. The man died in Hungary yesterday. He was in custody, so I've been told. People here in Montone worked with him. They set all this up as a way to send a message."

Alarm bells in her head were firing rapidly now. A message? What kind of message? Was this a mafia thing?

"I'm not sure I'm following. Wait," Sarah raised a finger and paused. She wanted to see if this old man knew more than he was letting on. "Do you know a man named Drake Bellamy?"

The old man looked away and then started away from her, using his cane to guide him.

"Come in about an hour and watch the funeral. Then you'll see what I'm talking about. It's disgusting but necessary. So they say."

"So who says?" she asked. "You didn't answer my question." But the old man was already ten feet away. He waved his hand to say goodbye.

Sarah moved from the area quickly, intent on finding Parkman.

Something was happening and it was connected to Hungary. A man died in custody and a funeral for him was being held in an hour in Montone. Too coincidental.

That's probably why that man in the pizzeria where she bought the water was dressed in black.

And why did the old man walk away when she asked about Drake Bellamy?

Maybe finding out who died in Hungarian custody would shed some light on what was happening here?

She headed down the cobblestone road she'd come up and searched for Parkman for almost forty five minutes. She couldn't find him anywhere. All the people in the town square had left and the shops had closed.

Montone almost seemed like it had turned into a ghost town in under an hour.

The funeral would be starting shortly. That must be the reason. Everyone was going to be present at the eulogy.

She started back to where the men had been setting everything up with the intention of finding the old Italian man. She would need him to translate the service for her.

But where was Parkman?

Chapter 15

People were assembled in the area in front of the stage. Sarah leaned against a stone wall and watched everything from the rear. She counted at least one hundred people. Men, women and children stood around, chatting to each other. At least eighty percent of them were dressed in black.

There was a congregation of men around the podium area. They stood by three vehicles that had made it up the narrow cobblestone roads. Things were definitely abuzz. Something was happening and it was big for this little town.

Sarah kept her eyes out for any sign of Parkman but couldn't see him. Had things gone south already?

She looked at the surrounding buildings. Windows as high as three stories up were closed with their shutters closed too. A survey of the roofs eased her concerns of snipers.

"Sarah, ready for the show?" the old man from earlier stood two feet away.

She couldn't help it. She actually jumped. "Yeah." She collected herself and then asked, "Does this happen often?"

"No, only when someone dies."

"I realize that. What I mean is, how often is this kind of spectacle taking place for a funeral?"

"Every time."

So much for getting a straight answer.

The old man started walking away.

"Wait. I could sure use you as a translator?"

He slowed and turned back to face her. "I'm performing the ceremony. I'll translate what you need to hear."

With that he turned and walked away.

He's performing the ceremony? What the fuck does that mean? Who is this old guy?

Things weren't adding up. He walked away earlier when he heard the name Drake Bellamy. He knows Italian, British English and American English. He's old and he's the one doing the eulogy. This old man knew about the dead man in Hungarian custody. What else did he know? Could he be the one she was looking for?

As the old man reached the stairs that allowed access to the platform where the microphone was set up, he tossed his cane to the side, righted himself and walked up the steps two at a time.

Shit, another Jack Tate. All this time the old man was the guy she was looking for.

Jack Tate was the alias Armond Stuart used on Sarah all those months ago when she didn't know what he looked like.

She quickly checked her surroundings. No one appeared to be watching her or getting too close. Give it a few minutes and then she'd leave. Something about Montone was getting under her skin. It seemed too intense, too scary, too closed in.

She never thought she'd feel on edge about such a beautiful place but it was giving off bad vibes now.

The old man had reached the microphone and started speaking in Italian to the crowd. People responded randomly. Some shook their heads, while others nodded and clapped.

What is this?

It reminded her of a cult or a ceremony of some kind.

Then she heard her name.

"Sarah Roberts. She's over there."

The old man was pointing. She felt the eyes of everyone devour her as they turned to stare. Then the thought hit her. *When did I ever tell him my name?*

Like an animal being hunted, she suddenly felt the urge to run. An equal urge to make those responsible pay in blood, rose in her too.

"Sarah has been the cause of all this turmoil," the old man continued in English. "Not only does she show up here, but she comes announcing the name Drake Bellamy. And look who she brought with her."

The old man pointed to the roof of a building on Sarah's right.

She looked up. On the roof of a three-story building stood five men dressed in black. In between them stood Parkman. His hands were tied behind him and he had a gag in his mouth.

When Sarah looked back at the podium two men dressed in black had moved in close to her. Each man stood on either side four feet away.

The hundred people who had showed up for the ceremony were slowly dispersing. Everything was quiet for a moment. Who would make the first move?

Sarah looked back up to the roof. No one was there anymore. They had moved Parkman away from the edge.

The old man had walked from the microphone and stepped off the podium. He turned and started toward her.

What was all this for? Could they have staged this whole event to capture me? Why, when all they had to do was take me on any street? There was definitely enough men and weapons to handle that.

He stood before her now. "Let's walk and talk. I want to know what you know."

Sarah shook her head. "Actually it's the other way around."

The old man had turned away but stopped and looked back at her. "What did you say?"

"I want to know what you know, asshole. I am here to close this immigration business down and if I can't succeed then I'm here to expose it for what it is."

He turned fully and addressed her. "Your reputation precedes you. I've heard all about your accomplishments. You can be quite dangerous. That's why we needed to be prepared. But now that you're in my grasp, I don't fear you. Armond informed me about you and your sister. We're prepared."

"Armond Stuart?"

Sarah started breathing heavy. Her anger was boiling over. These men would think it was anxiety or fear. That would be their mistake.

"Yes. He told me who you are and that you're hunting him. Did you know that he is one of my best customers? There is no way I could ever allow any harm to come to him."

Sarah began putting it all together.

"The Hungarian man who died in custody was István wasn't it? The man who told me where to find you, Mr. Tony Soprano."

The old man turned and walked away without another word.

In that moment something banged hard above, making her duck down. The shutters of numerous windows had been whipped open over her head. When she looked up she counted seven different men holding rifles with scopes on them.

"You've been watched since the moment you entered Montone," the old man said from about ten feet away. "Did you think you could just walk into our lair without any of us knowing you're here?" He slowed and turned to his men in the windows. "Kill her in the street like a rabid dog if she doesn't start walking in two seconds."

Sarah waited and watched. Two seconds wasn't very long. She stepped forward as the first bullet passed close enough to be heard as it cut the air by her head. Her next step was quicker.

Real fear of death turned her stomach. As angry as she was she couldn't accomplish anything dead, so she kept walking.

The two men dressed in black on either side of her stepped up closer and walked with her.

As she followed the old man new shutters opened and ones further away closed.

How many men did this guy have working for him?

They guided her down a sloping cobblestone road and onto the front steps of a church. Two large wooden doors were opened as she neared the entrance. She could no longer see the old man. He had already entered the church.

Sarah stepped into the centuries-old church and took in her surroundings. Long wooden pews sat facing the front. The roof was made of stone with huge paintings on all four walls.

She was shoved forward by one of the men behind her.

She stepped into the middle of the church and saw the front more clearly.

A large wooden crucifix hung on the wall at the front. What made her almost ruin her new underwear wasn't the cross, but who it bore.

Parkman had been tied to the cross, bound there by his wrists and ankles, his head fallen and resting on his chest.

Chapter 16

She couldn't believe what she was seeing. Why would they do that? Was this a group of human traffickers or some religious cult? How sick were these people?

She started for Parkman. Footsteps behind her sped up. She dodged to the right and slipped in between two pews at the exact moment one of the men in black who had been escorting her was about to shove her yet again. He lost his balance with the forward motion and fell to the stone floor.

Sarah hopped back out from the pew and kicked him in the stomach. She heard the air rush out of him as he fell over on to his back. In seconds she had the weapon out of his belt and up and aimed at the other man in black who was approaching fast.

"Back up!" Sarah shouted. "I'm going to untie my friend. I will be doing it whether or not you are still breathing."

The man in black raised his hands and nodded. Other men were filing in through the front doors of the church.

Sarah stepped backwards as she headed for the crucifix at the front. She turned at the last pew and ran up a couple steps to get to the bottom of the crucifix.

A quick glance back showed her that no one was moving. There were about twenty people assembled by the entrance doors now. The two men who had escorted her were standing side by side halfway up the center aisle, the guy she hit holding his stomach, leaning against a pew.

A ladder sat on the right.

That must've been the one they used to tie him up. Bastards.

She tucked her new gun into the waistband of her jeans and grabbed the ladder, constantly looking over her shoulder at the people watching her.

Once the ladder was set up, she climbed until she was face to face with Parkman.

"Hey, you okay?" she asked.

He nodded, but it was almost imperceptible. Then he whispered something.

"What's that?" she asked, leaning in closer.

"Don't worry about me. Talk to these people. While you're busy I will leave this place and bring help. Just leave me here. I have a way. Trust me."

"How am I going to get you down?" she asked, loud enough for everyone in the church behind her to hear. "Oh Parkman, what have they done to you?" Then she turned to descend the ladder and whispered, "Good luck," loud enough for Parkman to hear.

One last look up and again she saw the most imperceptible nod.

At the bottom of the ladder she turned to face everyone.

"You will all pay for this."

Tony Soprano, the old man with the cane, stepped into the side area of the church. It looked like he had come up from underground somewhere.

"Bring her to me," he said and then disappeared below ground again.

Almost everyone in the church advanced forward. Sarah raised her hands and said, "I'll go willingly. Just point the fucking way."

When she stepped back down into the main area of the church she counted almost ten guns pointed at her.

"Overkill isn't it?" she asked. She knew what they wanted. A scan of their faces told her how serious they were. She knew none of them would risk her serious harm as their boss wanted to talk to her. But she also knew they couldn't let her follow their boss armed and dangerous. The dangerous part they would have to live with but the armed part they could do something about.

She reached down slowly and lifted the weapon from the butt end. Once it was out of her waistband she handed it to the man she had taken it from. He grabbed it and motioned for her to move.

On the side of the church, where Tony had seemed to disappear into the floor, she saw a wooden door that opened sideways. It exposed a hole in the ground, with stairs that led down into darkness.

The crypt of the church.

Oh shit. Was this the crypt that Vivian had been talking about? But didn't she say that I still had five or six days left? Could it be that I never leave this crypt and by the end of the week they kill me?

She had no choice though. She had to descend the steps and enter the first crypt of her life.

"Thanks, Vivian, for the warning. I could've used more help here," she mumbled to herself.

Sarah took one step at a time, dropping below the stone floor of the church, her stomach dropping with her. A hallway turned to the right. She took it and walked four feet where she entered a vast room. The walls had large square stones that appeared to signify where people had been buried. On the side was another door that sat open. From where she stood she could see that it looked like an office of some kind. Soft amber light emitted from the room.

She took a deep breath, stepped across the crypt and entered the office. Tony sat behind a large metal desk that was littered with weapons and ammunition. She scanned the room, surprised that for this second they were alone. A red couch sat along the back wall. She stood on a huge red square carpet that had two chairs facing the desk. To the right of the desk a fire licked away at the new wood that had been added recently.

Okay good, Vivian said to use the fire. There's fire now. So how do I use it?

"Do you like my office?" he asked.

"A fireplace in a crypt? How did you work that?"

"I chose this room as it sat directly below the leper's hole. The smoke from the fire has been set to funnel through there and then outside."

"What's a leper's hole?" Sarah asked.

"Years ago the church would feed the lepers through a hole in the wall so they wouldn't catch the disease."

"Sounds humane."

"We're not here to discuss that though are we? Have a seat and tell me everything."

He pointed at one of the two chairs facing the desk. Sarah stepped forward and sat. Movement caught her eye from behind. She spun in her chair and saw her two escorts entering the office and moving to the couch along the back wall where they both sat, guns in their hands.

"I know about Drake Bellamy," she started after turning back around. "He has the original documents now and he gave me a copy. The attempt on his life in two weeks at the baseball game will fail. If I don't leave here alive, everything I have will go to the proper authorities and everything Drake has will follow. I came to tell you that it's over."

"You're a fool. Do you think I actually believe you?"

"I don't bluff."

"Well then, you are a fool. We're too big to bring us down. Too connected. We have employees in almost every government worldwide."

"If I don't have the goods on you then why didn't I come in heavy handed? Why come to Montone un-armed and allow myself to be taken so easily. Ask yourself that?"

Tony looked down at one of the weapons on his desk. "I'm a collector of weapons and ammunition."

"I can see that. You have enough to arm a small militia on one desk."

"I love guns, but more importantly I love bullets. Guns don't kill people, bullets do."

"If you say so."

She began going over in her head how possible an escape would be. She now knew how she was going to use the fire. She also knew what she would do next. It was all coming together fast. But getting upstairs and leaving a fortified town made of stone before any of the hundreds of Tony's followers or supporters stopped her, could prove difficult.

Something crashed above them. In unison they all jumped.

"Vincenzo, go upstairs and see what happened."

One of the men on the couch got up and ran from the room.

Parkman's escaping. Everything is right with the world again. My turn now.

"Let me tell you a parable of how I live my life," Tony said. "Maybe it'll help you understand how I am always one step ahead of you."

He paused to set the gun in his hand down and pick up another. She watched as he dropped the magazine out of the handle and began loading bullets into it from an open carton on the corner of the desk. Sarah adjusted herself in her seat to be ready when she felt the moment was upon her.

"Two men are hiking through the African jungle. They can feel they're being watched but they can't tell who is stalking them. A few moments later, out of the bushes on their right, a lion emerges and snarls at them. He appears to be ready to charge, fangs bared and his breathing is aggressive. One of the men sits down on a nearby rock and begins to open his backpack. The other guy stands there in shock as he watches his friend pull out a pair of running shoes and start to put them on. The guy watching says to his friend, 'Hey, what are you doing? Are you crazy? You can't outrun a lion.' His friend finishes tying the last lace and stands up. 'I don't have to outrun the lion. I only have to outrun you.'" He stopped arming the weapon in his hand and looked directly at Sarah. "And that's how I handle problems like you, Sarah."

"If I'm following you correctly, I'm the lion but you're going to be okay because even if someone goes down it'll be other people. People that are not as elevated as you, or as quick. In other words, you're wearing running shoes."

"Precisely. You will die in this crypt and I may or may not have a problem with the authorities. But even if I do, after you and Drake are gone, I'm isolated enough that it won't hurt me."

Sarah shook her head. "You really do sound like Tony Soprano, but I will tell you, you're not above the law. If I can't take you down I will just have to kill you."

He lifted his weapon and aimed it at her. "Big words for a captive girl. You've got some balls coming in here and threatening me. You still don't get it, do you?"

Sarah stared at him, watching his eyes for movement, on edge, waiting for him to shoot.

"You are being held here as my captive. You will never leave Montone. You will die here, in this crypt. And yet you talk big, like you're the one in charge. Can't say I've ever met anyone like you before. But before I shoot you, tell me one more thing."

"What's that?" Sarah asked, happy that her voice didn't crack. It really pissed her off to have a loaded weapon pointed at her.

The sound of gunfire came to them from upstairs.

Tony cocked his head. "What was that?"

"My backup," Sarah joked.

"Bullshit."

Sarah saw the gun waver a little. It moved to her left a notch and then the weapon erupted.

Tony fired a small caliber bullet from five feet away. The sound of the bullet cutting the air as it raced past her right ear, combined with her nerves, made Sarah dash sideways and fall from her chair. She hit the hard floor and spun around to see where the bullet hit. The guard dressed in black, the man she had taken the gun from upstairs, gasped for breath, his eyes wide. A neat hole had formed in the center of his neck, blood trickling from it.

His body went into convulsions and slid off the couch he sat on.

Sarah could barely hear, but she got enough from Tony that he was asking her to get up. She looked over at him and slowly got to her feet.

"None of my men ever get disarmed by their captives. The punishment for such ineptness is death. They all know it." He motioned with his gun for Sarah to take a seat.

She looked back one more time and saw the vacant stare on the man's face. He was gone. Saddened by being around death so often, she was somewhat relieved that now it was only Tony and herself in the room. Noise overhead would conceal what she was about to do.

"Sit," Tony said.

The only other chair was too far away from the fire so she turned and righted the chair she had just knocked over when she fell. By righting the chair she could place it in the most opportune location.

Her heart was racing, everything inside was aflame.

She was ready.

"So for this last order of business. Tell me about Vivian."

She waited for a moment, calming herself, preparing. "My sister comes to me and tells me how to kill people. Ever since Armond murdered her, she has been haunting him through me." She leaned forward and took a deep breath. *Any second now*, she thought. "Since real ghosts don't have a strong physical presence here on earth and they can't hurt or maim someone, Vivian decided to tell me what to do so we can get back at Armond and people like you."

"Oh really," Tony said.

She could swear she saw a twitch in his face under his left eye. Was that worry or fear? Did he believe her?

"What did Vivian say about me?"

"She was the one who told me about Drake Bellamy. She also told me how to bring you down and how to kill you."

Sarah put her hands on her knees and smiled at him.

"You're kidding right? I'm the one holding the fucking gun. If I pull this trigger, you're dead. How does that fit into your ghostly plans, you little bitch?"

"It doesn't," Sarah said as she lunged forward and with one big swoop of her arm, knocked at least three full boxes of bullets into the crackling fire and then dove behind the desk on her side.

Nothing happened. The fire continued to burn.

She heard Tony's chair slam back.

"Get up you fucking piece of shit!" he roared.

Fuck. What now? I used the fire. The door is too far away to make a dash for it. He's armed. I'm not. Fuck!

He stepped around and looked down her. She looked up at him and smiled.

She did what she was told. She used the fire. Now she had to believe. Trust the process. Vivian wouldn't have her killed so easily.

Tony Soprano raised his gun two handed. He looked like he was auditioning for a police movie.

"Funny how I'm the last one you see before you die," he said.

Sarah could see his finger leave the trigger guard and rest against the trigger.

"Wait," she said.

"Too late."

"No, that line you just said. That's my line."

"What?" Tony shook his head.

In that moment the bullets in the fire had heated enough and the minute amount of gunpowder in each individual unit began firing.

He spun around and ducked a little at the sound of bullets randomly discharging in the fire and ricocheting around the room.

Sarah ducked her head and curled into a ball behind the metal desk. Bullets continued to discharge. The desk vibrated a couple times as some lodged into its front or sides.

After a moment she opened her eyes and saw Tony on the floor beside her, blood coming from a wound in his eye. His other eye stared into space. He wasn't moving.

Vivian, you are a genius. I owe you.

The frequency of the popping sounds slowed. She reached out and took the gun from Tony's hand.

"Funny how I'm the last one you see before you die," she said. "Told you that was my line."

The intervals between popping bullets had gone to over twenty seconds apart. She risked leaning up and looking at the fire. Everything appeared normal. The cardboard boxes the bullets had been in were ash now. There were random spots around the walls where bullets had hit and scuffed. With all the ricochets Sarah was surprised she didn't get hit.

On the desk sat three other guns and six more boxes of ammunition. She loaded as many bullets she could, stored a couple guns in her waistband and one in each hand with bullets in her pockets and then moved to the door.

It was time to get Parkman.

She kissed her hand and touched the wall beside her as a gesture of respect to Vivian and then left Tony Soprano's office in the crypt, intent on murder.

Chapter 17

No one was in the hallway as she eased out. A couple of quick steps and she glanced around the corner that led to the stairs and out of the crypt. It was cool below the church, yet Sarah had broken out in a sweat. She couldn't count how many times she had someone point a gun at her with the intent of shooting and yet each time it was just as frightening as the first. Exposed to something routinely can often desensitize people, but for some reason she couldn't get used to having guns aimed at her with murderous intent.

More noise came from above. Someone was running. She heard a distant cry from outside somewhere. It sounded like a small war was taking place. She wondered how Parkman was involved and how he could have possibly gotten down from the cross.

Fucking assholes. Crucifying Parkman. Who does that?

She made it to the stairs without trouble. No one seemed to care about the noise the bullets had made in the crypt while they shot around the downstairs office.

Paying fierce attention to the square opening at the top of the stairs, Sarah made sure the safety on the gun in her hand was off and then started up the steps. Moving slowly, glaring forward, waiting for someone to stick their head down, she edged up. At the rim she paused and peeked over.

In the immediate surrounding only three people lingered. Two men and one woman were facing out square windows, guns in their hands. Sarah aimed at one of the men and considered firing. The stairwell could act as a trench keeping her hidden from return fire. In seconds she could easily take them all down while in relative safety.

She waited a heartbeat and then lowered her weapon. She couldn't just shoot someone in the back.

Moral dilemmas sucked. It's better to have them firing at me first and then I can shoot to kill. Makes me feel better. Yeah right, who am I kidding?

She turned slowly and looked at the front of the church. The tall wooden cross was empty. Parkman was gone.

Whatever he did seemed to have worked.

When she looked back at the three people, the woman was staring at her. Sarah raised her weapon and aimed it directly at her. The woman slowly lowered her weapon to the floor and left it there by her foot as she stood back up to face Sarah, her hands raised.

"I'm unarmed. Don't shoot."

Her voice made the men turn. They looked at the woman and then at Sarah and back to the woman. Finally their attention was diverted to the window again. To them, whatever was happening outside was much more important.

What the fuck?

"We are your friend."

"Bullshit," Sarah yelled. "Tony Soprano is dead and the one guard he had down there with him is also dead. It's over."

"Can I lower my hands?"

Sarah nodded. She rested her forearms on the edge of the stairs and kept her aim on the woman true.

"He was the head of a large organization that goes deeper than one man. Hundreds of criminals are employed by this group. They traffic people everyday throughout the world. We've been hunting them for years now. Only in the last six months have we been able to get this close to Mr. Soprano."

"Who are you?"

"My name is Rosalie Wardill. I'm the task force lead handling *Operation Border Control*."

"Come again?"

"We are a task force set up by multiple police and law enforcement agencies around the world. Our objective is to stop Mr. Soprano and his group of international immigration fraudsters. It has been over three years since our task force was put together and today we have made great progress because of you."

"Show me some kind of badge."

Rosalie slowly reached inside her black suit and came out with what looked like a leather wallet. She flipped it for Sarah to see, but she couldn't read anything from her distance.

"Wait. I will approach you. If anyone turns my way with a weapon or I see anything I don't like, I begin shooting and I start with you."

Rosalie nodded. "We're your friends. Nothing will happen."

Sarah ascended up the last few steps and after a quick check behind her she walked across the stone floor of the church until she was close enough to read Rosalie's identification.

Unless it was a quality counterfeit badge, everything checked out. Having said that, Sarah wasn't an expert on what to look for. She hadn't spent any time studying police badges as she had no use for the police. She disliked cops and law enforcement in general. They'd rarely stepped up in the past and done the right thing for her. Only Parkman could be trusted.

She lowered her weapon and flipped the safety on. "Okay. The gun is down but it stays in my hand. I don't exactly feel safe yet."

"Understood. Come and sit down. We need to talk."

Rosalie gestured to a nearby pew. Sarah nodded and stepped over to sit, her face aimed at the two men sitting by the square windows.

"Where's Parkman?" she asked.

Rosalie sat opposite her. "He's outside somewhere. We assaulted the city once you were down with Tony in his office. Parkman said you would use the fire, whatever that meant. We assumed it meant you would be okay because you would use our cover fire to make whatever move you were going to make. It's a relief to see you come up those stairs and not Mr. Soprano."

"I used the fire, but it wasn't yours."

Rosalie frowned for a second then her face flipped back to composed. The ultimate professional soldier. "Your reputation is quite something."

Always suspicious, Sarah looked away to keep an eye on the two men who were staring out the windows. They weren't firing at anyone, just watching from their concealed spots.

"My reputation? How do you know me?"

"A few months ago your name crossed my desk. It was regarding the compound bust in the southern States in your hunt for Armond Stuart. Armond is one of Tony's best customers. Many law enforcement agencies are hunting for Armond but he's one of the slipperiest perps we've ever come across."

"He's quite cunning, but I won't rest until he is brought to justice whether that's in front of a court or

God. Either one is fine by me. Every day he walks free is another day I'm disrespected."

"I understand. That's why we need you. We heard you were coming so we organized our team and planned the assault for your arrival."

Sarah almost lifted her gun again to demand more specific answers.

"What do you mean, you heard I was coming? How could that be? And how come you know so much about me? This isn't making me feel all cozy and cute. I just met you and yet you have the upper hand. Usually that pisses me off. Start talking and telling."

"Of course," Rosalie said in her best motherly voice. "A man named Rod Howley, an American, said you would be coming to Montone to meet Mr. Soprano today. He's with some American University that deals in paranormal research of some kind. This man said you were to be taken care of. When he says taken care of, I mean..." she paused.

"What?" Sarah asked, her stomach turning at the thought that the man she shot in the shin in Budapest had passed her name along like an old friend. All she kept hearing in her head was *property of the United States of America*.

"His message came to me directly. It was forwarded to me through my superiors. They took a risk contacting me like they did. Usually there's only one reason for that kind of contact. Abort the operation. But this wasn't an abort order. This was someone sending me a message and the message was about you. Can't say I wasn't elated to hear your name and that you were on our team, but the message came down like it was from the President of the United States himself."

Sarah breathed out through her teeth. How powerful was this guy? How connected? If he knew everything about her, where she would be going and when, and he had the power to delegate to a group of undercover operatives like this, than he was much more than she could deal with.

"I know, I couldn't believe it either," Rosalie continued. "Anyway, once you went downstairs, we took out the few men Tony had in the church, got Parkman down and tossed him a weapon. The three of us were left behind to debrief you. By the way, loved the quick action to disarm one of their men and run to Parkman. I've read your file, heard about your triumphs, but it's quite another thing to watch you in action."

"Is this where I'm supposed to thank you for the compliment? Because truly, all I'm doing is staying alive and sticking with the people I trust and at this moment Parkman's it. What's next?"

"The city of Montone will be ours in the next few minutes. After that we have six months or more of files and paperwork to sift through. That paperwork will effectively bring down all the people in each government around the world that are on the take."

Sarah was shaking her head. "I mean what's next for me."

"We need you to accompany us back to Budapest. At this point you and Parkman, but mostly you, are the only ones who can positively identify Armond Stuart's new face."

"Then what?"

"Rod said that he would meet up with you after that and the two of you are heading back to the States."

Sarah shook her head. "No fucking way."

Rosalie frowned. "I take it you two aren't associates?"

"If attempted kidnapping of an American citizen is thought of as being pals, then maybe we're acquainted."

"What? Then how does he know so much about you?"

"Long story. Maybe another time. If you've got Montone locked down, I need to meet up with Parkman and get something to eat. Kinda shaky with what went on down below in the crypt."

"Absolutely. By the way, taking out Tony Soprano was like taking out the master vampire. All his minions will soon follow."

"Why does everyone continually refer to vampires?" Sarah said, almost to herself.

"What?" Rosalie had half turned away, but looked back.

"Nothing," Sarah brushed her off.

"Tell me, how did you do it?"

"I didn't. Tony shot himself. I was unarmed. He had bullets in little boxes on his desk. I just knocked a bunch into the fireplace. When they began discharging, he was in the way. I wasn't."

"That's risky. You could have been shot too," Rosalie said, her eyebrows raised.

"I had a feeling I'd be okay," Sarah said, thinking about her sister's note.

Rosalie nodded and stood up. She walked over and addressed both men in their positions and then talked into a lapel mic. She looked at Sarah and waved her over.

"It's done. As far as we can tell the streets are safe. My men have about four men locked down in a stronghold. They're the last of Tony's crew that didn't surrender or get killed. My team are drilling into the stone wall of their stronghold as we speak. Everyone else is accounted for."

"Parkman okay?"

"Other than bruising on his wrists from the ropes when he was tied to the cross, he's fine. It was great to have him on our team. He saved the lives of a couple of my men today."

The four of them stepped from the church into the late afternoon Italian sun and watched as people ran left and right, cleaning up shell casings and bodies as they went. Blood stained the ancient stones around Sarah's feet.

A massacre took place here, she thought. *Something the ancient Romans used to do for sport.*

For all Rosalie had said and all that Sarah could see about her, something still nagged at her conscience. It was obvious the woman was telling the truth. A gun battle had taken place. The enemy was killed. Rosalie walked among the workers like she was the boss congratulating her employees. Everyone recognized her authority. Some even stopped what they were doing to salute her. A couple stared at Sarah. *More people who might know of her*, she thought.

Sarah was escorted around with the two men from the inside of the church who had been staring out the windows. The men she almost shot because they were looking away and she held the advantage.

But something still nagged at her. Rosalie had known Sarah was coming for Tony. She had been warned and then ordered what to do with Sarah afterwards. They had waited years to advance on Mr. Soprano, but the day they decided to move forward was the day Sarah was coming. Sarah, an unproven professional. She wasn't employed at any law enforcement agency. She hadn't had any formal training as these people had. Yet they waited for her.

Was it to see how far she got? Was she a guinea pig or fed to the lions? Any way she sliced it, Sarah wasn't comfortable with how it was handled. A full assault on the Montone compound with a professional task force would've been a better option, leaving Sarah outside eating gelato. It would've been safer for her and

Parkman. What if Tony had an itchy finger? Was her life worth nothing to these people? Or was she making a big deal out of it for nothing? And what was that message from Rod about *taking care of Sarah*? Did that mean take care of her like in pampering or take care of her like the mafia?

Not much would've stopped her from hunting Tony. Not after her sister's message. They must've known she would be quite the person to try to stop. But still.

And then there's Rod. How powerful was this man? How powerful could any man be?

She realized as she walked the tilting streets of Montone that she was a prisoner. This task force had their directive and that was to deliver Sarah to Budapest to ID Armond Stuart before being handed her over to Rod Howley.

The handover to Rod would never take place. But she'd allow them to take her to Budapest, because taking Armond down was her priority too.

Once Armond was dead, Sarah would disappear for a while.

Maybe go to Canada and meet that Drake Bellamy guy she'd been hearing about lately.

The paperwork these people had to go through would take too long to stop the hit on Drake at that baseball game in two weeks.

Decision made. She would deal with whatever she had to, to take down Armond, and then she would hide in Toronto and save a Canadian's life.

Pulling her thoughts together, she looked past a group of people and saw Parkman.

She looked down and saw the gun was still in her hand. She'd forgotten it was there. A quick pull on her jeans and the gun was stashed away.

Parkman looked up at her. Their eyes locked and she felt safe again but only for a moment.

They needed to talk. She wouldn't be a prisoner of these people forever and Parkman was the only one who could help her leave their custody after Armond was dealt with.

Planning an escape from Rod Howley was going to be tricky. The man was good. He was powerful.

But he wasn't as street smart as Sarah.

If she couldn't escape from him she would shoot him again but this time it wouldn't be in the leg.

It would be a killing shot.

Chapter 18

They removed Parkman and Sarah from Montone and put them in Hotel Rio downtown Umbertide for the night, with Rosalie's men guarding their room.

"What the fuck are we going to do?" Sarah asked in a whisper.

Parkman was trying to get the television to work. He smacked the top and then looked up at her. "I don't know. Maybe I could ask them to get us another television."

"No, not that. I'm talking about these people that are guarding us. You do know we're prisoners?"

Parkman turned fully and stared at her. "There's nothing we can do right now. They're feeding us, getting us new clothes and flying us both back to Budapest. Our luggage has been picked up and everything is right with the world again. We have a major task force on *our* side hunting for Armond now and we're in the lead as we're the only two that can ID him. In my opinion we couldn't have a better situation."

Sarah turned and plopped down on her bed. It was a hard mattress like any other European bed she'd felt so far. "You don't understand me. After this is finished they're handing me over to the people who kidnapped you. What are we going to do about that?"

Parkman turned away from her and stepped to the window. With his back to her he said, "You know, I could really go for a toothpick right now. Do you know how long it has been since I've had a toothpick."

"Parkman!"

He raised his hands. "Okay, okay."

"Deal with this with me or I do it all alone. I'm offering you the choice and you know how hard that is for me," Sarah paused and looked at her hands sitting on her thighs. "This is the first time I've had to deal with so many law enforcement types. You know me better than anyone, my parents included. I respond to a note from Vivian and walk away. I yearn for anonymity. I don't have that now and I could use your help."

Parkman turned from the window. "You're right. I'm here for you and I will help you get through this. We'll do it together because I know you're going to need my help."

Sarah looked up at him. "Why's that? Why do you know I'll need your help?"

Parkman walked over and sat beside her on the end of the bed. "I was taken by those Sophia Project men. What I learned in their company was that they use the University as a cover. They're actually U.S. Government men working a black operation. Something seriously top secret. It's also something that has given them clearance to the top. This Rod guy can make a call and the President would listen."

Sarah frowned. "How is that *even* possible? The top people in our country are elected officials."

"Sure, in the public's eye. Behind closed doors the powerful people are the ones with money and the war machine guys, the ones who protect the country. Rod and his team are green berets and mercenaries all tied into a group that have the power to do what they want when they want because they are an elite group."

"That still doesn't answer my question about how this could be possible in our country."

"Think of it on terms of when the first atom bomb was developed."

Sarah shook her head and leaned away from him frowning, "What?"

"When the States developed the atom bomb and dropped it on Japan, twice during that fateful August of 1945, people were shocked. A bomb that could destroy a city. No one else had that technology. Russia didn't get their first bomb until 1953 as far as I remember. Anyway, Japan surrendered and the war ended a few months later. This Rod guy is charged to deliver the next atom bomb. Something no one else would have."

"Are you trying to say that I'm an atom bomb?"

"Not at all. I'm saying that there are others like you out there. Hundreds of people with special gifts that can alter the future. You've saved lives with your gift. You're using it for the good of people at the risk of your own life. If someone like Rod could use that in their war effort, America could potentially win any battle they waged. It would begin a new era."

Sarah didn't like where this was going. "How's that? Vivian decides what to send me when she feels like it. And what of others like me?"

"Rod intimated that he had many other psychics working for them already. He talked about how well these people were taken care of so I would be assured of your comfort. He felt getting to me was important. Little did he know, eh?"

"Taken care of? There's that taken care of shit again."

Sarah got up from the bed and started pacing the floor.

"Taken care of? What are you talking about?" Parkman asked.

"He contacted Rosalie and told her we were coming today. He said to take care of us. Rosalie planned her assault for today to correspond with out arrival. That's another beef I have. Why would they do that when they know I'm not in their league."

Parkman leaned back on his arms and smiled. "Ahh, but you are. You're better than most of them and they know that. It was an honor to work with the great Sarah Roberts, I was told."

Sarah stepped away fast, walked across the room and dropped into the chair in the corner. "See, that's what I'm talking about. I don't want to be *known*. I don't want popularity."

"Too late. You can't do what you do for almost five years and not get noticed. You've been on the front cover of newspapers around the globe for what you did at the compound. You're being hailed a hero. There's no escaping it. People want to meet you. People want to understand you. It's human nature."

"Shit," Sarah said and slapped her hands together. "Shit," she said again. "Okay, first things first. Let's go to Budapest and nail Armond. Then we leave."

"It won't be that simple but I agree with you. Nail Armond and then drop out of sight."

Sarah looked directly at him and raised her hands, shrugging her shoulders. "But how?"

"You'll find a way. You always do. Ask Vivian what to do. She'll tell you what's the best for you. Come on, after all you've been through, all the crazy things you've done and you're still walking the earth. She has put you in harm's way but she always knew you'd walk away. I have faith. You'll figure this out."

Parkman laid back on the bed and closed his eyes.

"That's a lot of faith, Parkman."

"I believe in you Sarah. When this is done you'll get us both out of trouble and back to the States."

"Canada."

"Wherever," Parkman said, his voice sounding sleepy.

"Hey, get up. That's my bed."

"What, why is it your bed?"

"Because I fucking well said so. Now get up."

"Okay, okay. See what I mean. Sarah gets shit done. Sarah has it her way. Sarah always has."

She got up from her chair. "Don't patronize me."

"I'm not. You know me. I'm here for you. I didn't come to Europe for a vacation. We'll figure it out."

Parkman moved to his bed and promptly fell down. She waited a few minutes and laid on hers.

"Wait, why did you say Canada?" Parkman asked.

"Never mind."

In minutes Parkman's breathing told her he was asleep. It took her another hour to sleep and the whole time she couldn't get Rod out of her mind.

Things would be different when they met again.

There would be no taking care of Sarah.

She would be taking care of him.

Chapter 19

Someone was knocking on the door.

Sarah opened her eyes and jumped up. The morning sun blazed in through Hotel Rio's curtains.

She rolled off the bed and hustled to the door just as the knocker was trying to open it. The door got moved an inch inward before Sarah body-checked it with her shoulder, slamming it shut.

"What do you want?"

"Time to go. Orders from Rosalie. Truck out front taking us to Rome. You have fifteen minutes."

"Fine. Fuck off."

She had to pee a storm. After using the bathroom, she came out to see Parkman standing at the end of his bed fully dressed. His eyes still showed fatigue but other than that he was ready.

"How are your wrists?" Sarah asked.

"Fine."

"You ready for this?"

"For what?"

"The final chapter of Armond Stuart's pathetic life."

Parkman looked at her. "Are you ready?"

"Of course I'm ready. Been ready since Vivian began talking through me."

Parkman looked away and began gathering his meager things. "It's just...what'll you do when it's all over? You've been hunting this guy for quite some time. Odds are this will be the end of your vendetta."

"When this ends I'm going to lay low, disappear for awhile. Maybe I'll go back to helping strangers like I used to before this whole mess began."

Parkman looked up at her. "There's something you haven't considered."

Sarah shook out her hair and started playing with the ends. It needed a wash but they were out of time. She'd just have to tie it up. A part of her was still getting used to having so much of it. "What haven't I considered?"

"Vivian."

"Okay, seriously Parkman. Start making sense. This is what Vivian wants. She's the one who has led me to him all along. What's there to consider?"

"Will she continue sending messages once Armond is dead or in custody for his crimes? She sent you after him. Look to the future when he's done with. What then? Is her purpose fulfilled? Are you two done after that?"

Sarah looked away. The idea that her sister would stop talking to her hadn't crossed her mind. What *if* Vivian stopped? What would she do? Get a job? Marry one day? Have kids of her own? This was her life now. Saving people, averting tragedy, stopping criminals. She'd killed people. The life had changed her. There was no way she could go back. No way she could walk from this war and not be haunted from it. She owned physical and mental scars from the life.

But what if Vivian didn't contact her? What then?

"Sorry. I didn't mean to ruin our mood," Parkman said as he softly touched her arm.

Sarah pulled away. "You have a point. I'll deal with that if and when it comes. In the meantime Armond is on our radar and we have an international task force assigned to aid us in finding and neutralizing him. Let's do that and then we'll talk. Deal?"

"Deal. Now, let's get out of here and find me some toothpicks or I'm going to fucking lose it."

Sarah smiled as she entered the bathroom again and added some water to her mop of hair. She tied it into a bun just as someone knocked on their room door again.

"Five minutes!"

"Coming," she shouted back.

Three black sedans were waiting out front. Sarah and Parkman were directed to get into the second one. Rosalie sat in the back waiting for them. She signaled the driver and all three vehicles pulled out of Hotel Rio. In minutes they were on the E45 heading south toward Rome.

Other than idle chit chat, nothing new was covered. Rosalie didn't talk to Sarah like she did yesterday. The task force's mission of infiltration was over. Now the real job began for them. Other than dealing with Armond, they would be going after the rest of the criminals one by one, which had nothing to do with Sarah.

An hour into the ride south, Sarah watched the countryside race past the windows. Without turning she asked, "Tell me, what will you do about the people who have standing orders out there?"

Without looking, her peripheral vision caught Rosalie turning toward her. "I'm not sure what you mean. Explain."

Sarah turned to her and they met eye to eye. "I have reason to believe that a man will be killed in Toronto in two weeks. Tony told me about it when we were chatting in the crypt. If that order isn't rescinded then the men directed to take out their subject will go ahead. While your team is sifting through paperwork people will still be dying or worse."

"What do you want me to do? I can't know about all of their exploits without tracking them down through whatever we find on their computers and files. If you are privy to certain information then you should bring it forth and we will attempt to deal with it. But until I'm brought up to speed, there's nothing I can do."

"Humph," Sarah grunted and turned back to look out the window. She knew Rosalie was right, but that's who Sarah was at her core. If she knew something was going down, she would try to stop it. "Then I'll deal with it."

"What was that? Could you repeat your last statement."

Sarah looked back. "I said I will deal with it."

"You're not a member of any law enforcement agency. You can't act like a vigilante out there with no accountability. I have read your file but eventually someone will try to stop you."

"You mean like Rod Howley?" Sarah leaned forward. "You don't know me." She raised her index finger. "What member of the law ever put the people first?" Through gritted teeth she continued. "Armond used to be a cop. I hate cops. Always have. Mostly because they have rules to follow, accountability. The bad guys don't. So, pretending to sit there and preach to me that you've got a degree and you've studied law makes you better only shows me how much of a fucking ass you are."

Sarah could see that Rosalie was shocked. She tried to hide it as she leaned back in her seat. The sun beat in through the side window and cast a yellow line across her face.

Sarah continued. "I've been through things that would make the best trained operatives puke. I've puked. I was scared. But I persevered and did what I could to stay alive. I don't want recognition. Look what it's got me. Rod Howley wants me for his research. I've been shot numerous times and had more broken bones than I can count but I'm still here because I have to be. I have no choice. It comes from in here," she tapped her chest. "You've got to have it in here. This isn't about vigilante shit. This is about dealing with a criminal element that work outside the grasp of cops." Sarah turned to look at Parkman. He knew better than to cut her off or interrupt but he was a cop and a friend. She looked back out the window and said, "Sorry Parkman. You know that doesn't include you."

Rosalie said nothing. She turned away and watched the rolling hills of Italy on her side.

"I do have one question," Sarah continued. "If you think of me as inexperienced and acting like a vigilante, then why did you wait on your assault of Montone until I arrived? Why leave me alone, unarmed, in the crypt with the head of the organization? Was that the part of the *take care of her* message from Rod? Sure you've read my file and you know I've got skills, but anything could have happened down there. Tell me, what's really going on?"

"I don't have the information you're looking for. I did what I was ordered to do. I'm a soldier. I follow orders. Currently my orders are to deliver you to Budapest and use you to locate Armond Stuart and identify him. That's all you'll get from me."

Sarah nodded. "Fair enough. Now we understand each other. But remember one thing. You've got orders. I don't."

"What does that mean?"

"That's all you'll get from me."

Sarah looked at Parkman. He was acting like he wasn't listening, watching the traffic beside them. She looked back out her side. A sign went by saying they were just over a hundred kilometers from Rome.

The rest of the ride was done in silence. At the airport the driver passed through security and drove onto the tarmac where a private jet was waiting. All three vehicles emptied and a total of six people, including Parkman and Sarah, entered the plane. In minutes they taxied out and rose to 30,000 feet where they cruised for almost an hour and a half.

They made a quick descent into Budapest and then deplaned and entered two waiting black SUVs. Sarah could've sworn they were Rod's trucks. Something about the last twenty-four hours bothered Sarah deeply. She was a prisoner. A captive. She'd been held by assholes before and this was akin to it. The only reason she'd allowed it to get this far was because they had mutual goals. This was the best case scenario for hunting Armond. It wasn't just her anymore. It was a whole team of specialists backed by multiple governments.

The SUVs drove through Budapest until they got to an area Sarah started to recognize. Moments later they pulled up to the Best Western hotel and stopped.

"This is a joke right?" Sarah asked.

"No," Rosalie answered. "We have two rooms booked for you and Parkman here. Your luggage is already in your rooms. My orders are to deliver you here and you're to wait for contact. Once we have something we'll be in touch."

"That's it?" Sarah asked. Parkman had been mute the whole trip. *What's with him?*

"That's it."

"What's to stop us from walking away?"

"Nothing. As far as I understand it, Mr. Howley and his team would know. I have a feeling he won't let you stray too far. But even he doesn't have the power over our Armond mission. Too many countries want Armond stopped. It would look bad if the Americans jeopardized that. This thing we're doing here, with him allowing us to have you for an ID of Armond, is a favor from Rod, an olive branch."

The SUV idled in front of the hotel, everyone inside listening to Rosalie and Sarah talk.

"So what you're saying is I'm already Rod's. This is it. There's no going back. Deal with Armond and then Rod does with me as he sees fit."

"I'm following orders. Something you don't do."

"Exactly." Sarah opened the side door. "You'd do well to remember that."

She stepped from the SUV and Parkman followed.

"Sarah," Rosalie shouted from the inside of the vehicle.

She turned back and looked at Rosalie.

"Thanks for your help and I'm sorry," Rosalie said, real concern in her eyes.

Sarah used her right hand to close the door. She turned around and walked into the lobby of the hotel.

Ten minutes later Parkman was in his room knocking on the dividing door. Sarah opened her side and raised her eyebrows to ask what he wanted.

"What was all that back there in the SUV?"

"Testing her. Watching where her loyalties were. Now I know."

"Where are they?" Parkman asked.

"With us. She doesn't like this Rod guy at all. She has orders to follow. She has a job to do and she's happy we're on her side. But when it comes to the handoff to Rod we may need her, and I now know she'll help."

"You got all that from your conversation? How?" Parkman looked quite stymied.

"Just trust me on this. Deal with Armond and I'll do the rest."

"What's the rest? You gonna fill me in so I know what to prepare for?"

"I'm going to die. That way Rod can't come after me anymore. Once I'm dead, it's all over. And Rosalie is going to help me with it."

Chapter 20

Someone was knocking on the door and yelling something in the hallway. Sarah woke and rolled off the side of the bed. The alarm clock beside her read 4:18am.

Who the hell is making all that noise at such a ridiculous hour?

They had eaten in the hotel restaurant and retired early to bed. Parkman had asked if Vivian had said anything lately and Sarah had replied in the negative. He didn't ask how she was planning to die. Partly because he didn't want to know, Sarah assumed and partly because if she did in fact die, how would he tell her parents? He knew them. He was in Europe because of them. Parkman felt it was his personal duty to stay close to Sarah. To protect her.

The knocker rapped again.

"Coming."

Sarah got to the door and leaned against the wall beside it.

"What do you want?"

"We think we've located Armond. We have a lead."

It was Rosalie.

"We need you to come with us," she shouted.

"Okay. How much time do I have?"

"Will five minutes be enough?" Rosalie asked.

"Yeah," Sarah said and stepped away to get ready.

In four minutes she opened her hotel room door and moved into the hallway.

One of Rosalie's men sat a few doors down on a chair. He got up and gestured with his hand. Sarah followed. They made it to the lobby and out into a waiting SUV. The wind had picked up, blowing Sarah's hair into her face. She brushed it clear and reminisced on a day when she didn't have as much hair. A day when she used to pull it out. In her rush to leave she hadn't put it up and out of the way.

She sat in the back across from Rosalie as the vehicle got underway.

One thing above all that was getting under Sarah's collar was that she was unarmed. Since the Montone event they had taken her weapons like they couldn't trust her. She was the one they wanted here. She was an expert at taking care of herself. That had been proven and Rosalie knew enough about her to know that. Maybe they were worried she was uncontrollable? Perhaps it was more to do with escape and their ability to limit her chances by removing any advantage she'd have?

She looked around. "Where's Parkman?"

"He's not joining us on this one," Rosalie said.

"Why's that?"

"Only one of you is needed to make an ID. Actually I think he's heading home to America today."

He hadn't said anything last night at dinner. "Does Parkman know this?"

"No. But as I said, only one of you is needed for Armond and Rod isn't interested in Parkman."

"Is there really a lead we're following up here or is this just a way to separate us?"

"There's a lead."

"Then tell me about it," Sarah said as she leaned against the door while the SUV turned a sharp corner. The driver wasn't wasting any time. Wherever they were headed they were in a hurry.

"A strip joint, the Palace Night Club, had a complaint called into the Rendorshag, Hungarian Police. A couple girls showed up without the proper documentation. Other, legal girls, got pissed off about it because the ones who showed up are obviously too young to be working there. The report called in said that these younger ones were busy all night, taking away foreigner's cash from the Hungarian girls who should be making a living as they've done it legally."

"Management called this in? Doesn't make sense."

"Why not?" Rosalie asked.

"If Armond has anything to do with this then it's happening because management is getting a kickback. They're bought. That's how it works with him."

"I see what you mean. For the record it was an anonymous call but we do suspect it was other dancers who called it in. The police are holding the youngsters until we get there."

The SUV crossed over one of the large bridges that spanned the Danube River. Sarah looked out at the lights of Budapest at night. The sun would be rising soon and she was en route to a strip club. What had her life come to? And where was Vivian in all this? Why had there been no message lately?

"Okay, here's the drill. We will handle the questioning. We will deal with the girls and get them home safely or wherever it is they end up after tonight. During the taking of their statement, we'll attempt to get a location from them. Apparently their boss was there ten minutes before the Rendorshag showed up. This is the closest we've been to Armond in a long time. We think they'll furnish us with a good description too."

Sarah nodded. She had to accept this. They would be in charge. This was their gig and she was just along for the ride. She was an observer. After all she'd gone through, she was an observer as others sought Armond. *Fucking great.*

"Are we clear?" Rosalie asked, evidently worried Sarah would get too involved.

Then why did they bring me?

"How do you know this is tied to Armond? Sounds a little small time even for him."

"We know. He did this years ago to get fast cash when we were on his tail then. After a couple weeks he fled with his pockets full and another new identity in the States. Now," Rosalie leaned forward as the vehicle slowed. "I need to know you'll follow directions. This is our gig. You're along in case we get a visual. Clear?"

"Clear. But I'm not waiting in the SUV. And when this is over you buy the coffee."

Rosalie nodded.

The SUV pulled up to a building. Sarah looked out the window and saw a large drop off. Down below she could see a train station of some kind with many tracks leading in and out of the station.

As everyone filed out Sarah waited and then edged out herself. She left the door open and leaned on it as she took in her surroundings. This was a part of Budapest she hadn't gotten to in her month's stay. It seemed older, more decrepit.

In the distant sky the light blue indicated the rising sun was coming along.

She looked around to the front of the strip club and saw three little police cars. Rosalie's SUV was the only other vehicle.

Where did management park? Was anyone else there other than the young girls?

Something didn't make sense.

A loud metallic bang startled her. She looked toward the trains but didn't see any movement this early. A couple people were walking around down there but no trains were moving.

A flash of light caught her eye. As she made to turn the metallic bang came again but this time it was closer.

Much closer.

Sarah whipped her head to the front of the SUV. A small hole had formed in the hood.

A bullet hole.

She ducked behind the open back door.

Who the fuck is shooting at me? Was this a setup?

Thoughts raced through her mind. The flash of light she'd seen was a weapon discharging. She looked left. Movement in the second floor window of a brick building across the street told her where she'd seen the flash. Whoever had shot at her was packing up. They were moving fast.

The angle from that window to the hood's bullet hole was a perfect line.

Whoever the shooter was he wasn't very good. You missed asshole and now you're going to pay for it.

Sarah jumped to her feet and bolted for cover across the street. With her pulse rate jumping and her back against the brick wall she ran along the building working her way to the entrance of the shooter's building.

No way would he come out the front door. Unless he thinks I'll think that and do it anyway.

She charged for the back. A small fence meant to keep people out had a hole in it just large enough for a six year old to walk through. Sarah dropped to her hands and knees and crawled through, standing up on the other side.

The sun had gained more ground illuminating the area enough that she didn't need any light.

Why hadn't Vivian said anything about this? What about a friendly warning? Fucking sucks that I've got this talent but it doesn't come when most needed. Unless she knew he'd miss and telling me would only cause me to be too cautious? Something to think about later.

She reached for her belt line. No gun.

Shit.

What now? How could she stop a gunman unarmed?

Shit, fuck!

She heard someone coming.

The shadows covered her as she stepped back and crouched behind a garbage bin. The smell almost made her gag but she held a hand over her mouth and waited.

What an idiot, she thought. *The guy could've walked out the front door.*

He wore a black jacket and black pants. He had a long black bag slung over his shoulder. Sarah watched as he stepped out slowly and edged along to the corner of the building. He peeked toward the front. Satisfied that he saw no one, he turned toward Sarah and walked to the back fence where he jumped over it not six feet from her.

He hadn't been close enough for her to attack without a weapon so she had to follow. In the semi-dark he could have a handgun readily available. Something Sarah wasn't going to risk.

She stood and watched him run around the corner of another brick building. She hopped the fence in the same spot he did and gave chase.

At the corner she looked around with care. He was hustling up the street through a construction area toward a black vehicle that appeared to be a Cadillac.

Sarah ran, keeping to the shadows as best she could. The Cadillac was still about fifty yards away from him. She was gaining fast, her running shoes giving no sound off the cement they pounded.

She felt in her element. This was what she was good at. Decisions made in the deepest moment of stress. Decisions that meant she could be hurt or killed. She relied on her quick mind and skill. Reveled in it. She held a certain confidence that the outcome would benefit her.

Or am I too self-assured, too confident?

Now was decision time. Get a plate number and let the guy drive off or attack and make sure he couldn't walk away?

In the second she thought the question, she answered it.

Ridiculous. Like I'm going to get shot at and let the guy just drive away. Fuck that.

The shooter reached the Caddy and fumbled with his keys.

Sarah picked up her step as she heard the chirp of the car's alarm deactivating.

She was close now.

An orange and white construction bar that suspended a makeshift yield sign leaned against a hydro pole.

In one quick motion Sarah lunged for it, grabbed the pipe and swung her body in a circle with the metal pipe coming with her on a wide arc aiming at the vehicle. The shooter was just turning the Cadillac on and dropping the car into drive when the pole hit his windshield.

The glass didn't break inward but it shattered into tiny pieces that stayed stuck together.

Sarah lifted the bar and spun around to smash the driver's side window.

She felt near hysteria now as at any moment the gunman could pull a handgun and shoot her in the belly. The only defense was to keep him jumping back from the onslaught of the bar.

On her next windup the shooter managed to get the vehicle moving.

She swung hard, with everything she had, knowing that it may be her last hit. The pipe hit the driver's side window again.

This time it entered the window.

The car shot forward, pulling the pipe from her grasp. The Cadillac rolled ahead and then jumped the curb. Five feet or so along it bumped into a light standard and stopped.

Sarah ran for the car door. She grabbed the handle and yanked hard.

It opened, spilling the driver onto the sidewalk. He moaned and reached for a cut on his cheek that was bleeding.

She must've have made solid contact with his face. When she stepped around him, her hands ready to punch, her feet to kick, she saw his face had a small dent in it below his left eye.

Did I break his cheek? Or as my mother used to say, did I break his face?

She saw his good eye looking up at her. It was wide and scared.

She looked around. The street was empty.

In a quick motion Sarah dropped to one knee and started to search his waistband for a weapon with one hand held to his throat. In seconds she came upon a small pistol in his jacket pocket. After ripping it out, she checked if it was loaded and flipped the safety off.

She turned to address him. His right eye seemed wider. How afraid of her was he? By appearance only, she was just a small girl. Nothing to be feared by a medium built male. Unless he'd been told who she was.

"You're not going to tell me who hired you? I mean that's what I'm assuming here."

He didn't respond.

Her newfound weapon was held in her right hand. The safety was off and she knew he knew that. A gentle movement brought the gun to his mid-section. She eased it into his stomach and pressed the barrel hard, hoping when she used the gun most of his clothing would muffle the shot as a pillow would.

"Gut shot by a carjacker. You'll probably live but a hole in the stomach can mess you up for the rest of your life. I'm talking hard alcohol and spicy food. That'll fuck you up for a long time. And eating with a broken face could be challenging too. But what do I care?"

She leaned in close and whispered in his ear. "Three, two..."

"Wait," she heard him mumble. She could tell he spoke without moving his lips. "I was told," he started but the pain wracked him. He moaned louder and tried to curl into a ball. Sarah held him back.

She leaned up and stared into his face. "Tell you what. You get an ambulance and no more damage to your person as soon as I know who sent you and I'm satisfied with the answer. Each lie gets a bullet for your efforts. Oh, and I know you know who I am, meaning you know I'm not fucking around. Now, talk or die. Your choice, asscock."

"I was told...you might shoo uh. I was told to make sure you don't wah away."

"By who? Who told you? Remember, this answer is important. Your stomach is depending on you."

He stared a hole through her. "He say you would know him. He say his name was Jack Tate."

Jack Tate, also known as Armond Stuart.

"Okay, you've done well and you've saved your stomach."

She leaned back and sat on the sidewalk beside him. Then after a moment she lifted the gun and shot the man in the right foot, dead center. The report was loud with no suppressor on the quiet street but the man was louder. He screamed which caused his cheek to flare up. She watched as he turned and passed out on the concrete beside her.

"That was for shooting at me. You coulda killed me. Now you will limp for a long time to remember what you did today."

She grabbed his belt and undid it, keeping an eye on her surroundings. Not a single car had passed them in the few minutes they'd been there. Maybe people skirted this street due to the construction.

Or maybe Armond is here and he's keeping traffic away. Come on Sarah, he's not a God.

After a moment she had the belt wrapped around his leg as a tourniquet. She saw the bleeding in his foot was slowing.

I sure like to wound people in the leg or foot. That's getting to be my signature. I only kill to save my life. Anyone else who deals with me has trouble walking afterwards.

Sarah stood slowly, taking the entire area in. The first sign of life was an old man with a cane. He seemed to be looking in a store window.

Odd time to be window shopping.

A moment later he began walking slowly in the other direction. He didn't seem to have noticed the Caddy sitting at an odd angle on the sidewalk. Nor did it appear that he heard the gun and resulting shout.

The sun had gotten higher making shadows stretch. The wind of earlier had died down.

Run or stay?

Jump in the Caddy and pick up Parkman before they even know she's gone or stay and attempt a break later? Staying meant she may walk into more traps set by Armond. Staying also meant she would have to deal with Rod Howley. Leaving meant less assurance she would see Armond go down and she'd still have to deal with Rod. At least with staying she'd have witnesses when she faked her death. People who would report to Rod. People who were professionals that he'd believe.

She decided to stay, as Armond was her priority above everything else.

She sat back down and kept the pistol handy. She'd wait for them to come looking for her. No way was she letting the shooter out of her sight.

After ten minutes she loosened the belt and then tightened it again. She reached inside his jacket to search for a wallet. She found one in an inner pocket. Inside she found no identification. *Big surprise.* But there was a few hundred dollars in Hungarian currency and a note on a lined piece of paper. She opened the note to see a small grocery list.

What the hell is a palichinta?

Her hand started with the familiar numbness.

No way. Now?

She frantically searched for a pen. The shooter had one in the same pocket the wallet was in. She grabbed it and leaned over the paper as a full blackout came upon her.

"Sarah? Sarah, are you okay?"

She snapped awake. *How long was I out?*

Rosalie was leaning over her. Two of Rosalie's men were attending to the shooter, one of them on a cell phone directing an ambulance to their location.

Sarah nodded at Rosalie.

"What happened here? We came out of the strip club and you were gone. One of my men thought he'd heard a gunshot but we didn't know where from so we started a block to block search. When we got here an old man with a cane was approaching. We got him out of here and tried to wake you up. Did he hit you? Are you hurt?"

Sarah listened to her and sat up, blinking in the morning sun.

Where's the note? What did Vivian want?

"I'm fine. I must've blacked out. Everything's okay with me. This guy tried to shoot me outside the front of the strip club."

"What? How did this happen? Are you saying this was a setup to get you out here?"

Not only can she run a team of international agents she can think on her feet too. Impressive.

Sarah recited everything from the first ping she heard from the shooter's gun until she blacked out, omitting why she passed out.

"So we're being played." Rosalie seemed quite disturbed by this prospect.

"Don't let it bother you too much. Armond plays everyone. You're no different."

Rosalie turned to glare at her. "You don't understand. I put a lot of time into this undercover job. My team and I were in with Tony. There's no way Armond could know who we were until yesterday when we raided Montone. If he knew, he would've blown our covers long ago. In such a short time, how could he know so much?"

Sarah used the wall of the building to stand up. Two police cars were arriving. An ambulance brought up the rear.

"Armond is a professional. He has remained elusive because of how good he is, how resourceful. He hides in plain sight. When my sister sent me to find him, he ended up becoming my colleague using the name Jack Tate without my even knowing it. There were times when we were alone in my car, but I didn't know him and how good he was at the time. I barely got away with my life thanks to Parkman."

"Thanks to me you almost lost your life tonight. I'm lucky he missed."

Sarah found that comment odd. *"You're* lucky he missed?"

Rosalie looked sideways at her. "Yeah, my orders are to keep you safe, protected. I'm to deliver you to Rod when this is over. I don't do that, I'm finished."

Sarah stepped away. "Then quit now."

"What?" Rosalie called after her.

Sarah moved away and around the Caddy and the commotion the Paramedics were making with the shooter. He was coming to and moaning loudly again.

She needed to find the note Vivian gave her. Unless it was still in her hand when she was passed out and Rosalie grabbed it.

She searched her pockets. To her relief she found it in her back right pocket.

She unfolded it and scanned the words.

Shit!

Rosalie had stepped out from behind the Cadillac. *No doubt wanting to keep me close,* Sarah thought.

She motioned for Rosalie to join her as she folded the paper and pocketed it again.

"You know that old man with the cane?"

Rosalie nodded.

"That was Armond."

"How do you know that?"

"Do you know anything about me?"

"Yeah?"

"Then you know my sister tells me things and she just told me the old man was Armond. He'd stuck around to watch me die. When I chased the shooter to his car he followed. After everything went down I saw him across the street but he appeared to be walking the other way. Then I passed out. You show up and usher him away. He was about to make his move when you got here so take some consolation that you did save my life after all." Sarah said this without conviction. If she'd really been in danger Vivian wouldn't have taken over.

Rosalie talked into a mic telling her men to scour the area for the old man with a cane.

"Did your sister tell you anything else?"

"She told me it all ends in a crypt on Friday."

"A crypt," Rosalie repeated, evidently thinking over what it meant. She looked away from Sarah. "Most of the men involved in the immigration racket use crypts all over Europe as a meeting place. Too hard to record them talking. Cell phones almost never work buried in that much stone. Wiring anything down there can only be done with external cords making it obvious where electricity is. They have many other reasons for using crypts but that's a few of them." She seemed in a daze as she recited some of her knowledge, thinking over what Sarah was telling her. She looked at Sarah again. "Did your sister tell you where? Any other details?"

"Just that it has something to do with vampires."

"Vampires?"

One of Rosalie's men called for her. The police needed a statement from Sarah.

"Stay here. I'll deal with the police." She raised a finger. "Sarah, we need you. Let me think about this crypt thing. I may have an idea what your sister means regarding the vampire angle, okay?"

Sarah nodded and stepped away to wait on the opposing curb.

She pulled the note out and reread the ending of it.

Vivian explained in the note how messages were sent for Sarah to change or alter an event. If something was to happen that didn't require any meddling then she wouldn't interfere. She knew the gunman would miss so she'd said nothing. Vivian apologized for all that she'd done to get Sarah into this violent life. She expressed her love for Sarah and her sympathy for what was going to happen at the crypt but there was nothing she could do about it now.

Fate was in charge this time.

Nothing at all could be done with destiny.

Chapter 21

An hour later Rosalie sat across from Sarah at a small bakery. Sarah lifted her coffee and sipped.

"Thank you for finding a place that sold American coffee," Sarah said. "Everywhere I go all I can find are cappuccinos and espressos. I had to go to a McDonald's to get one of these but this one is so much better."

Rosalie nodded.

They sat in a corner booth with Sarah's back to the wall. She wasn't going to let anyone get the drop on her again. She watched the windows and scanned the cars parked along the road. Her eyes were drawn to the random people walking by. Having men hired to kill her had caused a new level of paranoia.

She looked back at Rosalie. "You're lost in thought. Pray tell."

"I think I know the crypt you mentioned earlier."

Sarah set her cup down and leaned in. "Where?"

"It's in Esztergom."

"Where's that?"

"Just north of us. About an hour."

"What's special about this Crypt?" Sarah asked.

"When you said vampires, it clicked. The place is called *Esztergom Basilica*. It's the largest church in Hungary. The crypt there is huge and it's the resting place of many famous people. Bela Lugosi, a Hungarian actor by the way, filmed part of the original Dracula in that crypt."

Sarah sipped her coffee and leaned back. "How would you know that kind of detail?"

"I toured it five years ago when I was first stationed in Hungary. We knew then that they were using crypts as meeting places so I went as a tourist to over a dozen in the country. The Esztergom one is quite impressive. It sits overlooking the Danube River."

A plan began forming in Sarah's head. "How close to the river?"

"Oh I don't know exactly, but you could hit a golf ball from the main dome and make the water. On the other side is Slovakia. It's a long climb up narrow winding steps to get to the top of the basilica but it's a gorgeous view of the city. The crypt itself is magnificent. Inside the church area they have the largest painting in the world that's painted on one canvas."

"You sound like you know the place well."

"I only bring it up because of the vampire connection. And it makes sense that this crypt is important to Armond. It would be an ideal place to hide.

There are entire areas of the crypt cut off from the public by iron gates. After you told me about the crypt this morning, I had one of my men make an inquiry." She looked at Sarah more intently. "Did you say the event would happen Friday?"

Sarah nodded, gripping her coffee with both hands now. Something about what Rosalie was saying felt right. This had to be the place. This was where she would make her stand. Whatever happened wouldn't be good though. Each time Vivian brought up the crypt she apologized to Sarah. That wasn't very consoling.

While Sarah scanned the outside looking for an asshole with a gun and a hope in hell, Rosalie continued talking.

"On the first Friday of each month the church is closed to the public for mass. This happens in the late afternoon, early evening. Based on what you've said, we think Armond will be there this Friday when the church will be closed."

Sarah took a couple big swallows of coffee to warm her insides. She felt cold, and the coffee wasn't helping.

"So you believe in what I do?"

"What do you mean?"

"You know I receive messages from the Other Side and then act on them. I told you about the crypt and that it has to do with vampires. You've taken this on, investigated the place and set the time. That tells me you believe in the Other Side. That tells me you believe in me."

Rosalie looked away.

Could I be too intense even for someone as strong as Rosalie?

Sarah watched her fidget with a fingernail and then look back up.

"I believe in what you are, yes. It's just hard because I didn't believe until I met you. The fact that you showed up in Montone because of something your sister told you was miraculous. It took years to get the kind of information you got in a note so it's kinda hard to dismiss it. I still don't *want* to believe but I have no choice."

"Good. That means you'll help me escape."

"Escape?"

Sarah could see the expression on Rosalie's face. She didn't like those words.

"Am I a prisoner?" Sarah asked.

"Well no, not really. Not in the traditional sense where charges are to be laid, but you are here, aiding us in a criminal investigation."

"Then what?"

"We're to hand you over to the American authorities. They've made arrangements to take you home once this is over. That's it. My understanding is that you're not in trouble at all. Rod said you were considered a hero. You've saved countless people."

Sarah drained the rest of her coffee. "And I want to continue doing that but I can't if I go with Rod."

"So what are you saying? Spell it out for me."

"You'll know when the time comes and you'll know what to do. Just make sure you check your conscience before acting. Do what you think is right."

Rosalie's phone chirped. She held up a finger for Sarah and reached for the phone. After reading the screen she looked up.

"Parkman is pretty mad. He wants to see you right away."

"Sure, he wakes up and I'm gone without a note. He's probably worried. He did travel to Europe to watch my back."

"Okay, let's go. We'll drive you to the hotel but only to pick up your things. From here on in you stay with us. I can't let Armond send another sniper after you."

"Gee thanks," Sarah said as she rose from her chair. "I don't really like the idea of being picked off either."

"Are you always this sarcastic?"

"Only with people I care about or work with."

"How do you treat the bad guys?"

"I don't *treat* them, I just shoot them."

They made it back to the Best Western hotel in good time. On two different occasions Sarah was sure they were being followed. They were using the same vehicle that took a bullet in the hood. Rosalie had said that the bullet had gone right through to the pavement, damaging nothing in its path.

While jumping from the vehicle, Sarah scanned the cars passing them. Something was bothering her. Armond was getting desperate. He'd hired a guy and then showed up dressed as an old man. He had gotten close. Too close. Now he would make sure there was no more fucking around as he meant to kill her and make it final. But everywhere she looked in the immediate area looked normal. She still felt in a heightened state of alert. After what happened that morning she had to be more aware. With the way Armond worked, at any time a man could walk right up and shoot her in the face.

She turned to Rosalie who was getting out of the vehicle.

"Give me a gun."

"No way. You're here in advisory capacity only. You're not a member of the law enforcement community. I can't arm you."

Sarah shook her head. "You saw what happened this morning. I was lucky there was a bar nearby to break the car's window. Don't be difficult. Give me a gun." She reached out and held her hand up.

Rosalie stood across from her on the pavement, looking her up and down. "Even if I wanted to, I couldn't. What if you shoot somebody?"

"I plan to."

"You're not helping."

"No, you're not helping. You know the alternative."

"What's the alternative?"

"If you won't give me a weapon, I will take one."

"Sarah, are you always this difficult?"

"You should see me when I'm pissed. Now, I've asked nicely. Do this or my cooperation goes downhill fast. Seriously, think about it. I have a guy like Armond out there somewhere wanting me dead. I have had the damnedest time trying to stay armed in Europe and I have almost been killed a few times because of it. Get me a gun for protection or I start taking care of myself. These aren't ultimatums or threats. This is me. This is who I am. I get a gun or fuck you and your advisory role bullshit."

Sarah could spell shock on Rosalie's forehead. She had never heard Sarah talk like this. They'd chatted after the Montone incident and then this morning after the attempt on her life. But now things were being amped up.

I need a weapon and fuck anybody who thinks different, she thought.

Rosalie's mic on her waist beeped. She ignored it.

"Okay, say I *want* to give you a weapon. How would I do that? Whose name would I use to register it under? Do you want a police issue gun so it can all be traced back to me? Whose career do you want to end?"

"The better question is whose life do *you* want to end? Mine or the bad guy's?"

She knew it would come to this. As much as she wanted to do the right thing, working with cops had rules. They couldn't give her a weapon as much as Santa Claus couldn't hand out Easter eggs. Just didn't happen and wouldn't happen. She was better off on her own. Always had been and always would be.

She heard Rosalie's mic beep again.

"You better get that," Sarah said as she stepped away.

At that same second a piece of stone chipped off the wall behind where Sarah had been standing. It startled her enough to turn and stare at the wall.

In a rush, the realization that a bullet had smacked into the wall, thereby missing her head because she turned, hit her like a meteor. She spun, ducked and dove for cover as another bullet pinged off the side of the vehicle.

As she landed on the hard cement she heard Rosalie yelling over her mic, "We're under fire." Sarah nestled up against the rear tire of the SUV. After assessing the trajectory of the bullet to figure where the shooter was, she confirmed he was somewhere across the street. The shooter sat low this time, and not in an elevated position.

She looked at Rosalie who had crouched down by the front tire of the SUV. "Gonna rethink your position on arming me?"

"This isn't the time—"

Another ricochet shot past Rosalie's head cutting her off.

"I knew we were being followed," Sarah offered.

"Why didn't you say anything?"

"You guys are the professionals. Thought you'd know. I mean, how else could Armond keep tabs on me? He's not a God. He has to follow us to continue trying to kill me."

"Why the hell are you so important?" Rosalie sounded pissed as she let off her frustration. She looked across the expanse of the SUV's wheelbase for all of three seconds before reaching into an ankle holster. She tossed Sarah a small caliber weapon.

"I want it back. You Americans have a right to bear arms so I know where this desire for a gun is coming from. I will cover it in my report as we are under fire. Just don't kill a citizen or worse."

Sarah looked back at her. "What's worse?"

"Killing me."

Another shot rang out. A car on the road turned hard, its wheels protesting on the pavement. Sarah heard its tires squeal as it careened off something solid. It came into view and hit the wall of the hotel ten feet in front of the SUV they were hiding behind.

"We have to move," Sarah shouted.

"Why? We're covered here."

"The shooter is attacking drivers, trying to get them to ram this SUV we're hiding behind. We need to move and now."

Another shot rang out. This time Sarah heard an engine revving. The gunman must've missed, spooking the driver.

Lucky us.

"On my count," Rosalie shouted.

"No, now!" Sarah shouted as she got to her feet and ran for the hotel doors, head down.

A gun began firing bullet after bullet. It sounded like a speed metal drummer double kicking. She made the door and half fell, half dove into the cover of the hotel lobby. Gratefully, Rosalie fell in behind her. They sprawled along the tile floor of the lobby of the Best Western. As far as Sarah could tell Rosalie hadn't been hit. The driver was still in the SUV. She had no idea if Rosalie's vehicles were bullet proof but she guessed that they weren't as there's still a hole in the hood.

"How did they miss? That gun was on rapid-fire," Rosalie gasped.

"I have no idea but I wonder how much more my heart can handle. This has been a dangerous day. I don't like days like this one. This kind of day bites ass."

She could feel her mouth getting away from her. The anger at always having to run and duck and hide could weigh on someone.

262

Footsteps pounded down the hotel stairs. A door banged open.

Rosalie and Sarah both raised their weapons in unison and got ready to plug the bastard coming through the door. It was Sarah who yelled first.

"Wait!"

Parkman stood there, gun in hand. He was smiling.

"Got him," he said. "Lone gunman across the street. He was sitting in a black car. Some Russian model. Dead now. Didn't you hear me unloading on him from our room?"

Sarah looked at Rosalie. Rosalie looked at Sarah. Knowing how close they came to being killed and having thought the barrage of bullets were coming from their attacker made Sarah feel like a defibrillator had been applied to her chest. She was sure Rosalie felt the same as her chest was heaving up and down rapidly.

"We didn't know," Rosalie tried. "We thought..."

"Oh you thought the rapid fire was the shooter?" He stopped smiling. "Sorry. Didn't mean to scare you."

"If it had been the shooter," Sarah said. "We would've had a much higher chance of getting hit, so I'm happy it was you, Parkman. Saved my life again." Sarah got up off the floor. "How many times are you going to do that?"

"Don't know," he shrugged his shoulders. "As many as I can, I guess. Hey, where'd you get the gun?"

Sarah pointed at Rosalie as she applied the safety and stashed it. A quick look around the lobby counted four people. The desk clerk and what looked like a manager in a suit were behind the counter, only their eyes and forehead showing, and a couple were crouching behind a sofa in the corner.

"We good now? Minden jó?" the suit asked.

Sarah nodded. "Yeah, bad guy dead. Everything back to normal."

The guy in the suit shook his head and swiped his hair back using both hands. He was evidently quite upset. In his broken English he said, "No, not normal. Please, everyone leave. No stay my hotel. Please leave. Get things and go. Not good for business."

Rosalie had gotten up off the floor. She glanced out the door and then turned to the manager.

"We will leave. My associates will pick up their bags and we will leave." She turned to Sarah and pointed at the gun. "I'm gonna need that back."

"Come and get it."

Rosalie stared at her. "Are you challenging me?"

"If you think I'm stepping outside at any time in the next week without a gun then you should join the circus because you'd make a good fucking clown."

"Sarah, you don't understand. I can cover you when there's a guy shooting at us but I can't cover you in any report just for carrying a weapon. I'll toss it back to you if you ever need it."

Rosalie put her hand out. Sarah could feel the hotel employees watching them along with the couple by the couch who had stood up now.

"Rosalie, what you don't get is that I don't care about reports and whether you can cover me or not. All I care about is my ass and making sure that it stays where it is. I'd sure hate to get it shot off. That'd really piss me off. So, I keep the weapon until this is over. That's it. This isn't a negotiation. We don't talk about it anymore. If you still feel you want it, come and take it. My pissed off meter is rising and I'm ready."

Rosalie looked at Parkman.

"He isn't going to help you," Sarah continued. "I know *he* wants me armed. Now, your move."

In her peripheral vision Sarah saw Parkman shrug his shoulders at Rosalie.

Rosalie stared a moment more. Sarah could tell the issue was over. She hadn't acted.

She turned to Parkman and then started toward the stairs. "Let's get our things."

Fifteen minutes later they had checked out. Rosalie's men were outside dealing with the local police. A tow truck had shown up to remove the car that had careened off the road. Parkman was told he would need to make a statement.

Knowing Rod's men would be close, Sarah squinted into the sun as she looked for the familiar fedora hats. Sure enough, three men stood in the shadows across the street, watching everything. One of them lifted his hand to his mouth and spoke into it.

As much as she hated them it was good that they were staying close. She needed them at the crypt on Friday. Her plan was coming together in her head. Unless Vivian said something different, Sarah knew her plan would work. It had to.

Be killed or remain a prisoner.

Although, after surviving two attempts on her life in one day, it was clear that being a prisoner wasn't very good for her health either.

Chapter 22

Rosalie arranged for everyone to be driven out of town. She'd asked that Parkman ride in another vehicle so if they were attacked again it would limit the assailant's odds at getting both her witnesses.

Sarah could tell they were heading north. She hadn't talked to anybody or asked where they were going. She needed some time to think.

The big question for her was: could she pull the trigger if given the chance? She could've when he confronted her in the Mormon Temple all those months ago. She tried to, but got careless.

She looked out the window of the SUV and watched as the Hungarian countryside raced by. Seeing Armond again would stir up a lot of internal shit. Knowing he'd raped and murdered her sister, how could she *not* shoot him when given the chance?

She felt the vehicle slowing. They were pulling into a gas station. For Hungary she was surprised at how new and modern looking it was.

They pulled up to the pumps and stopped.

The driver turned in his seat. "Grab a coffee. We have five minutes."

Sarah opened the door and looked around before jumping out. An open field was off to the left. Behind her sat the highway and to her right was a small building that appeared to service the main gas station. Nothing looked threatening and no bad guys lurked in any shadow as far as she could see.

Parkman walked up. "You going in?"

Sarah nodded.

They walked together and got to the door without being shot.

Whoopee.

Sarah took a quick look around the convenience store. The only person in the store was the clerk behind the counter reading a magazine.

"Feeling paranoid?" Parkman asked.

"You could tell?"

"Yeah." Parkman got to the coffee dispenser machine first. "You're watching everything intensely. They tried twice today. They'll regroup and try again later. Relax for a bit."

He placed a cup under the spout and chose a coffee with cream. Sarah looked back out the gas station's windows. Her driver was standing at the back of his vehicle holding the gas hose. The SUV Parkman had been in was further down at the next pump, also being filled.

"Do you know where we're going?" Parkman asked.

Sarah turned to the coffee machine, selected a large cup and hit the black button.

"We're going to a city called Esztergom."

"What's there?"

"Another crypt."

"The crypt Vivian told you about?"

"Looks that way."

A screeching car tire made them both turn around. Sarah spun so fast she knocked the coffee out of Parkman's hand, spilling it across a row of magazines.

Neither of them paid it any attention as three vehicles shot off the highway and into the gas station. The lead vehicle drove around the front of the lead SUV and stopped. The other two fell into formation, blocking all the SUVs from moving.

Rosalie's drivers both dropped their respective gas hoses and ran for the passenger doors, trying to get in.

"Regroup and try again later eh?" Sarah said.

Parkman grunted under his breath. He turned to the clerk who had looked up and was standing there frowning. "You got a weapon under the counter?" he asked.

"Mi az?" *What's that?*

"Gun? Bat? Bar? Knife? Anything to…"

A loud crash emanated from outside. All three of them turned, Sarah already yanking Rosalie's gun out.

"Shit," she heard Parkman exclaim beside her.

The lead SUV had just been rammed by the second vehicle. The driver hadn't made it inside his vehicle yet. He was knocked into the gas pump beside the vehicle as he was reaching for his weapon. The attacker's car reversed and rammed into the SUV again. This time the SUV bumped up and into the gas pump, the driver crushed between it.

Gunfire erupted from Rosalie's vehicle. Return gunfire came from the car in the back.

"This is getting old. How many times are they going to try to hit us in one day?"

"Until they complete the job," Parkman said, his face deadpan.

Sarah watched in stunned silence, gun in hand. Where to move? Which way to run? They were trapped inside the gas station. The lead vehicle that blocked the front SUV was ten feet from the doors Sarah and Parkman had just entered. Walking outside right now would be suicide.

"Find a weapon Parkman and meet me outside."

"Stay alive, Sarah, or I'll punch your corpse. I'm serious."

"Got it," she said as she ran behind the counter and past the stunned clerk. Armond's men had done this before. In the States when Esmerelda was driving her and her newfound friend Jack Tate to safety, his men had pulled over and shot two police officers to get to them. People like the men out front had no regard for life. They held no belief system. All they put forward was their desire for the almighty dollar and the only way to stop them was to kill them. To exterminate them. Cops couldn't do it. Members of the law enforcement community could only kill while engaged in a fire fight. But Sarah could do it and get away with. Sarah could do it and enjoy it, knowing she was ridding the world of scum.

An old quote from an early 90's band called Jane's Addiction crossed her mind. *Some people should die.*

She got to the back door and slammed into it, knocking it open and tumbling out into the sunshine at the rear of the building. She had no fear of being shot as no one had had a chance to get around to the back yet. She spied a line of four large 18-wheelers parked side by side, all idling. One of them started moving, edging out and turning towards the ramp that would take him back onto the highway.

She turned and started along the wall of the gas station. She heard more gunfire from the front. It reminded her of Fourth of July celebrations. Lowering at the waist, gun held out in front, she slowed as she got to the corner.

She could see the gas pump was dislodged now as the attackers had rammed into it a few more times when she was running around to the back. She could see her driver sprawled out on the pavement beside his vehicle, not moving, blood on his abdomen. Rosalie was crouched down behind her SUV. From where Sarah stood it looked like Rosalie was adding bullets to her gun's clip.

A quick assessment of the carnage told Sarah that there were three vehicles and three attackers. One was dead on each side by the looks of it. If she were to walk out from where she stood, there would be nowhere to hide. She would be an easy target and the last thing she would ever do was make it easy for them.

"Hold them down," she whispered. "Hold them down."

She turned from the front and ran back with everything she had to the rear again. She passed the open back door and continued running to the long trucks. Gunfire erupted at the front as she made it to the first rig. It was a Peterbilt with a long nose. Perfect for what she wanted.

She hopped up the steps and peeked inside. The cab was empty. She tried the door. It opened on the first pull. There was no way she could drive anything this big or intense. Too many gears. The only way this would work was if the driver was present and since she didn't see anyone in the gas station he had to be...

She jumped into the driver's seat and turned to rip open the curtains. A man lay wrapped in the fetal position, sleeping away while a gunfight took place not seventy feet from him.

"Get up!" Sarah yelled and jabbed him with her gun. "Get up now or I shoot you and go to the next truck!"

He grunted and turned, his eyes red, but staring and open now.

"Wha...wha?" he managed.

Sarah gestured to the steering wheel and the gear shift. "Drive this thing."

He rolled over to lean toward her and asked again in Hungarian what she wanted.

"Drive!" she yelled and jammed the gun under his nose.

More gunfire erupted in the distance.

Shit, I'm losing this fight. Vivian, where are you?

The truck driver had raised his hands. He moved to get off his sleeper bed but before he could Sarah had to move out of the way. She kept the gun trained on him as she got onto the driver's seat with her feet and frog hopped over to the passenger side. The driver maneuvered into his chair and stared at her again.

"Hol?" *where?* he asked, using his right hand to gesture out the front window, his shoulders rising.

Sarah pointed to the front of the gas station. There was only one exit and it was right in front of them. To drive around to the front of the gas station would be going the wrong way.

The driver showed his confusion. Sarah knew he had to be thinking she was kidnapping him and his truck when all she wanted was a large battering ram. But whatever he thought, she had to get him to work faster because she was running out of time. *Better yet,* she thought, *Rosalie is running out of time if she's not dead already.*

Sarah raised the gun, flipped off the safety and with her left hand showed him three fingers. His eyes widened as he stared down the barrel of the weapon, no doubt losing most of the weight of sleepiness in that moment.

Sarah slowly lowered one of her fingers and then waited another second to lower the next one. He quickly figured out it was a countdown. When the last finger dropped so would his head.

She moved the gun up against his cheek and started to lower the last finger.

Whether he spoke English, Hungarian, or Swahili, he understood her quite clearly.

He raised both hands in the air in a gesture for her to hold on and then set the truck in gear and started it moving. Instantly he yanked hard on the big steering wheel and turned it toward the front of the building.

She knew he had no idea what was happening but he would find out soon enough.

The truck was slow to get moving. It felt like forever, but finally they were coming around. As they got closer she heard gunfire again and felt relieved. The fight was still going on. That meant someone on her side was alive. She never thought she'd be so happy to hear gunfire.

They cleared the building and Sarah could see off to their left the backs of the attacker's vehicles. One of the hit men was crouched behind his car. He looked up at the sound of the rig and turned on the balls of his feet to fire at it.

A hole formed in the windshield. In that second the driver lost all his ability to cope. He panicked and tried to spin the wheel away. The rig lurched to the right. If they continued on that path they would cross a grassy median and end up on the highway going the wrong way.

Sarah anticipated him losing it and making the wrong decision. She dropped her gun in that second and dove across the cab, her left shoulder hitting him seriously hard as the cab had just bunny hopped to the right. She scrunched him into his door as she spun the wheel back as fast as her hands could manage, but it was too late. They were already passing the attacker's car.

She kept on turning anyway, knowing the trailer, at least fifty feet of rolling metal, would follow.

Sure enough, it did.

She felt the collision as well as heard it. Metal screeched across metal. The cab was tilting a little to the right. Sarah stopped spinning the wheel and jumped back to her seat. The driver looked petrified, both hands on his chest, his whole body shaking. Not ten minutes before he was sleeping. Probably dreaming about fields of sunflowers and flitting around like he could fly and now he was ramming cars with his rig and being shot at. She understood how that could fuck him up a little.

There was no time to console him. Bad guys could still be out there. She reached over and yanked his keys out of the dash and then grabbed her weapon from beside her and ripped open the door, gun held out.

She dropped to the ground and studied under the rig.

No movement.

Carefully, ever so slowly, she stood up and edged around the front of the cab. Behind her she heard cars racing by on the highway. Miraculously not a single vehicle had tried to enter the gas station in the time the three attacker's vehicles had entered.

When she reached the corner of the rig she looked around it cautiously. No one was in sight. There were bullet holes in the sides of all three SUVs. The lead one that she'd been in was tilted almost on its side as it now sat on the gas pump.

She looked left and saw that the gunman had been trapped between her trailer and the car he'd been hiding behind. He was dead, his upper half sprawled out on the back of his car's trunk.

"Rosalie!" Sarah shouted.

"Over here."

"You okay?"

"Yeah."

"Are there any more?"

"There were three of them. I clipped two," she shouted back.

"I got the last one over here."

Rosalie stood up from behind the hood of the SUV she'd been in, her gun held out in front of her.

Parkman opened the front door of the gas station convenience store and stepped out.

"From where I'm standing, they're all dead."

He held a chair in his hands. Sarah dropped her gun into her waistband and asked, "Is that supposed to be a weapon?"

"It's all I could find," Parkman shouted back.

"They weren't tigers. That chair wouldn't have held these guys back."

"Well, at least it was something. I was thinking I could've thrown it at them."

"Ahh," Sarah nodded. She motioned for the driver of the rig to come down and join them.

"Rosalie, Parkman, let me introduce you to this guy here," she said as the driver stepped down beside her. "It was his rig that got the last guy. I'd wanted him to ram the vehicle but that's okay. We still got him."

Rosalie walked over. "All of us need to get in that truck."

"What?"

Parkman had set the chair down and was walking closer.

"We get in that truck and leave before anyone gets here. The police are going to want a statement. They aren't going to like this. My colleagues will come in and clean it up. We have to stay on the move. Being in a nondescript rig will be better than more SUVs or any other vehicle that tips these assholes off to who we are or where we are. This is getting crazy. How many times in one day can they try to kill us?"

"They're after me," Sarah said. "Leave Parkman and me to deal with this. You go home."

Rosalie looked at her for a moment. "That hurts. I just lost good men here. Men I went undercover with. Your driver, I've known him for ten years. I will *not* be going home. I will see that Armond pays for what he has done. I'm just as determined to see this to the end."

"Okay, then let's get out of here. The crypt awaits," Sarah said. Sure people died. That went deep for her too. But they've all lost people. Her sister was raped and murdered by Armond and nothing anyone could do would bring her back or remove the horrible image of what that must've been like. Before this was over, more people would die. She would mourn later. What she wasn't going to do was feel sorry for anyone. This wasn't the time.

"Hey," Parkman stepped forward. "You two think they'll try again today? I mean, we're not cats. We only have one life to live."

"Yes. I think they'll continue until we're all dead. Using this rig," Sarah gestured up behind her, "will slow them down though. Rosalie is right. Let's move now."

"You know there's one thing you're not considering," Rosalie said.

"What's that?" Sarah asked.

"These men entered the lot and engaged me and my drivers. During that time you and Parkman were in the gas station."

"What's your point?"

"If they were truly after you, why engage us? We're trained professionals. Why not just drive up, walk into the gas station and shoot at you two?"

"Maybe they want to remove the *professionals* first. Take out my *bodyguards* and then leisurely go after me."

"Don't take offense Sarah. I have a point and that is, I think they're after me as much as you."

"Why?"

"Because I orchestrated the attack on Montone. Tony Soprano is dead along with his organization. Over time, their group will be finished and people like Armond are super pissed about that. I think they're here for me as much as you."

Sarah mulled it over for a second. "Good point. I think you could be right."

She turned, walked around the front of the cab and jumped up into the passenger seat. She looked down through the cab and out the open driver's side door.

"You guys coming?"

Chapter 23

The driver didn't protest much. Sarah caught him looking at the bullet hole in the windshield from time to time, sizing up how close it came to hitting him. Rosalie spoke Hungarian so communication became a non issue.

Within minutes they were underway, with Sarah and Parkman sitting back on the driver's bed while Rosalie directed the driver to Esztergom.

Parkman fumbled in his pocket and produced a little package of something. Sarah looked over and saw him tear it open and yank out a toothpick.

"Got those at the gas station?" she asked.

He nodded. "Haven't been using them much lately but I sure need one today. Good thinking on using the rig earlier."

"Thanks."

"Sarah?" Rosalie turned in her seat. "You guys okay back there?"

Sarah nodded.

"Good. Give me a minute. I'm going to call it in and request more men."

Rosalie got on the phone, stated a couple of numbered codes and then spoke in what sounded like German. When she was done she turned to the driver, pointed out the windshield and gestured at an exit and then turned back to Sarah and Parkman.

"They're going to send two parties. One will clean up the gas station mess and deal with the police and the other team will meet us near the Basilica tomorrow afternoon at 17:00hrs."

"The team meeting us at the crypt are to do what?"

"Whatever I need them for. To secure the perimeter, to assault the crypt if there's a problem. They're coming in a helicopter that'll land on the Slovakia side of the Danube River. No one on the Hungarian side of the river will even notice their arrival."

"Is there any proof that Armond will be in Esztergom?" Sarah asked.

Rosalie shook her head. "Just you, kiddo. Just you."

Sarah leaned back on the bed. *You got anything for me Vivian? Is this the end? Will it finally be over? Are you going to tell me why you are sorry?*

The driver moved the rig onto a narrow street and explained something to Rosalie. She turned in her seat and said, "this is it. We get out here."

The three of them filed out and the rig started moving almost instantly.

"He's in a hurry," Rosalie said.

"I'd be too," Parkman said. "After what just happened."

They crossed the street and stepped into the shadows of a line of trees, all three of them scanning the area to make sure they wouldn't be attacked by surprise.

"I've always wondered how many men Armond has working for him. Or does he hire mercenaries as he goes?"

"We believe it's a consortium. This large group of individuals and companies that pool together to reach their common goal of immigrating whomever they want for a price. That also means young girls. The documents were perfect because they actually came from the normal branches of government that produce them."

Rosalie was leading them down a street just slightly off the broken sidewalk.

"You don't think walking the way we are won't attract attention?"

"Who cares what people think? If the bad guys show up I want to be a little hidden first and not out on the open side of the street."

"Fair enough."

They continued on in silence. Three more blocks up Rosalie gestured for them to stop. Sarah turned at what Rosalie was staring at. The Esztergom Basilica stood in regal form with its three domes held high in the air.

"Wow, it's gorgeous," she said.

"Yes, it is," Rosalie responded.

Parkman gasped behind her.

"Come on. Let's take a tour. The place is full. Armond's men won't make another attempt with a church full of people."

The three of them entered at the side door. They walked into the vast room filled with majestic art and the largest organ Sarah had ever seen. Rosalie was right. The place was filled with tourists, gawking and taking pictures. They toured the entire room and took the narrow twisting stairs to the top for a look above the city. Finally Rosalie led them back down and into the crypt. Just as she had explained, areas were cut off by gates to keep the public out. The entire time Sarah walked through the insides of the building she studied all the hiding places. Where could she run if she had to? What exit door would work best? She tried to memorize the crypt. The stairs she came down appeared to be the only ones giving access to the crypt. Maybe Armond and his men knew another way?

When they were done, Rosalie proposed dinner. They got up the stairs, out into the lowering sunshine and into a trap.

Seven men wearing fedoras stood in a semi-circle around the doors leading outside.

"Come with us," Rod Howley stepped away. He started limping toward the back of the church which offered a view of the Danube River. The gunshot wound in his shin that he received in the back of the SUV at the

Budapest airport hadn't done a lot of damage if he was already walking.

Sarah's stomach dropped a little. This guy was incredible. It lowered her spirits to see him here already but she knew he would be coming. How and when she hadn't been sure of but now that he was here she could focus on tomorrow and what had to be done.

The fedora men trailed behind Rosalie, Sarah and Parkman, with Rod leading them. The rear of the church had two very large doors. They were at least ten feet from the doors when Rod turned around to address them. It was clear that even Rosalie respected his authority.

"Tell me Sarah, what has your sister been up to lately?"

Sarah glanced at the men behind her and then back at Rod. "You brought your motley crew with you to Esztergom to ask me about my dead sister? You could've just called."

"Enough with the jokes. Tell me what's happening? Why are you three touring this basilica?"

"I don't have to tell you anything," Sarah said and turned to spit on the ground. She wanted him to know he left a bad taste in her mouth.

Rod smiled, his brow creasing. "I see you still don't fully grasp the situation."

Parkman stepped up beside her. He was so cute when he fell into protection mode. She smiled on the inside.

"I guess I don't. Why don't you tell me?"

"You are the property of the United States Government. At this moment you are on loan to Rosalie and her team. Whatever it is you're planning has been given the go ahead as we are watching to see what Vivian's role is." His gaze turned to Rosalie. "I understand your objective is locating and terminating or arresting a man named Armond Stuart?"

Rosalie nodded.

"I also understand that Sarah has seen him up close. My government has agreed to aid in this investigation. If your mission is complete or not, at midnight tomorrow evening Sarah comes with me."

"Says who?" Sarah asked.

Rod turned toward her. After a moment's pause he looked back at Rosalie. His smile was gone. "Your support team is landing over there," he turned and pointed at Slovakia. "I understand you are getting a quality assault team. This is good because Sarah cannot be involved in the assault. We need her unharmed."

Rod stepped up to Rosalie and pulled out a weapon so fast even Sarah didn't respond in time. She reached for her own and in the second her hand clamped on the butt of her gun, several hands lifted her off the cement.

Confusion reigned for a moment. Moving body parts and scuffling feet. The only things that weren't chaotic were Sarah's thoughts. She looked at Parkman who was now on the ground with two men holding his arms back, a knee jammed into his right kidney.

A man stood behind her yanking her arms to their limits. The pain was instant and caused an internal rage that could only be quieted with violence.

She took a deep breath and ducked her head, lifting her feet up like a horse would buck. Knowing full well she could do a face plant because her arms were being held back didn't stop her from kicking at her attacker's face with everything she had.

The man holding her wasn't prepared. Both her feet smacked each side of his face in unison, knocking him teetering back, his fedora hat lost to the breeze.

Her hands were freed but not fast enough as gravity yanked her down. She landed on her right shoulder, pulling her face up just in time, saving a broken cheek or nose.

She instantly rolled and hopped up to her feet.

Two more men advanced. Sarah raised her hands and gestured for them to continue.

Come and get it.

"Wait!" Rod yelled.

The two men stopped and stared at him.

"I said unharmed. Leave Sarah alone."

Sarah looked at him with something greater than violence, something in league with absolute rage. A large knife with a brass knuckle handle was held in his grip, the blade pressed against Rosalie's cheek.

"Drop the fucking knife," Sarah said.

Rod ignored her. *Mistake after mistake*, Sarah thought.

"Rosalie, you're a professional," Rod said. "The gas station gun fight could've seen Sarah hurt or worse, killed. You have her on loan. Your orders are to take care of her."

"Hey asshole," Sarah said. "Last chance. Drop the knife." She edged closer. The two men on Parkman continued to hold him. The man she kicked was getting off the ground slowly, holding his face. The other men stood and stared at her as ordered leaving her untouched. Rod continued to ignore her.

"You will be destroyed, your career over and then I will come in the night and kill you myself if anything happens to Sarah. Do we understand each other?" Rod asked.

Rosalie nodded as Sarah felt her shoulder flaring. Would it hold up when she jumped Rod? She never bluffed. He'd had two warnings. When she said last chance she meant it. She only hoped her shoulder wouldn't pop out.

With two quick steps she was beside Rod. Using her right hand she shot a fist up under his left arm and into his armpit. At the same instant her foot came down on the back of his knee. The armpit shot was meant to weaken, if not temporarily paralyze the arm and the back of the knee was meant to make him drop fast, which would remove the knife from Rosalie's face almost instantly.

She missed a little on the knee, her foot landing on the top of his calf muscle. The kick had the effect she wanted anyway as Rod dropped to the ground like a pro. He landed, rolled and sprung back up in some kind of stance, the knife held out in front of him. The armpit shot worked, though. His left arm dangled a little. He shook his hand to get it feeling right again.

His men were on Sarah in a flash. Multiple hands grabbed and prodded. Nothing pissed her off more than being held down by men. She squirmed and fought, but their grip was too intense.

"Sarah!" Rosalie shouted.

She stopped fighting and looked up, breath heaving in and out. She was sure her face was red with the fire that stoked her insides.

Rod was sliding his knife into a leather sheath.

The men who had held Parkman were standing up.

Then the three pairs of hands on her arms and legs all let go in unison. She stood to her full height and stared at Rod.

"Cause and effect," Sarah said, her teeth clenched. It had been a long time since she had felt this much rage.

He smiled at her. That fucking smile. "I actually think I'm beginning to understand you," he said. "You're saying we all have to be accountable for our actions. In your eyes I can see that you are going to try to make me pay for pissing you off. I need to be accountable. Is that right?"

"Absolutely. You will pay and the price I charge is fucking high. You have just bought a ticket on the fuck you train and I'm conducting you to hell."

He collected himself, shook his shoulders, dusted off his right knee from when it had hit the cement and massaged his left hand. After a moment he gestured to his men with a nod and all seven of them stepped back a few more steps.

"We have had a very bad day," Sarah continued. "It started quite early with a sniper trying to pick me off and Armond showing up to finish the job. Rosalie saved my life. Then at the hotel, gunmen opened fire and Rosalie gave me a weapon. Parkman saved the both of us. Finally, the gas station. It was Rosalie again who, along with her team, kept the gunmen at bay until I could commandeer a rig to finish the last one off. We have been attacked all day. This was the most I've been shot at in one day and you with your fucking knife and your ragtag group of fedora-wearing fuckwats show up to try to intimidate us. You jump on Rosalie as if she's the one fucking up? If it wasn't for her I'd be dead so you can take your asswipes and fuck off. We don't need you here."

Rod nodded. There was nothing left to say. He started limping toward the front. As he passed Rosalie, Sarah heard him whisper *take care of her.*

Parkman stepped up to Sarah. "That was very brave. You could've gotten seriously hurt."

"Do I ever think of the consequences? Besides, he doesn't want me hurt. I can fight him and his men with impunity."

Rosalie stepped up to them as she watched Rod and his men leaving. "You didn't have to do that. Rod's just angry. He can't touch me. He's not that powerful. I know his kind and who he has to answer to."

"But he was touching you. And he had a knife. That's all the provocation I need."

"For what it's worth, thank you." She looked down at the ground and then off in the distance.

"What is it?" Sarah asked. "Something bothering you?"

"How does he know about my team and where they're landing? If he knows, could Armond? Those plans were just arranged."

"Maybe your phone is bugged?"

"What scares me is how powerful he is. There's above the law, and then there's Rod. He does have a boss, but he thinks he's a God and when you have that kind of complex, you really can do what you want. He's the kind of guy that if he goes too far, everything gets covered up.

No government could admit to knowing him. He could get away with murder and he knows it."

Sarah started walking toward the front of the church where all the tourists were. "That makes me feel really good."

"Sorry Sarah. Oh and I liked your *fuck you train* comment. Truly, I almost burst out laughing."

"I was serious. I will not go quietly."

"If there's anything I know about you Sarah," Parkman said from behind her. "It's that you will not go quietly."

Chapter 24

They checked into Hotel Esztergom and registered under their own names. All three of them knew the false name trick wouldn't work on Rod, Armond or any other group of professionals looking for them, so Rosalie said they'd just use their real names. They rented two rooms and stayed in one together, leaving the other room empty and available if they needed it. Sarah held out a hope that if they were to be attacked at the hotel, the attackers would go to the other room first, thereby giving them a chance to all get up and get ready.

They had chosen to do a rotating sentry shift with Parkman having first watch, Rosalie next and Sarah last.

Sarah and Rosalie lay down in their own beds. Parkman settled into the corner chair with the lamp turned toward him.

"Wake me at two in the morning," Rosalie said.

"Don't worry. I will. I want some sleep too."

"Rosalie," Sarah said. "I'm a bit concerned about tomorrow."

Rosalie leaned up on her elbow. "You, concerned? About what?"

"You made a good point earlier. If Rod knows about the team coming to meet you, then why couldn't Armond? If everyone is converging on the crypt for tomorrow afternoon's mass, then wouldn't Armond just stay away? I mean he's got to know something is up. This could be a waste of time."

"I've thought about it too and I'm sure he knows. But could he pass up the chance to have all of us in the same building at once? If I was Armond and I knew that Rosalie and Sarah were going to come to my backyard, a backyard I know intimately, then I wouldn't stay away. I'd be there with guns on."

Sarah looked over at her. Parkman sat in his chair, a gun on his lap. "How do you feel Parkman?"

"You know what I'm going to say. Let Rosalie's team converge on Armond. Once they secure the crypt, you can come in and ID Armond. Nice and simple and you don't get hurt. That is if he shows up."

"I have to say," Rosalie chimed in. "I like that idea."

"Well, I don't see that happening," Sarah said. "What about Rod? When and how is the handoff supposed to take place?"

"You're not a package and there's nothing set yet. We deal with Armond and then I'm sure Rod will be around to collect you. His team will be close. They'll be watching."

Sarah thought about it for a minute and then crawled out of bed. She walked over to the desk and pulled out the chair. A pen sat beside the little hotel pad of paper. She grabbed the pen and held it up.

"Sarah?" Rosalie asked. "You okay?"

In her peripheral she saw Parkman wave Rosalie off.

She lowered her head and dropped the pen down to scrawl fast. After a moment she lifted the pen along with her head and gasped.

I hope that was convincing enough.

She set the pen on the desk and neatly folded the paper before returning to bed.

"What was that all about?"

"Nothing," Sarah said, knowing full well that she'd be called on it again.

"Sarah, what did you write?"

"I didn't write anything. Vivian did."

"Can I read it or will you read it to us?" Rosalie asked.

Sarah looked at Parkman and then at Rosalie. "You're not going to like it. Things like this could ruin your day."

"I don't care. We know that when Vivian says anything it's important and vital."

Sarah slowly unfolded the paper. She looked back up before reading it. Parkman had a confused look on his face. He'd seen her in a blackout state before and she was sure he could tell that she faked it. She looked back down at the paper.

"Vivian says that we are being watched by Rod and his team. She also said that they're listening to us right now."

"What? How are they doing that?"

"When he brought the knife to your face at the back of the basilica he planted a listening device on your person."

Rosalie jumped out of bed and grabbed her jeans that were folded on the dresser. After a quick search she came up with a little button-like piece of metal. She held it up for Sarah and Parkman to see and then set it on the floor and broke it with her shoes.

Then she ran to the hotel window and peeked through the curtains. After a moment she turned to them and nodded slowly.

"They're across the street in a black van. I just saw one of them step out and look up at our room. Probably because I broke their bug. What else does the note say?"

She couldn't believe it. She had been right. There was no other way for Rod to have known as much as he had without having bugged Rosalie.

Without appearing too elated at her confirmation Sarah looked at her scratchy handwriting. "It says that Rod has ordered Rosalie killed after Armond is neutralized."

"What!?" Rosalie gasped. "How could he do that? He doesn't have the authority."

She stomped across the room and grabbed her pants, intent on putting them on.

"Rosalie, take it easy. Calm down," Sarah sat up on the edge of her bed. "Stop what you're doing and come sit near me."

Rosalie looked at her for a long moment. Then she dropped her pants and sat on her bed, facing Sarah.

"I'll kill him first," Rosalie said.

"He doesn't want anyone to know that he has me. I think he even has plans for Parkman."

"But why?"

"Because I'm one of the rare ones. I actually can talk to the Other Side. He needs me. But he will never get me."

"How can you be so sure?"

"Because you're going to help me and in doing so you will stay alive too."

"What's the plan?"

Sarah explained what she had in mind. Rosalie listened and only gasped twice.

"Do you really think you can do that?"

Sarah nodded. "Absolutely."

Rosalie turned to Parkman. "Are you on board with this?"

"Of course," he said and smiled at Sarah, as he knew exactly what she was up to.

Rosalie was her wild card. Sarah had thought that Rosalie would definitely help when given the chance, but between how powerful Rod was and Rosalie's respect for Rod's authority, she wasn't sure anymore. She needed Rosalie's commitment. She needed to know where Rosalie stood. And she needed to know that tonight and not in the heat of the moment.

Sarah leaned back in her pillow, sleepiness weighing her down. The exhaustion of the day had caught up to her.

"Parkman?"

"Yeah?"

"You can relax. No one is going to hit us tonight."

"True. Not with Rod's boys out front. They won't move an inch now that they can't hear in here."

Rosalie laid back down on her bed. "Sarah, are you really going to be able to pull this off?"

"Yes," she said, her voice softened by sleep.

"Do you know how fucked up this is?"

"Yup."

"That my life would depend on your death is ridiculous."

"I know," Sarah said. "A lot of people will die tomorrow. Don't think of it as being special. Think of it as being smart."

"It's smart to die? You're not making sense. Are you asleep?"

"Almost…it's smart because we will live, *because* we're dead," Sarah said and passed out.

Chapter 25

Dull light slipped through the hotel curtains. Sarah opened her eyes halfway and squinted at the window. She looked to her right and saw the alarm clock said it was 10:48am.

Turning in her bed she saw Rosalie still sleeping and Parkman sprawled out in the corner chair.

She crawled out of bed and took a peek out the hotel window. Overcast skies threatened rain. The van was still across the street and most of the hotel parking lot had emptied.

She closed the curtains and turned around. Parkman's eyes were open.

"That was quite something last night," he whispered. "I've never seen you do anything like it. A fake blackout?"

"I made a good guess with the listening device and I got Rosalie on our side without question."

Sarah walked over to Rosalie. She was still out cold.

"Can you trust her not to waver?" Parkman asked.

Sarah nodded. "Not really, but I'll have to try." She walked past Parkman headed for the bathroom.

"You're not the trusting kind so I get that. But why now? Why her?"

"We don't have a lot of options. With her, our odds of success increase. If things go sour, she could die as *Vivian* predicted." She made air quotes with her fingers. "Either way, I turn out looking authentic don't you agree?"

Parkman nodded and pulled out a toothpick. She closed the bathroom door and jumped in the shower.

By 11:30am all three of them were showered and discussing plans.

"There's not much we can do until late this afternoon," Rosalie was saying. "My team doesn't show until then."

"We could use disguises. Take a crypt tour and disappear behind one of the roped off areas," Parkman suggested.

"No. They monitor everything. Alarms would sound."

Sarah walked over to the window again. The clouds were letting go. Rain covered the empty cement of the parking lot, coming down hard.

"Then what's the plan?" Sarah asked.

"I'm not sure yet," Rosalie said, her chin resting in her hands. "We have to assume Armond will be here today or tonight. I wanted to wait to meet my team and *then* deal with whether we go in quietly or as an assault. The only problem with an assault is that more people usually die versus doing a covert operation, and this is a national monument. Many treasures are going to be wrecked. The Hungarian Government won't look too kindly on us shooting up their largest church."

"With that many tourists and a mass being held, I think we all dress up in nice civilian clothes and go in armed to the teeth. We walk around and locate Armond or some of his men. Then we phone in a bomb scare and have the place emptied, with real police on hand to deal with the public. We stay in the building watching for Armond. If he doesn't leave, your men lock the exits up and we do a search until we find him."

Sarah turned from the window as she finished speaking. Rosalie was staring at her. "Sarah, that's brilliant. I'll propose that."

"Propose that? Aren't you in charge?"

"I am. But this team has their own chain of command. If they feel there's a crack in my idea, sorry, your idea, they will work with an altered plan or they may come with one of their own."

Sarah walked over and sat on the bed, facing Rosalie. "Be clear on one thing. I don't have a boss. I work for no one. That's what has kept me alive for so long. I do exactly what my sister tells me and I stay alive. *You* have to be accountable; I don't. So do whatever you want with your team, but be assured, Armond doesn't get away this time. He either gets taken into custody or he is killed. Understood?"

Rosalie nodded.

Someone banged on the hotel door so loud all three of them jumped. Sarah dove across her bed and retrieved her gun. Parkman was standing, his hands in front of his face, and Rosalie was still fumbling for her weapon.

"Who is it?" Sarah yelled.

"Hotel management. Check-out time has passed. You have to leave."

"Five minutes."

"Okay."

She heard his footsteps retreating. "Damn. Our nerves are rattled." She rolled over onto her back. "I thought a good night's sleep would have calmed me."

Parkman was sitting back down. Rosalie was putting her weapon away.

"We need to be more on the ball. One of us should have heard someone approaching the door."

Parkman nodded at her.

"Okay. Let's get out of here and get some food. I'm starving and we have a lot to do tonight."

"I have a feeling everything will work out," Rosalie said. "It's going to be a great day."

"Yes. It's a good day to die."

After a late lunch of Hungarian goulash, the trio crossed the bridge into Slovakia. They drove in two rented cars that Rosalie had picked up, Parkman driving one and Rosalie the other.

They met with Rosalie's team and were debriefed on how extraction would work once the target was confirmed. With or without Armond they would all fall back, cross the bridge and make it to the helicopter. The plan was to fly to a military airport in Romania since Romania wasn't part of the Schengen Agreement. After that they would fly Parkman and Sarah back to the States or wherever they wanted to go on a military jet. They didn't work for Rod's group, nor did they recognize his direct authority.

Sarah was warned that Rod could have orders sent to them through their chain of command, but he couldn't order them directly. Any orders coming their way they could avoid for a short while. Rosalie stressed that it was vital to get Sarah and Parkman out of Hungary as soon as this was over, and that Rod wouldn't be looking too hard for her as he would think she was deceased.

To Sarah's relief the team of professional soldiers were dressed in civilian clothes. It had been decided before they arrived to attempt a surgical extraction. There would be no military assault for one man. This was supposed to be a group of law enforcement officers arriving to arrest an international criminal. The only difference was that these people were an elite group; one that could handle situations that would rattle a Green Beret.

Armond, you have no idea what's coming, Sarah thought to herself as they pulled up to the front of the Esztergom Basilica.

They filed out as a group near the back of the parking lot. The rain was still coming down as they all separated and went their different ways. Radio communication had been established between the six-man team and Rosalie. Parkman and Sarah were considered civilians and only here for positive identification. They were supposed to stay close, but were ordered to fall back if a firefight took place.

Fat chance, Sarah said to herself.

She was still upset that her bomb threat idea was thrown out. They said that no one would attempt to bomb such a large and heavy building made of stone unless they had a seriously large device. Otherwise the damage would be minimal.

Sarah argued that there'd be no bomb, therefore no working theories on damage. The point of the bomb scare was the fear of it.

The team leader said that Armond would be able to see past that and know it was suspect. She could still hear him saying, "We will go in and attend mass and look around. He'll turn up."

Bullshit.

Parkman stayed close to her as they entered the basilica. Rosalie had fallen behind and was coming in a few minutes later.

As Sarah entered the main church she could see that everything appeared the same. People stood throughout the interior. Others were sitting on the pews waiting for mass to begin.

Parkman started off to the back and Sarah followed. She couldn't believe how upset her stomach was. Usually when walking into a dangerous situation she had her wits about her, adrenaline ran high and she felt ready. But tonight was different. Maybe it was the rain bringing her mood down? Or maybe it was that she finally gets to see the end of Armond?

To escape Rod she planned on faking her death. The ramifications of that went deep. It meant her parents would think she was gone too. A part of her knew that was going to happen when she came up with the plan but she hadn't thought about how it would all work out after the fact. Her focus was on Rod and how she couldn't live with him poking and prodding her like a lab monkey. Maybe after six months or a year she could attempt to contact her parents to let them know she was okay. Her dad would be pissed but he'd get over it. She knew her mom would cry and just be happy she'd returned. Maybe Rod would've moved on by then?

Yeah right, she thought. *I'm going to have to be dodging him for a long time.*

She watched as Rosalie entered the church and started for the front. After a moment Sarah saw more of the team enter. They'd all introduced themselves by name when they met at the helicopter. Sarah couldn't remember any of their names but one.

Bennett.

Bennett had been the name of the first girl she'd saved from a kidnapping five years ago. Mary Bennett.

Mary had even helped her out once all those years before.

And now a man named Bennett was on the strike team to bring down Armond Stuart. Funny how things worked.

She looked for Bennett but couldn't see him anywhere.

"What are you looking for?" Parkman asked.

"Bennett."

"Why?" He looked at her sideways.

"Because of his name. Mary Bennett was the first girl I saved from a kidnapping. Earlier, when we met the team, Bennett stared at me longer than the others. It didn't creep me out though. It was like he knew something about me. Maybe he read something in the papers and was now seeing Sarah Roberts in the flesh. That kind of feeling."

"I'll watch for him and tell you when I see him. But I'm sure it's nothing. Maybe you felt he was watching you more because you recognized his name—"

Parkman was cut off by an alarm. A high-pitched siren was resounding throughout the building. Sarah had her hand on her weapon, waiting to draw it but seeing no immediate threat.

"What the hell is that?" she yelled to Parkman.

He shrugged his shoulders.

The siren stopped as fast as it had started. A voice over a loud speaker said, "Could everyone please leave the building. Please find the nearest exit and leave the basilica. This is not a drill." The message was repeated in Hungarian.

"What do we do now?" Sarah asked. "This is fucked. I thought we decided against a fire drill or a bomb threat."

"Maybe they went ahead anyway. They don't think of us as equals. They could've done it without consulting us."

Sarah watched as the people who had come for mass were converging on the exits and leaving the building. Rosalie was standing by a column, watching her and Parkman. She gestured with a shrug of her shoulders too.

Someone stepped up close behind Sarah. She spun around and drew her weapon as she looked into the eyes of the team leader.

"Put that away. Do you have anything to do with this alarm?" he asked.

"No. I thought you did."

"Okay. We'd better get you outside in case Armond or any of his men also evacuate. We're going to want you two out there to ID them. We'll stay inside and start a room-to-room search in the crypt."

Rendorshag, the Hungarian police, were entering through the main doors and showing people which way to go. The inside of the church was almost empty. Since the stairs to the crypt were near the main entrance on the left, Sarah hadn't been able to see if anyone had come up from there. Armond could already be outside.

She nodded to the team leader and started for the doors with Parkman following.

Near the doors she saw Bennett. He was standing back behind a pillar, watching her and Parkman advance on the exit.

"Don't look now, but there's Bennett at three o'clock. He's watching us. This is getting strange."

After five steps Parkman said, "I see him too."

They neared the doors. The police said something in Hungarian. Sarah shook her head and said, "Angol". *English.*

"You appear to be the last two. Please come with us."

"Go with you? Why? We're leaving the building. Mass was cancelled."

"We understand. It's this way," the cop gestured and walked away.

Sarah and Parkman followed. They reached the outer doors and stepped into the rain. People had gathered under the overhang and a few others were collecting under a tree to wait out the drill.

"Come with us," the police officer said again.

Sarah looked at Parkman. Her eyes asked him what the hell was going on.

"Where are you taking us?"

Both officers were wearing thick bullet proof vests.

Were they here for a bomb scare or expecting something more like a gunfight?

The officer turned to face her. "We have a few questions for you. We'd like to check your passports. We are Hungarian police officers. At this point you have no choice. It will only take a few minutes and then you can return to the church once it's been swept. Now, follow me."

The officer walked away from them toward the parking area. Sarah could see his little police car. His partner waited behind them. Parkman started walking and Sarah followed.

This is weird. What are the odds they'd be subjected to a routine inspection of their documents during such a time?

The officer in the front lowered his head because of the rain and turned to them. "We had a bomb threat. Most of the people we saw leaving the building we recognize. You two are the only ones we don't know. This is all normal while the basilica is swept."

Fine.

They got to the cruiser. The officer opened the back door. "Get in."

Sarah waited for a moment, standing in the rain as it soaked her hair.

"Please get in. It is raining. We can do this easier in the vehicle."

Something was wrong. No way was this routine. Every radar bell she had was pinging, telling her to run. She looked around. No one was watching them. All of Rosalie's team were still in the building. Things were going downhill fast.

"What if we decide to not get in?"

"Sarah..." Parkman started but didn't finish.

The officer had pulled out a gun.

"Get in the backseat of my cruiser or I kill you in the street like the filthy dog you are. Armond is waiting in the crypt to see you."

Chapter 26

The driver's partner had slipped in beside Sarah in the back seat, a weapon pointed at her side. Parkman was ordered into the front. He was reminded that any hero shit would not only get him killed but would guarantee Sarah got a bullet too.

They should be warning me, Sarah thought. *People always underestimate the girl.*

They drove away from the basilica, the cruiser's wipers trying in vain to keep the windshield clear of the incessant downpour.

"Where are you taking us?" Parkman asked. "You are men of the law. I'm an American police officer. Are you even aware of what you're doing?"

"Shut up!" the driver glanced at him and then turned back to the windshield. "Janos, shoot the girl if this guy talks again."

The man beside Sarah nodded into the rear view mirror. Sarah looked at the back of Parkman's head. He stared straight ahead.

This was bad. She couldn't come this close and miss Armond. Her whole existence had become focused on one true goal, and that was to stop the madman who hired these thugs. She was worried her luck had run out. How many times had she been shot and hospitalized? How many broken bones? How many injuries, cut skin and bruises to stop this one man? And yet she still walked upright. She was basically healthy and wanted to keep it that way.

Vivian had apologized. What was that all about?

Would this be it? Was she supposed to die for real? Wouldn't her sister have warned her?

The police officer turned the car onto the green bridge connecting Hungary to Slovakia and raced across.

What is Rosalie going to think now?

They took a hard right. A sign on the side of the road had the number 63 on it. A red building went by that had *Steak House* written on it in English. Sarah could barely make out the words through her rain soaked window. The driver drove another hundred meters and then turned in between two houses and stopped.

Sarah looked at her backseat companion. The weapon he held stayed aimed at her.

The driver turned to Parkman. "You. Out."

"I'm not leaving Sarah."

Parkman spoke. Sarah waited for the bullet, ready to attack. None came. Her hands unclenched. These people don't keep their word. *Janos, shoot the girl if he talks again*, the driver had said only moments before.

"You have no choice. This doesn't involve you. Get out. No hero shit. Last chance for it to be done nicely."

She hadn't been looking behind the vehicle as she was paying serious attention on the guy beside her. Two men walked up beside the police car. They were in uniform. It appeared they were police officers too. Neither one looked like they were wearing kevlar.

"Parkman. We have company."

As she saw his head swiveling, his door was ripped open. Hands grabbed him around the lapel. Even though she saw his own hands cling to the doorframe, he was pulled from the vehicle as if he had no strength.

"No!" Sarah yelled and grabbed her door handle. It was locked. She reached up and tried to find the knob to unlock it and then realized she was in the backseat of a police car. She couldn't get out unless they unlocked the door from the front. But neither could her backseat companion.

Arms flailed outside her window. Parkman was taking serious blows to his body. The driver eased along the front seat until he was at the passenger door leaning out to watch the fight.

In the confusion, while the men outside fought and the driver stuck his head out the passenger door to watch, Sarah got ready.

She felt a shift in the seat beside her. The guy leaned forward to see more of what was happening.

She did her best to judge the location of his throat without looking directly at him. The kevlar came right up to his collar. She would have to make sure she did it right the first time. There would only be one chance.

She raised her left arm to rest on the back of the front seat. She too leaned up to pretend to watch. A quick check using her peripheral vision showed that her elbow was around a foot from the guy's exposed throat.

She waited. He edged closer still. The driver leaned further out the passenger door, his attention diverted.

With all the speed she could muster Sarah shot her elbow in a backward thrust at the guy's throat. It held all the pent up anger at Armond; all the times she had been placed in dangerous situations because of him, all the times she had been duped by him, all the anger at having lost a sister…it all went into the blow to the throat that drove the cop into the back of the seat, his head banging the blind spot between the back and side windows.

Her right hand reached under and wrestled the gun from his weakened grasp as he lost his fight for air. At the same moment the driver shouted something outside to his comrades. A quick look up told Sarah that he hadn't seen anything.

The men outside were almost finished, but grunts and groans were still coming from the fight, masking the backseat choking sounds.

The cop in the front seat spoke again in Hungarian. The fight was over as the two cops outside stood up.

The guy beside her had turned blue. She was sure she'd collapsed his trachea. He grabbed at his throat and gestured wildly but couldn't catch a breath or make a sound other than the choking kind. She kept her left arm across his chest so he couldn't lean forward to warn the driver.

They'd stopped hitting Parkman and were pulling him away from the vehicle.

Oh Parkman, I seriously hope you're okay. They will pay for this.

The driver leaned back in the car and slid along the front seat after slamming the passenger door shut.

The guy beside her had stopped making noise. The driver put the car in gear and went to start reversing. He spun in his seat and looked at Sarah. His eyes widened when he took in the situation. The car stopped as he hit the brakes.

She was holding the gun up on the back of the seat aimed at his face.

"Unlock the back door. Slowly."

She saw him reach for something. A clicking sound confirmed the door was unlocked. She reached to her right without looking and opened it.

"Good. Now, one more thing. Where are you taking me?"

He shook his head.

"Not a good answer. I'm the one with the gun. Where are you taking me? Last chance."

The driver turned a little and looked at his partner. He looked back at Sarah.

"Back to the crypt in the basilica."

"So you kidnapped us to bring Parkman over here?"

"Yes, and to give Armond a chance to neutralize your assault team."

"Why not leave Parkman and neutralize him too?"

"He would never have left you without a lot of noise. Too much trouble. Our orders were to remove anyone who was with you and bring them here. Then return with only you. By that time everyone else would be dead."

"Is that why you're wearing vests? Because of the assault team?"

He nodded. "Everyone has one tonight."

"Tell me your name."

"Why?" he asked.

"Ballsy to be defiant when I'm the one with the gun. Tell me your *name*." She emphasized the last word by pressing the weapon into the skin of his throat.

"Peter."

"Okay Peter. As you said, everyone else will be dead. But it won't be only my side because I'm going to end this thing tonight."

He frowned. "You can't win. Whether you shoot me or not, Armond will kill you tonight and everyone else you brought along. No one can stop him."

"I'll take my chances," she said and fired her weapon.

The bullet entered the center of his neck right below the adams apple. His eyes widened and his hands rose to the wound. Blood began trickling out and down his chest. After a moment he slumped in the driver's seat.

"That was for my friend Parkman. No one delivers him to a beating like that and gets away with it. No one."

She looked outside but couldn't see anyone. The rain continued to pelt the car. It must've masked the sound of the gunshot well enough because no one came running to investigate.

She needed to find Parkman. She needed to make sure he was okay before going back to the crypt.

She eased out of the backseat, the gun held in front of her. A quick look up and down the small alley revealed no one. It was getting dark and the rain wasn't showing any signs of letting up.

She started down the alley the way she'd seen the two men pulling Parkman.

At the corner she looked around slowly. Both men were standing inside an open garage door. They had the trunk of a car open. Sarah could see the edge of Parkman's elbow from where she was.

"Hey guys!" she yelled from her hiding place, deepening her voice as best she could. She looked behind her to make sure she was alone. *No more surprises.*

When she looked back around the corner with one eye she could see both men were staring in her direction but neither one had stepped out into the rain.

"Peter and Janos said to bring the American cop back to their car," she shouted, trying to sound as masculine as she could.

She watched as they looked at each other. One of them shrugged his shoulders and reached into the trunk to pull Parkman out.

How stupid can you get? They don't even question why a woman's voice is shouting at them? Maybe her voice was convincing enough? Or maybe it was saying the names Peter and Janos that did the trick.

Parkman was lifted out. One guy took his arms and the other his legs as they started carrying him back toward her.

I'm sorry this happened to you, my friend.

She waited until they were five feet from the corner before stepping out, her gun raised with both hands.

Two quick shots from such close range dropped each man. It happened so fast that neither one of them got a chance to reach for their weapons.

She ran to Parkman and brushed the rainwater from his face.

He blinked and then shut his eyes again. Blood covered his face. He was still bleeding around his mouth. Bruises were already forming and his left eye looked like it would be swollen shut within hours.

"I'm sorry," she whispered.

He grunted something.

"What?" She leaned in closer.

"Get Armond...finish this." *This* was pronounced *dis.* Sarah could see a couple teeth were missing in the front.

"I will, but I'm not leaving you here. Can you walk?"

She saw an almost imperceptible nod of his head.

"Okay, let's get you to your feet, fucker. And next time don't let them hit you so much."

She turned him over and wrapped his arm around her neck.

"Man are you heavy. What the fuck do you eat? T-bones for breakfast?"

When he grunted it almost sounded like laughter. To Sarah it was musical.

"What happened...to dem?"

"They're all dead. Every one of dem." She said it his way. He was alive. He would heal. Everything was all right in the world. The people that stood for her would make it through. The only real person she trusted took a hit for the team. She would go to the edge and then jump for him. He proved his allegiance. She would prove hers.

Something loosened and moved inside her. It opened, blossomed and sprung new life. She felt it in her soul. It was filled with life, love and trust. What Parkman did and what he was made of moved her to a place she never thought possible. She was feeling again. It had been so long that it felt foreign.

In that moment she knew she would die for him. There could be nothing more noble.

But first Armond has to be exterminated.

They shuffled to the police car, arm in arm. Sarah gently placed Parkman back in the passenger seat he'd previously occupied. When he was seated and secure she raced around to the driver's side and yanked the dead cop out of the front seat and onto the wet pavement. Then she began undressing him. It took too much time but she got the kevlar vest off him. She tossed it at Parkman and then opened the backdoor to work on the other cop.

After she'd removed his vest she left him in the backseat, got behind the wheel and started the car.

"What about...?" Parkman asked, pointing to the guy in the backseat.

"He's coming with us."

Parkman moved his head sideways a little and raised both bloody hands in a questioning gesture.

"Because I want Armond to see what happens to the people he sends after us."

Sarah dropped the police car into reverse and backed down the alley. She eased onto the street and started back the way they had come, hoping some of Rosalie's team were still alive. As they began to cross the bridge back into Hungary she flipped the police siren on. She didn't want anyone getting in their way.

Parkman muttered something beside her.

"What was that?" she asked.

"I could use…a too pick."

Chapter 27

Sarah drove into the empty parking lot of the Esztergom Basilica, siren blazing. The only vehicles were three other police cars. She killed the siren half way up the lot and pulled to the far right. There were eight large pillars at the massive front of the basilica. She drove to the far right side of them and, keeping her vehicle in the shadows, edged onto the grass where she stopped and turned the police car off.

"Put that thing on. I know you're in pain, but I can't leave you here without it on. Sorry about the blood on it." She pushed the kevlar vest in his lap.

"Are you going to be okay?"

He nodded.

"Stay out of sight. When this is over I will come and get you and we will drive to the helicopter and get the fuck out of here. Got it?"

He nodded and started to slide an arm into the vest.

Sarah lifted her T-shirt over her head and then donned the vest, slipping the T-shirt back on over top.

"Sure hope this thing works," she muttered to herself.

"Me 'oo," Parkman said.

She looked over at him, knowing this might be the last time they saw each other. After a moment of silence she leaned in and kissed his cheek. She saw his good eye open a little in surprise.

"I love you Parkman. Thank you for what you do. You've helped me in more ways than you know."

"I uv oo too."

She raised a finger. "Just be clear. Love as in a brother and not sexy-time shit." She almost giggled. She felt young and free.

He smiled as best he could and nodded. "Of orse."

Sarah saw the teeth that were missing. A little blood still trickled out of his mouth.

"We'll get you to a doctor as soon as this is over."

He nodded.

She turned and jumped from the vehicle. In her right hand she held the cop's gun and in her waistline she had Rosalie's ankle gun stashed. The rain had eased a little. She didn't have to wipe as much off her face as earlier. Her shirt was soaked and her pants felt like she'd gone swimming in them.

With her hand low at her side she headed around to the back of the church. She wanted to find another way in. Using the front door was like shouting out *I'm here motherfuckers, come get me.* She wasn't in that kind of mood.

Kill Armond and leave. That's it. Time to go to Canada and take a break.

After turning the corner she heard a car door shut behind her. *Good, maybe Parkman was moving into a more secure location.*

At the back of the church she turned the corner. She saw no movement of any kind. Maybe they were all in the church. It was full dark now, and difficult to see. A few small security lights were affixed to the side of the church but they didn't give off a lot of light in the rain-darkened night. She had to move slowly. This was the end game. There could be no mistakes.

She passed the two large back doors of the church. As she came up to the corner she heard a solid thump behind her and nearly jumped out of her skin.

"Shit." She whispered. "What the fuck was that?"

She turned toward where she thought she heard the noise. Faint gurgling sounds came from about ten feet in front of her. In the dark she couldn't make anything out.

"Identify yourself," she said, her weapon raised, safety off, finger in place.

She stepped closer.

"Identify yourself," she said again.

More gurgling.

Her eyes adjusted. She saw the faint shape of a man lying on the ground about four feet in front of her. He was ·wearing the clothes of one of Rosalie's team members.

After checking around her immediate area to make sure this wasn't a trap, she leaned forward and knelt down.

"What happened? Where is everyone?"

She could barely see his eyes roll to her. Then she heard a final release of air. She reached up under his neck but felt no pulse.

"Shit."

She stood up and raised her gun. *Where the fuck is everybody? And where did this guy come from?*

Five feet from her another heavy thump shook the ground. She ran over and saw another of Rosalie's team. He was still alive but going fast.

"What happened? Tell me."

"They…" he gasped, fighting for air.

"Try to tell me. I'm sorry, but try."

"Roof…throwing…" two big gasps and then he said, "off roof," he lowered his head and rolled away a little, his body still.

Sarah stood and looked up at the roof. She could see flashlights roving around. A dark figure was out on the edge. Then whoever it was stepped back from the edge.

Sarah ran toward the building. Not three steps away, another thump smacked the ground behind her. She turned back to see who it was. He was close enough that the security lights illuminated his body. This man was dead before they threw him. Three bullet holes could be seen in his chest area. He lay at an odd angle, his right arm twisted behind his head in a way that arms weren't supposed to go.

Anger rose inside her beyond anything she had ever experienced. The people who had come here to see that justice was done were being thrown off the roof of a church as if they were vermin. Real human lives were being thrown away like trash. Someone's brother, son or father lay at her feet.

She almost felt paralyzed with anger. All thoughts of accountability and consequence disappeared. There was no way Armond could live through this. Even if she died, it didn't matter. This was more than catching a criminal mastermind. This was war and Sarah felt ready for battle.

As she turned to head back to the church another body thumped to the ground a few feet away. She didn't stop to look; there was no point. The only thing that mattered was Armond.

Maybe I'll wound him and then throw him off the roof.

She came around the corner and strode up to the main doors of the church. They were propped open. She saw no one in the area.

They must all be on the roof. The building was evacuated and everyone sent home. He thought his men were handling Parkman and me so they needn't worry about us while they deal with Rosalie's team. Brilliant and stupid. What they didn't count on was me coming back alone, armed and ready. And pissed the fuck off.

She stepped into the church and looked down the steps that led into the crypt. Should she go down there and wait or go upstairs and attack one by one until she kills Armond? The smart thing was to lie in wait. Safer. Attacking meant, putting herself at greater risk.

Fuck it.

She moved forward into the main church. Something moved above her. She ducked a little. A straw broom swung down, attached to a rope of some kind. She stepped sideways, easily avoiding its arc. She must've tripped a wire or something as she entered.

Great. Now they know I'm here. So much for stealth.

She stepped past the doorway and looked up to see where the broom had come from to make sure it wasn't thrown by an attacker.

That was her undoing.

Something hit her hard below the right knee. She shouted out in pain and crumpled to the floor. Before she could turn around, a heavy black boot stepped on her right forearm and the gun in her hand was ripped away.

Rough hands seized her and tore the other weapon out of her waistband.

She was lifted into the air and carried toward the line of pews by three men. She couldn't protest much due to the throbbing pain in her leg. She gritted her teeth and mentally chastised herself for being so stupid.

They had meant to make her look up so she wouldn't see them standing behind the door. They used a broom because they didn't want to kill her yet and now here she was a prisoner of Armond Stuart. Again. But this time, even if she could escape, she couldn't run very far.

Fucking great!

The meat claws of Armond's men set her down hard. She cried out at the pain in her leg despite herself. It felt like it was broken.

Wire wrapped around her wrists. She felt them tying her to a pew.

"What the fuck you gonna do? Preach to me?" she asked through gritted teeth. A sweat broke out on her forehead. Her hands felt clammy scrunched together.

One of the men looked up at her, paused what he was doing and then looked away.

"Fucking pussy. Beating up on a girl. Your mother know what you do for a living?"

He wound up and backhanded her across the face.

Oh shit. That fucking hurt. I gotta watch my mouth until I can get out of this.

"Don't talk to them," a voice said above her. "They don't speak English. Only Hungarian."

She looked up and into the eyes of Armond Stuart. He was standing in a raised pulpit wearing a priest's vestments. The pulpit was attached to the side of a rounded pillar. Stairs could be seen behind the pillar where access to the pulpit would be gained. She figured they were used for sermons as the church was so large the priests would want to come closer to the people to be heard better.

"Are you enjoying your last evening alive?" Armond asked.

"Why are you dressed like a priest? Gonna change from young girls and start in on young boys now?"

She struggled with her hands a little. The brutes who'd tied her up had stepped away. Two of them had left the area. The one who slapped her was standing at the end of the pew watching over her.

"Your sense of humor is courageous. I could order that man to sever your head right now and be done with it. So I think that your death has everything to do with me because I'm the one who is going to kill you. It's time, don't you think Sarah?"

She stared up at him. He was bigger than she remembered. Then it donned on her. He was wearing a kevlar vest too. "Sure. Who knows. You stall and I might get out of this hogtie and run past your gorilla and chase you through the church until I catch you and jam my thumbs into your eyes and through your brain. So I guess, sure, it's time. You have the advantage. Take it. Come and get me."

"You know," he said, arms out in front of him. "You are a pain in the ass and naturally I don't like things in my ass. You're a large fucking dump that just won't flush. You should be dead by now. I don't trust anything that bleeds five days a month and never dies. It's too bad you aren't on my side; I could've used someone with your brains and skill."

She felt the swelling in her knee as the joint stiffened. How many injuries had she had in her life because of the man preaching to her right now?

"I've still got one more card to play," she said.

The curiosity on Armond's face was evident. "Oh, really. What's that?"

She shook her head, eyes down to the floor. "No way. I'm a gambler. The cards stay close to me. I'll reveal it when I need it. And man," she looked back up at him. "Wait until you see this card. I mean it's the fucking ace of spades this one. And it's going to really mess with you."

"You're bluffing for real this time. You're actually full of shit, Sarah. I have this church surrounded. The Rendorshag work for me. Rosalie's team have been neutralized. Didn't you see them falling from the sky?" He stopped and looked sideways like he was thinking. Then he looked back at her. "How did you like my bomb scare idea? Well it wasn't exactly my idea. I stole it from you. We have been listening to you since you toured the basilica yesterday. You should've seen Rosalie's face when I popped up out of this pulpit and shot four of her men before she even had a chance to pull her weapon. It was over before it started." He paused and looked around again. He seemed agitated. "Wait, where's Parkman? How did you get away from my men?"

He was playing her. He wouldn't let random people drive up to the basilica and go unnoticed. He just said the basilica was surrounded. He knew she would be in the rear of the building when he tossed Rosalie's men over. So they'd been watched the whole time. That meant he had Parkman.

Damn!

"I see you're working it out. That's right, your American cop will die in the crypt tonight. After all the shit he pulled at the compound, he's lucky that I'm just going to kill him. You too, for that matter. But we must hurry this along."

Armond turned from her and walked down the steps at the back of the pulpit. He came around the pillar and opened his arms like he was talking to a great many people.

"The number of assholes I have killed in my lifetime could fill this room. What's another couple?"

He turned to the animal at the end of the pew and spoke in Hungarian. The brute walked briskly to Sarah, grabbed her under the arm and half lifted, half pulled her from the seat. She staggered along as best she could, doing her best to stay off her right leg.

A tinge of real fear spiked her stomach. What if Armond killed her? Could it be over so easily? It couldn't end that way. Not after all she had done. Not after all she had gone through. Wouldn't Vivian have warned her? Or was that the apology part of Vivian's message?

She was dragged toward the side exit door and the stairs that led to the crypt. Armond stayed ten feet ahead.

As they neared the open front doors Sarah was sure she heard something outside. A scuffling sound or the sound of a weapon's safety.

It all happened so fast.

The man holding her let go. Sarah fell to the floor and sprawled out flat, her right shoulder taking the hit as she couldn't put her hands out in front.

Guns were fired. Bullets raced by over her head.

She snuck a peek when the guns went silent. Armond was hiding behind a door to her left. The guard who had been holding her was dead, blood oozing from a wound in his forehead.

Who the fuck is shooting if they have Parkman? Has Rod Howley finally showed up?

Someone was yelling outside.

"What?" Sarah shouted.

"Stay down Sarah. It's Bennett. They've killed the whole team. I'm the last one."

She stole a glance at Armond. He was speaking into a cell phone.

"Watch your back!" she shouted. "He's calling in more men."

Gunfire erupted outside. She frantically looked at Armond. He stepped out from behind the door, cell phone to his ear. He was grinning like a fucking asshole. The whole ear-to-ear shit.

"Got him." He snapped his phone shut and stashed it in his front pocket. "My men just told me the problem has been neutralized."

He walked up to Sarah, reached down and yanked her to her feet. She almost fell back down because of her leg. Repulsed by his touch, she reared back trying hard to dislodge his hand.

"Take it easy. Your sister wasn't as much of a fighter as you are. And I'm not even interested in your pussy. I just want you dead."

Something clicked in Sarah's head. In a distant place, deep in her consciousness she felt her sanity shift to the edge of reality. She would never be the same. It felt like she'd had a stroke but only the good side of her was paralyzed. The angry, violent side got energized.

Armond dragged her to the stairs and started descending them, pulling her along. He mumbled to himself. He yanked harder, almost knocking her over, and then mumbled something else.

She wondered if the best thing was to throw herself at him. He'd tumble down the stairs, but so would she. Tied up the way she was, broken bones and death were probable. Armond on the other hand might walk away with bruises.

She'd wait. Her moment would come.

They reached the bottom. He dragged her to a gated area and then past that and into a darker chamber.

"Here is where you will lie for eternity."

They entered a room with candles burning. Along the walls she could see large squares that had words written on them in different languages. When she had toured the crypt with Rosalie and Parkman, what seemed like a lifetime ago, this area had been sealed off.

In the center of the room sat an old wooden table. He dragged her a little further and then tossed her down to the floor. She leaned up against the wall.

"Was that guy Bennett your ace of spades?"

"No."

"So what's this last card you have to play?"

"You'll see."

Armond pulled his weapon out and aimed it at her. "You know, I'm sick of your games. I'm pissed that you're still alive. Every day you live is another day I'm upset."

She struggled to sit upright. "You know, I was thinking the same thing."

"I should just shoot you now. Be done with it."

"I thought that's what we were down here for."

He shook his head and lowered the weapon. "No. I have better plans for you."

He turned away and started touching the wall around one particular square.

"I had this stone removed. Once that was done I took the remains of some asshole clergyman out and tossed them in the garbage. This will be your new home." He stopped and looked her. "For eternity."

After a moment he clicked something under the stone and drew it out on wheels.

"See, I even had my men install these wheels so that I could do this alone without having to lift the slab myself."

From where she sat she couldn't see inside the square hole. All she could tell was that it was dark.

Something akin to real fear washed over her. Was this the end? Would he get away? But rational thought escaped her. She was ready. Something would happen. There was no way it could be this easy for him.

Gunfire erupted above them again.

"Aw shit! What the fuck is going on? I thought everything was handled."

He flipped open his cell phone again and dialed out. After a moment he stepped to the doorway to get better reception.

Armond raised his weapon at her and said, "Stay put. I'm only seven feet away. I won't miss."

Then he started talking in Hungarian on the phone. After a couple sentences he flipped the phone shut and swore to himself.

"Okay, I have to go upstairs. That Bennett fucker is proving to be a real asshole. We're down to only a couple men left."

"Don't worry about me. I'll wait here for you," Sarah said.

"I'm not worried about you. You're dead."

Armond raised the weapon from about five feet and pulled the trigger.

In that second Vivian took over. Her right arm went numb, her body slack.

Before losing consciousness she heard Armond's gun fire four times.

Sarah felt each and every bullet hit her body in the chest area.

Then she was gone.

Chapter 28

She woke with a start, gasping for air. Each intake of breath screamed pain throughout her ribcage. She almost shouted out loud in frustration. Her eyes watered, her face felt flush.

Sarah groaned and tried to collect herself. Four bullets in the chest.

Thank you God for the kevlar.

Frantically she looked down at her vest. There were four small holes in her shirt where the bullets had made contact with the kevlar. She wriggled her hands but they were still tied too tight.

The pain was intense. At least half of her ribs had to be broken.

She tried to move but couldn't. Everything she did screamed pain.

"Either get up and walk out of here, or stay and die," she grunted to herself.

Finding resources where she didn't know she had them, Sarah leaned against the stone wall and forced herself to her feet. Sweat broke out on her brow and threatened to run into her eyes. For a brief second she felt lightheaded. She paused and breathed in deep. A woozy feeling came and went.

"Don't you fucking faint," she whispered.

She looked around but there was nothing sharp to cut her wrist restraints. The gate that closed the section off was metal, the color of rust. Near where the gate connected there was a hook for a latch. She ambled over, taking careful steps to avoid any more internal damage. A broken rib bone could be tearing into muscle tissue. The last thing she wanted was to survive being shot by four bullets point blank to the chest only to die from internal bleeding because she wanted to walk away.

She got to the gate and waited again. She needed to breathe but each breath was testing her pain threshold. The pain had an odd soothing effect on her. She reasoned that it should feel good even though it didn't because it meant she was still alive. Her heart was still beating.

Gunfire erupted above her. Two shots then silence. Then two more.

Time was running out.

She turned and hooked her bound wrists onto the latch and then pulled away, hoping to loosen the binding as one would take the tine of a fork to a knotted shoelace. The wire dug into her wrists as she pulled, but she ignored it as best she could. After a couple of pulls, she loosened it enough to struggle back and forth attempting to free her hands from their restraints. They felt better but it wasn't enough.

Someone was running around upstairs. She heard shouting.

One more attempt with the latch pulled an edge off the twine. She wriggled her hands frantically, keeping her breathing even. The pain subsided a little.

Maybe it's heavy bruising and not broken ribs. Maybe only bruised bones. Hopefully.

She undid the last of the twine that bound her wrists and pulled her hands to the front.

"Ahhh," the pain renewed as her chest contracted. "Shit, that *fucking* hurts."

Adrenaline pumped. Endorphins kicked in.

She was ready. It wasn't over.

She turned for the stairs and started to climb.

With each step she reminded herself she was that much closer to killing Armond. She had to. There was no other option left. It motivated her to take another step and then another.

She made it halfway up the stairs. No one seemed to be in the crypt behind her. Whoever remained alive was upstairs fighting.

Before climbing any further, she kissed her right hand and pressed it against the rock wall.

"Thanks Vivian for taking over and making my body limp. I have no idea how I would've fared if I'd tensed up."

Her right knee was feeling better the more she used it. She was climbing with both legs, only limping a little.

She reached the top without encountering anyone. There was a small turn to the right and then a few more steps to enter the hallway that turned right to go into the church or left to the outside.

With no weapon and not many options to defend herself she took the last few steps very carefully.

A gun went off outside making her duck.

Damn the pain.

The sudden movement shot rivers of agony through her chest. She held the wall and waited.

Another gunshot outside.

What the hell's happening? Who's shooting who?

She climbed the rest of the way and stepped into the open. The man who had tied her up and who Bennett shot still lay face down. She approached him. A quick pat down gave her both her guns back.

Lucky me.

She stood up and limped to the inner wall. Slowly she edged around and peeked into the church. From where she was standing it appeared empty. The action was outside. She turned toward the main doors and shuffled for the exit.

To her surprise the first person she saw was Armond Stuart.

He was hiding behind a small brick wall across the walkway near the entrance to a refreshment store for the tourists. He was looking up the walkway toward an assailant. His hand held a weapon.

Sarah had a clear shot. She took careful aim.

He looked at her. His eyes widened.

She fired.

Perfect.

His gun hand was knocked sideways, his weapon thrown from his grip.

He screamed out in pain.

She fired again. Then again. Each shot she aimed for the center of his chest, making sure she didn't miss the kevlar vest he wore. He wavered on his feet.

She stepped forward and shot Armond a fourth time.

He fell to his knees and then onto his back in front of the tourist store's front door.

Sarah walked across the opening. Whoever was exchanging fire with Armond wasn't her enemy. She had no fear of being hit.

As she stepped up and stood over Armond she reached back and placed the gun in her waist line.

She wouldn't be needing it anymore.

"I shot you. You're dead," Armond breathed out through clenched teeth, his eyes wide.

Sarah could tell by his gasping that he was going through exactly what she had.

She stepped up close and kicked him in the chest with her left foot. He shouted out in pain.

"Sarah!" someone yelled in the distance.

She ignored them as she got down and sat on Armond's stomach, straddling him like a horse.

"Yes, you shot me," she said. "I shot you so now we're even. But there's another matter to clear up."

"What?" he managed.

Real fear was in his eyes. His breath panted in and out, his face shining in the little light that came up from the security lamps. She could see that he knew it was over. His reign had ended. He'd made mistakes.

"My sister. Vivian. My trump card."

Sarah reached behind her and pulled her gun back out. She twisted around and took careful aim so as not to shoot herself in the butt.

The nozzle gently touched Armond's crotch.

"No!" he shouted.

Sarah fired. The bullet tore a hole in the vestments he still wore. She leaned over to get a better look.

"Perfect," she said. "That's for all the girls you've raped. All the lives you've stolen." She had to raise her voice over his inhuman screaming wail. "All the innocence you tore from everyone you have ever touched and this is from me to you!"

Sarah placed her right hand on his throat and started to push. With her left hand she set her weapon down and applied her thumb on his eye socket. Both hands pressed in amid his shouting. He wiggled under her but couldn't shake her off. She pushed harder.

And then someone tackled her from the side, knocking her into the wall by the tourist shop.

Before hitting the wall and coming to a stop on the ground she was already clambering for her gun. She grabbed it, brought it up and aimed at Rod Howley.

"You don't want to do that."

She could barely hear him as Armond screamed on the cement between them.

Sarah decided to shout too. The pain from being hit became a form of torture. "Give me...one good reason. Wait," she said and raised her free hand. "I actually don't need any fucking reasons. I wanna do it."

He raised his hands. "If you kill me it doesn't end. You have a file now. My successor will know what I know. He will hunt you down but this time they won't be as nice as I've been. This does not end with me. It ends with you." His eyes turned to pleading. "Come in with me Sarah, willingly. I will make sure you're comfortable. Then after six months or so you can go back to civilian life. Does that work?"

She pretended to think about it when really all she needed the break for was to get her breathing under control and manage the pain. Then she said, "I don't go anywhere until he is dead." She gestured at Armond.

The pig on the ground in front of her turned his head a little, following her voice. He looked at her with one eye already swelling shut, the other filled with malevolence. Blood pooled below his crotch area. He was in need of medical attention or he would bleed to death.

"Fine," Rod said and brought his hand up. In it he held a large handgun. It was a kind of sidearm Sarah hadn't seen before.

Rod fired from two feet away blowing the top of Armond's head clean off. He fired again, this time aiming at the throat. A hole the size of a cantaloupe opened up above Armond's collarbone, half his throat vanishing into the cement.

Sarah looked into his turned face and saw his good eye register the shots. Then he slumped toward the ground and Armond Stuart took his last breath.

I'm free! I'm free! He's finally gone!

She felt an exuberance she'd never felt before. To know that her sister's murderer was dead and to feel so good about it was almost enough to make her feel guilty. Her eyes watered a little. It was over.

The wicked witch was dead.

"Now, get up and come with me," Rod said. "Everyone's dead. There's just you and me. We'll leave together."

"Everyone's dead?" she was sure when she heard someone yell her name not a few minutes earlier that it was a voice she recognized. It wasn't Rod who had yelled.

Someone's still alive.

Whoever they were Rod was trying to get her away from them.

"Is that how this is going to work?"

"I'm not following."

"Whoever is still alive will be killed so there's no witnesses to this carnage?"

"But Sarah, no one is alive. Everyone was killed."

She looked into his eyes under the brim of his hat.

"Then who was Armond shooting at?"

"Me." He stood up and holstered his weapon. Then he adjusted his hat and looked down his nose at her. "Let's get you out of here before the real police show up. Now that Armond is gone, they will come and they're going to be pissed. If we're still here we will have too much explaining to do."

Rod reached out a hand to help her up. At that moment someone stepped up behind Rod.

It was Bennett.

She saw a weapon silhouetted in his hand.

"Ok Rod, you got me," Sarah said as she reached for his hand.

She saw Bennett place the cold steel end of his gun against the back of Rod's neck. Rod froze.

"So, everyone's dead are they?" Sarah asked. "Six months or so and then back to normal life? Who the fuck do you think I am that I would believe *you*?"

"Step away from the girl," Bennett ordered.

Rod stood up and raised his hands but not in supplication. He adjusted his fedora again and then lowered his hands. The hand cannon he'd killed Armond with had disappeared.

"Now what?" Rod asked.

Sarah chimed in as she was getting to her feet. "Watch it, he's packing."

Bennett found the weapon easily and disarmed him, tossing the gun at least twenty feet away.

"In the crypt there's a slab pulled out from the wall," Sarah said. "It's on little wheels. Lock him in there for the night. His men will retrieve him in good time."

Bennett nodded. "You heard her. Let's go." Bennett motioned with the gun.

"You haven't heard the last of me," Rod said to Sarah as he started walking back into the church.

Sarah followed to the top of the stairs and waited. She grabbed her gun and held it like she'd hold a rosary. Could never be too sure.

Where's Parkman? Did Armond really get to him?

She waited what felt like a long time before she saw Bennett coming back up the stairs, his gun put away.

"You okay?" he asked when he got to her.

"Other than the bruising and possible broken ribs from four bullets in the chest and the sprained right knee, I'd say I'm doing fine. Actually, scratch that, I'm fabulous. Armond is dead."

"Yes he is. Come on. Let's get you to the chopper."

"What happened to your team?"

"Ambushed. It was chaos. We had no choice. I was the only one they didn't see. When you and Parkman left with those police officers I was behind a pillar and that's where I stayed. They took my team upstairs and threw them all off the roof."

"I know. I'm sorry."

"We all knew the risks when we signed on."

"Sure you do, but you're human first. You feel."

He looked over at her. "You're right. I'm blocking it now, but tomorrow it's gonna hurt like a son of a bitch."

They exited the main doors with Bennett in the lead. She could see his training in everything he did. He cleared the entrance and then allowed her to step out. He moved along the wall in front of her, going her speed and keeping an eye behind them the whole time.

"Rod's secure in the crypt?"

Bennett motioned with his hand to stay quiet. Then he leaned in close to whisper. "Rod may have more men close by. We'll talk in the chopper."

Sarah nodded. Then pulled him close and whispered. "Do you know what happened to Parkman? I need to know before we leave the area."

"I don't know but I did hear Armond say that he was dispatched. I'm sorry."

Sarah looked down at the ground. *Oh Parkman.* It was over. Armond was dead now. Parkman, her best friend, her only friend was gone. Bennett couldn't confirm it but Armond had.

Parkman knew they were to fall back to the helicopter. She would hold out hope until they lifted off. She would get Bennett to delay as long as he could.

Come on Parkman. Wherever you are, get up. Meet me at the chopper.

They were nearing the rear of the basilica. Bennett looked back at her.

"Are you crying?" he asked softly.

"Keep moving. Let's get out of here," she said as she wiped her cheeks.

They hit the grass at the back running as fast as Sarah could on her bad knee. She only stumbled once on the wet grass. The rain had completely stopped and the moon was high now. Her eyes adjusted fast. She stumbled a couple more times due to the undulations in the ground.

Within ten minutes they had reached the edge of the Danube River. Sarah looked back up and saw the massive dome on the hill.

Oh, Parkman. Please. Hurry.

A quick run up the street would take them to the bridge. They could cross it on foot and be at the helipad fifteen minutes after that. Sarah looked at the river. Streetlights illuminated the area. Boats lined the side, tied up and bumping softly with the current.

They continued up the street, Bennett watching everything.

"I used to know a girl named Bennett."

"I know."

That surprised Sarah. "You know? How?"

"Mary Bennett is my sister."

She stopped walking.

"Sarah, we have to keep moving. We have to cross the bridge and get into Slovakia before the Hungarian authorities show up."

"Mary is your sister?" She couldn't believe it.

"Okay, I'll tell you briefly. As I understand it from her, you saved her life once. Armond's men tried to kidnap her about five years ago. You stepped in. She helped you once with your father Caleb but she actually felt she got you in more trouble. I signed on for this team years ago to stop people like Armond. I do the same thing you do but without the psychic angle. When I heard Rosalie needed help and that you were here I made sure I was on the assault team. Armond was the target but you were always my priority. Now we're even. You saved my sister and I'm going to save you from Rod Howley. It's in honor of who you are and what you do and also in honor of a brave and courageous woman who died tonight. Rosalie Wardill."

Sarah was stunned. She had no idea that something she had done years ago would come back to benefit her.

"I guess that's karma for you. Thanks," was all she could say.

They started walking again.

A gun went off somewhere. Both of them ducked and ran to the river side of the road.

"If they're firing at us we can jump in one of these boats for shelter. If they aren't—"

He was cut off as part of his head behind his left ear opened up. He spun around and fell into the boat moored below them.

Sarah felt a punch in her back and stumbled.

Before getting below the edge of the road and into the shelter of the boat another punch hit her from behind knocking her forward.

She plunged over the edge and hit the front of the boat.

The forward momentum caused her to roll off the fiberglass and into the Danube River, disappearing from sight.

THE CRYPT

Chapter 29

She opened her eyes. The water pressed down on her. It was cold, chilling her to the marrow. The kevlar vest had saved her life again but now it was killing her as its weight became too much, dragging her deeper. She didn't have the energy to swim to the surface. She felt her consciousness fading fast.

With the last of her strength she removed her shirt and let the kevlar vest fall from her body. The cold on her exposed skin chilled her further.

Am I dying? Is this how death touches us with its cold fingers?

She couldn't tell if she was sinking anymore or rising toward the surface. All she knew was that she was moving fast with the current.

Something brushed against her butt. She turned to look but couldn't see anything in the dark water of the river. Her lungs announced their capacity had been reached. Her chest heaved, the pain immeasurable.

Her arms flailed. She wanted to scream at the unfairness. She wanted to scream for Vivian. She just wanted to scream but opening her mouth was a temptation she couldn't afford. If she opened her mouth, water would fill it and she'd inhale as her lungs were demanding.

Was this why Vivian apologized?

Something brushed her again as consciousness wavered.

In her foggy mind she realized it was weeds brushing her as she traveled past them.

Maybe she was near the shore?

Panic set in. Her lungs shouted at her. The pain from where the bullets hit her dulled a little as a new pain increased. Lack of oxygen attacked her like no other assailant in her life had.

Sarah fought with all she had left.

There was a light above her. *A streetlight?*

She fought for it, arms pinwheeling. Her own voice screamed inside her head. She would not open her mouth.

A thick weed caressed her arm. She grabbed at it and held on.

Her feet touched mud.

She opened her mouth and let her lungs evacuate. On the inhale her face broke the surface. She pushed with her feet and landed half in, half out of the Danube River on the Slovakia side.

When she hit the mud on the shore, her body was still underwater up to her shoulder blades.

It was there she passed out.

Chapter 30

Vivian stood beside her. Sarah knew it was her sister. She could tell. The similarities were too close.

Am I dead? she asked.

Vivian shook her head. *We've come a long way you and I. Even though we didn't get to spend a lot of time together when I was alive, I miss you. You are what I would've always wanted to be. Strong, courageous and brave.*

Sarah leaned up and stared at her. *And here I'm the one respecting you and what you do to help people out of car accidents and burning buildings.*

Sarah, if I could've only been half the woman you've turned out to be I could've saved myself that day. Girls don't understand. They think the guy will let them go. They play nice because they are *nice. They blame themselves. Not you, Sarah. You deal with it and make the assholes pay. I love you for that Sarah. I love you.*

Vivian, I asked you if I was dead. You didn't answer me. Am I?

Vivian shook her head. *Not yet. It's not your time. We have work to do. Parkman is on his way.*

Parkman! He's alive?

Vivian nodded. *And so are you. I have to go now Sarah. Be well. Take care. I've got a message for you about Drake Bellamy. He needs you. Head to Toronto. Armond is dead but it's not over. Are you okay with that?*

Sarah looked at her sister and wondered what life would've been growing up with her. She longed to play games with her, talk about boys and do what sisters do. Because of Armond and people like him they never got that chance.

Vivian seemed to be floating. Her hair fell in golden locks, her smile a caress of light, her eyes a brilliance of love.

I'm okay with whatever you throw at me sis. I love you. Let's do this together. You and me.

Gotta go now. Love you too.

Something hit her face hard.

"Sarah, wake up!"

Parkman.

She rose from a deep place. It felt like she was swimming from the bottom of the Danube River again.

"Sarah!" It sounded like Parkman was crying.

"Wha..." was all she could say. Pain ripped through her as she coughed up water.

"Oh, Sarah."

More water came out. After too many pain-wracked coughs she curled into a ball and began moaning.

"We need to get to dat cho...er," Parkman said. He was talking weird. His *that* was pronounced *dat.*

She opened her eyes and saw his face.

"Parkman, you're alive," she coughed. "Shit. That fucking hurts." She looked up at him again. "Your face is fucked."

"I know, I know. Get up. No more fucking around. We have a cho...er to catch. And what happened to your shirt? Why are you swimming in your bra?"

She didn't answer his question. It was too painful to talk that much. After pulling her shirt off to remove the kevlar vest she had lost it in the river's current.

Sarah did her best to get to her feet with Parkman's help.

They walked up the embankment. Parkman had brought one of the police cars.

"What happened to you?" Sarah managed to ask.

He was helping her into the passenger seat when he said, "After putting on the vest you gave me I got out and crawled under the car. I was in no position to fight. I waited there until it was quiet. After crawling back out, I saw Bennett take you over the hill. I went to follow but then Rod came running out of the church. He started firing his weapon at you two. I saw Bennett hit the boat and you hit the water. I would've killed Rod but I was unarmed so I ran back for the car and here I am."

He slammed her door shut and ran around to the driver's side. After getting in he said, "I thought you were dead."

"I was."

He looked at her sharply.

"I saw Vivian. She looked amazing. We talked. We need to go to Canada."

"First things first. We need to get to that chopper. Rod thinks he killed you. He's down at the edge of the Danube River where he saw you go in. Let's get you out of here before he confirms otherwise."

Parkman threw the car into gear and raced out to the helipad. Within fifteen minutes they were in the helicopter. The pilot took some convincing, but he lifted off knowing that no one else was coming.

After fifteen minutes in the air, Sarah was shivering from the cold. Parkman had wrapped his shirt around her exposed shoulders. She looked at him and shouted over the noise the rotors made, "I love you Parkman."

He leaned forward, reached into his back pocket and produced a small plastic container. After flipping it open he pulled out a toothpick and placed it in his mouth.

"Cinnamon flavored. No more running out for this guy. I'm packing," he said and slapped the container.

Sarah leaned back, exhausted.

"Oh, and Sarah?"

She looked at him, her eyes half-lidded.

"I love you too."

About the Author

Jonas Saul, best-selling author of thrillers and horrors, lives in Italy where he is working on his next novel. Visit his website at www.jonassaul.com for more information on his new releases.